THIRTY FEET UNDER

WILLIAM WODHAMS

THIRTY FEET UNDER

A Mystery

Published by ECW Press
665 Gerrard Street East
Toronto, Ontario, Canada M4M 1Y2
416-694-3348 / info@ecwpress.com

Cover design: Michel Vrana

LIBRARY AND ARCHIVES CANADA CATALOGUING IN PUBLICATION

Title: Thirty feet under : a mystery / William Wodhams.

Names: Wodhams, William, author.

Identifiers: Canadiana (print) 20250320150 | Canadiana (ebook) 20250320169

ISBN 978-1-77041-854-7 (softcover)
ISBN 978-1-77852-544-5 (PDF)
ISBN 978-1-77852-543-8 (ePub)

Subjects: LCGFT: Novels.

Classification: LCC PS8645.O34 T45 2026 | DDC C813/.6—dc23

This book is funded in part by the Government of Canada. *Ce livre est financé en partie par le gouvernement du Canada.* We acknowledge the support of the Canada Council for the Arts. *Nous remercions le Conseil des arts du Canada de son soutien.* We would like to acknowledge the funding support of the Ontario Arts Council (OAC) and the Government of Ontario for their support. We also acknowledge the support of the Government of Ontario through the Ontario Book Publishing Tax Credit, and through Ontario Creates.

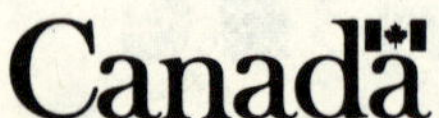

Canada Council for the Arts Conseil des arts du Canada

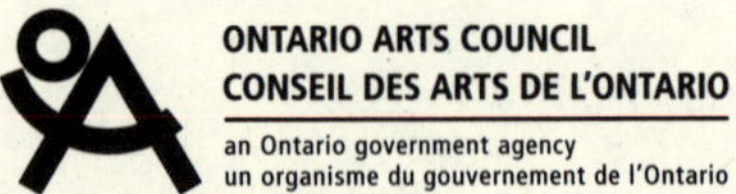

PRINTED AND BOUND IN CANADA

PRINTING: MARQUIS 5 4 3 2 1

For Ann, Patrick & Scott

CHAPTER ONE

If Matteo Bologna had been a more observant man, he might have noticed the pale white foot sticking out from under the desk where Sofia usually sat. He might also have noticed the slightly chipped, blush-red nail polish, the black pointed-toe shoe off to one side, and the splashes of blood on the floor. But he wasn't, and he didn't.

He did notice that Sofia wasn't sitting in her chair at the reception desk, as she should be at this time of the morning. And that the wooden door that served as the entrance to the museum, the one on the wall behind her, had been left wide open. She must have gone to the kitchen for coffee, he guessed. Understandable, but still, she shouldn't have left the room unattended. Somebody could have walked straight in and out with some of the museum's gifts. Matteo made a mental note to ask her to be more careful next time. She was still new, and seemed decent enough, so he would do it in a nice way. Maybe compliment her first before pointing out the risks involved in leaving the museum doors open and practically inviting criminals in to have their way. Hanging his coat on the rack, he put on his green-and-blue guard's hat and jacket and walked into the Great Hall.

The museum was housed in the magnificent old Gandolfi Castle, and Matteo's eyes followed the rough stone walls up to the ribs and archways far above his head. He took it all in and let out a long sigh.

Over the course of its illustrious 980 years, the castle had served as a home to a regular procession of royals and religious leaders, a state treasury, the seat of no less than six papal councils, and the center of government nine times. It had withstood the ravages of countless attacks, two earthquakes, several crusades and sackings, and one eight-month siege when it was just forty-two years old. None of this had left any significant damage on its medieval walls.

He imagined that the thousands of stonemasons, carpenters and slaves who built and renovated the castle over the centuries would be disappointed if they saw it today. The once proud and formidable fortress had been abandoned, ignored, and left alone to rot. Left alone, that is, until ten years earlier, when the town's council decided to turn it into a museum and embarked on a half-hearted restoration, which was still ongoing. The mayor, who was also Matteo's brother-in-law, had hired him as the museum's only guard. The large and well-supplied armies that once defended it had been replaced by one single, slightly overweight and fastidious middle-aged man.

Matteo walked down the hallway, his feet silent on the stone floors. He passed the kitchen and was surprised that Sofia wasn't there. Maybe she had gone for a walk? She had done that before, but not while she was supposed to be at the front desk! He really must have a word with her. She was being irresponsible, that's what it was.

Seven of the castle rooms had been renovated so far. They housed a mash-up of ancient art works and artifacts, most of them discovered in and around the castle's hundred-plus-acre complex, which was "steeped in history" (according to the museum's brochure). Other items on display had been donated or purchased from various collectors and dealers. He stepped into the Great Chamber, which had been the castle's private living and sleeping quarters. Today it held a scattering of wall hangings, kitchen utensils, household items, and a few vases and statues.

He saw the three men before they saw him.

Two of the men were lifting a marble sphinx out of its display case. They saw Matteo and froze. The third man, who had his back to Matteo, turned around.

"Who are . . . what are you doing?" Matteo asked.

The third man offered a broad smile. "Hello!" Matteo noticed he was dressed differently than the others. They were in ragged T-shirts and jeans while he wore a white silk jacket over a pink shirt. He walked towards Matteo and held out his hand. "We are taking this beautiful sphinx in for a little maintenance. Some tender loving care, you know, so it will remain beautiful for another thousand years." He kept his hand out and Matteo grudgingly shook it. "And who might you be?"

Matteo eyed the three men warily. "I'm the museum guard. And you're not supposed to be here."

"Don't tell me they didn't call you? I'm so sorry. My goodness, this is awkward. They told me they'd called you. We're with Dimitra's Conservation Services."

"Who are they? And how did you get in?" This, Matteo thought, was all Sofia's fault. She should have been at her desk. "You've got to have some kind of ID or something, you know. You can't just . . . you can't just waltz in and—"

"A thousand apologies. This maintenance was scheduled months ago. Our mistake. Someone should have called."

Matteo had never heard of anyone doing maintenance on the museum's artifacts. "Where is your ID?"

"Certainly. Of course." The man put his hand in his jacket and fumbled around. "I believe it's right here."

While he was digging around for his identification, Matteo wondered how they had got in here in the first place. If they came in through the front door, they would have had to speak with Sofia. She must have let them in. But if she did, why wasn't she here, watching them? She wouldn't just let them wander around like this, would she? "Did you speak with Sofia?"

"The charming young lady at the front door?"

The man grinned. It was the way he grinned, something about the look behind his eyes, that made Matteo's throat tighten.

Until he saw that grin, Matteo hadn't really believed there was anything wrong. He believed they were conservationists, just like the man said, but hadn't called ahead as they should have. He was wondering if he should send them packing, just to teach them a lesson about the importance of planning. But after he saw that grin, he wasn't so sure of himself. Who were they really? Why wasn't Sofia here? His heart started pounding faster, as if his body were telling him something his brain hadn't figured out.

"Where is Sofia?"

"I'm afraid she's had an accident."

If Matteo had been trained as a guard, he would have known what to do. He had asked his brother-in-law about that years earlier, when he had first taken the job. Asked him if he shouldn't take some kind of defense training, or firearm training, or something. Just in case. But his stupid brother-in-law had just laughed that smug laugh of his and said he'd never need it, that no one would ever try and rob this broken-down old castle. When Matteo looked down and saw the man pull out a gun instead of his identification, he knew he had been right. He couldn't wait to tell his brother-in-law just how wrong he was, right to his face, when he got the chance.

The man pointed the gun at Matteo's forehead. "I'm afraid I've misplaced my papers," he said.

Matteo looked at the gun and back at the man's face. The man's grin grew wider. Matteo realized it wasn't a grin at all. It was something else. Something like the smile of an amiable psychopath.

It was the last grin Matteo would ever see.

CHAPTER TWO

The Wentworth Museum was set in the Wentworth House in Yorkshire, England. The house had been built early in the eighteenth century and owned by a series of earls, princesses, and other assorted royals and wealthy merchants before being transformed into one of England's greatest art museums.

Kate scrolled through the job description. The museum had an international reputation, an impressive collection of ancient and classic art, and an eye on growth. The position of Wentworth Museum curator had everything she was looking for, including a pension, benefit plan, and a generous paycheck. There was only a single, yet formidable problem: She lacked twenty-eight of the thirty-two essential prerequisites required for the job.

"Hey, you still there?" said the nasal voice on the phone.

"Yes! Yes, I sure am," Kate answered. "I'm sorry, I was just . . . I had another emergency. What were we talking about?"

"Are you listening? I'm reporting a stolen Boston Bruins Stanley Cup ring." The voice was loud enough that Kate pulled the phone away from her ear. "It was in my display case yesterday. I wake up today, it's gone."

"What kind of a ring?" Kate wasn't certain she knew what a Stanley Cup ring was, but she was certain she didn't want to find out.

"A Stanley Cup ring! Don't even tell me. You don't know what that is?"

Kate took a long, deep breath. "Sir, you've contacted the FBI's Art Crime Team," she said. "We investigate stolen art. This Stanley ring . . . would you describe it as art?"

She had applied for jobs in several museums after graduating at the top of her class in art history at Columbia. But her best friend at university, Natalie, was working at a museum in London, and it sounded like it was all meetings and politics. Kate wasn't sure that's what she wanted to do with her life. Then she read an ad for a job on the FBI's Art Crime Team. Kate didn't even know there was such a thing as an FBI Art Crime Team.

"That ring is a piece of Americana, and it is art. If you knew anything about hockey, you'd know that. And it's been stolen, and it's your job to find it. Bobby Orr played on that team. Gerry Cheevers. Wayne Cashman."

"Yes, sir. I understand." She tried to sound like she was sorry. "I could file a report. But for your information, the object missing must be worth over three thousand dollars just to get listed in our stolen art file."

"I paid thirty-five grand for this. You don't even know who Bobby Orr is, do you?"

Before Kate joined the Art Crime Team, just over three years earlier, she'd had visions of grand, exciting adventures. Traveling to foreign countries, strolling through ancient museums and meeting rich, eccentric collectors, rescuing important works of art from the bad guys. She imagined interviewing mysterious suspects and discovering piles of pillaged gold and diamond artifacts big enough to fill King Tutankhamun's tomb. She saw herself being interviewed on television, giving lectures to learned guests in expensive suits, flying around the world to art crime symposiums.

Instead, she got a small desk, a business card that read "Kate Taylor Graduate Intern," and an aging computer. She was sent files full of hundreds of missing artifacts that she would post on the FBI's stolen art online database and search for, usually through social media sites and other online marketplaces. When she wasn't doing that, she was taking phone calls or responding to the dozens of emails that came in every day from hysterical victims reporting lost and stolen art—or what they thought was art—including everything from Rolex watches to Tiffany lamps to paintings of cowboys on horses. When did overpriced watches become art?

Maybe she shouldn't have been surprised. They had told her, more than once, that being an agent wasn't like what you saw in the movies. That it would be a lot of paperwork, computer work, and endless meetings. And she accepted that. Fine, it wasn't going to be all Indiana Jones. But still. There could be a little Indiana Jones.

Kate scrolled through the careers site for the Wentworth Museum again. Maybe she should apply for a job as a Visitor Experience Team Member. The only qualifications required were "confidence and enthusiasm," and she had plenty of that.

"You still there?" the voice on the phone asked.

"Yes, I am still here." Kate fought the temptation to add the word "unfortunately." "Can you describe the missing object?"

An hour later, the missing piece of "Americana" had been duly added to the other fifty thousand items listed in the database. Kate put her hands behind her head and looked out the window. Her big FBI job had turned into this: an overeducated, thirty-two-year-old desk clerk trying to solve the Case of the Missing Hockey Ring.

A creaking door swung open behind her.

"Kate?"

Camilla. Her boss. Otherwise known, at least to Kate, as The Robot. Probably had another big case for her to work on. Perhaps a missing football helmet, or a baseball signed by, well, somebody big. Another missing piece of Americana.

"Yes?" Kate called out.

"Could you take a call from the Italian police? There's an agent named Luca on line two."

"The Carabinieri?"

"He's with their Art Squad," The Robot said. "He said it was urgent. Of course, they think everything is urgent. At any rate, it's a Zoom call. I'll send you the link."

Yes, please. She certainly could take it. Anything that wasn't a stolen hockey ring or a cowboy painting, she was all over it.

A moment later, Kate clicked the link and her screen was filled with a sky full of stars over a rocky shoreline and dark green lake. There wasn't anyone there. It looked like one of those fake Zoom backgrounds people use, except it wasn't fake.

A few moments later, a voice called from off-screen. "Kate?"

"Hello? This is Kate. Is that Luca?"

Luca sat down, leaned into the screen and smiled. He had long, curly hair that was blowing softly in the breeze, as if someone were holding a fan beside him. His face looked like it had been cut out from the cover of a romance novel. Big, sad blue eyes, a warm smile, and a strong, square chin. He set a glass of something orange on the table.

"Yes, it's Luca. Ciao. Apologies, I had to run to the bar," he said. "Thank you so much for taking my call."

"Anytime," Kate said.

"I'm with the Carabinieri, and we could use your assistance."

I'll be on the next plane, Kate thought. Order me a drink. "Understood. How can we help?"

Luca nodded, looked around, and picked up his glass. "Thieves broke into a castle yesterday. It's one of those old castles—eleventh century, give or take—that has been turned into a museum, in a little village called Gandolfi, which is, say, an hour north of Rome. The thieves shot the guard and the ticket agent and stole an ancient marble sphinx." He drank from his glass. "We are almost certain the sphinx is on its way to the U.S."

This was more like it. A real, actual, international art crime. Even better—antiquities. "Understood," she said. "Is that all they stole?"

"Si. That's all."

"Understood." Quit saying "understood," she thought to herself. It sounds stupid. Think of another question. "Actually, doesn't that seem unusual? That they didn't take anything else?"

"Good question," he said, smiling. "Yes, it is, as you say, unusual."

Yes. That was a good question. Way to go, Kate. "And they only had one guard watching the entire museum?" she asked.

"Just one."

"Isn't that unusual?"

"Not so much," he said, sipping his drink. "As I'm sure you know, there are something like forty-five thousand castles in Italy. It would take several hundred armies to protect them all. We do the best we can with what we have." He leaned back in his chair and turned his face up to the sky. "It is extremely, umm . . . I don't know how to say it. Troppo? Too much? Over—"

"Overwhelming?"

"Yes. Too much overwhelming."

He didn't look overwhelmed. He was sitting in a gorgeous outdoor café with a beautiful view, drinking an aperitif. Still, she understood what he meant by being overwhelmed. After all, there were only three people in the entire New York office of the FBI's Art Crime Team and there was just too much for them to keep up. She was forever buried in a rising ocean of files, emails, and phone messages she didn't think she'd ever have time to respond to. "Of course. I'm sorry. We're all overwhelmed. I didn't mean it that way."

"Don't be sorry." He leaned back into the camera. "Tell me something. Who are you?"

"I'm Kate. With the FBI."

A voice called from off camera. "Excuse me sir, would you like another?"

"Yes," Luca answered, even though his glass was still half full. "Grazie."

"What is that?" Kate asked.

"Aperol," he said, lifting the glass and toasting her. "It's too early for champagne."

Too early? It was four o'clock in New York. Which made it somewhere around ten o'clock in Italy. How is that too early for champagne? At ten o'clock in Chester, where Kate grew up, people were already getting ready for bed.

"Tell me about the sphinx they stole."

"Like I said, it's marble. Approximately two thousand five hundred years old, possibly three. A lion's body, human head, big wings, a little over two feet tall. A few little cracks, but otherwise it's in excellent condition."

Kate was thinking, there must be hundreds of sphinxes in Italy that fit this description. She kept waiting for him to say what made this one special, but he didn't. "Where did the museum get it from?"

"A woman named Angelina Bernardi left it to them in her will."

"You've contacted Interpol?"

"Yes, of course, we've contacted just about everyone, all the standard procedures. Now we're contacting you."

"Why do you think it's coming to the United States?"

"Because the United States is the world's biggest market for stolen art. Don't most of Europe's looted treasures end up in America?"

He was right. "That's true. But Russia, China, England, they're all smuggling more every day."

"Yes, but the U.S. has held the lead over the last few hundred years, and they're still on top." He held up his glass in a toast. "Auguri! America first! Congratulations are in order."

"Thank you," Kate agreed, toasting him back with her coffee mug. "The United States has become very good at pillaging. No one really gives us enough credit for that."

"Oh, do not worry. We give you lots of credit. And if you don't mind, we'd like them back one day."

"I'll be sure to ask."

A sparrow landed on Luca's table and looked around. "Piccolo amico," Luca said to the waitress. "A drink for my friend here." The bird beat her wings and flew away. Luca leaned closer to the screen. "The thieves will want to move this piece quickly. They likely have a buyer already. If it's coming to your country, it'll probably be there in the next day or two."

"We'll do everything we can."

"Thank you." He smiled. "Give me your email, and I'll send the photographs right away. It was nice meeting you, Kate with the FBI. Please keep me informed."

"No, thank *you*. And don't worry, I will."

He ended the meeting, and Kate stared at her blank screen for a few moments.

Was he real? Or did they create some kind of hologram out of the lead actor in a Hollywood rom-com?

The photographs of the marble sphinx arrived in her email a few minutes later, showing the serene, smiling face of a woman on a muscular lion's body with one majestic wing flowing over her head. Kate guessed it was from early in the Hellenistic Age. Sphinx statues like this had often been used as guardians of ancient graves, protecting the final resting places of the upper classes from potential intruders. Still, there wasn't anything particularly notable about this one, unless . . . maybe she had been guarding someone especially important? Kate looked closer. The face on the sphinx looked beautiful and dangerous. Like she would attack if you got too close.

Kate ignored all the other files she was supposed to be working on and started searching right away, scanning through page after page on Facebook, Kijiji, and every other online marketplace where stolen art was sold. There was nothing resembling an ancient Greek sphinx. She had looked through these sites before and knew she could be there for days, even weeks, before she found anything—*if* she found anything. She didn't even know if the thieves had listed it online. Luca mentioned they might already have a buyer. What if they'd already sold it?

The stolen art market was worse than the illicit drug trade, Kate thought. No matter how many criminals they arrested, more poured in to take their place. The money was too good, the penalties for getting caught too weak. No matter how many pieces they recovered, thousands more disappeared—objects stolen from museums and private homes, or antiquities dug fresh out of the ground and smuggled out of the country they belonged to. No government agencies had been able to stop the thieves, or even slow them down: not the FBI, Interpol, or even Italy's famed Carabinieri Art Squad. And those were rich countries. Most countries simply didn't have the resources to make more than a token effort. The illicit art market had been estimated at over ten billion dollars a year, and trending in the wrong direction.

A few hours later, she shut off the computer. It was late, and she wasn't going to solve this tonight. She picked up her coat and got ready to leave. The Robot had gone home, which left only one other person in the office. Geri. Senior Agent Geri, Geri Gumshoe, Geri the thirty-year veteran, Geri the guy who got most of the interesting cases—at least the cases that didn't go to their head office in Washington—just because he'd been around longer. Geri was in the middle of a battle with troops of well-armed Russians on his computer. It sounded like he had just been blown to bits, so he didn't hear her when she said goodbye.

• • •

On the way to her New Jersey apartment, Kate picked up cheap sushi (the one food you should never buy cheap, she thought, but did anyway). Inside, she lay down on the couch and opened her laptop. Checked emails, scanned the news and Instagram, and turned her laptop off. Cleaned the apartment up, though it didn't take long to clean 528 square feet. Thought about going out for a walk, but it was getting dark, and even after three years she wasn't completely comfortable walking around this neighborhood at night. She turned the computer back on and looked at the photographs Luca had sent and thought about the sphinx. Then about Luca.

It was after ten o'clock when her phone rang. No Caller ID. Kate only knew one person who used No Caller ID. "Hi, Mom."

"Sweetie! How was your day?"

My day, said Kate, was pretty much like every other day. Next came what's with the weather, how are your friends from school doing, how much she misses Dad, the approximate number of birds and squirrels in the yard, all the noise the neighbors make, the status of her knees, her brother, and the inevitable "Have You Met Anyone?" A sensitive question to Kate, who, after three years here, still had not "met anyone"—or anyone she wanted to meet again. Still, it was nice. Talking to her mother was like listening to a song you've heard a million times and still can't get enough of.

"Well, I did meet someone," Kate told her. "And guess what? I'm married! I met this man on Saturday and we got married the next day. And here's the crazy thing. I think he might be Mormon, because—and I honestly did not know this until late yesterday—he's got five other wives. Five! Which I think he should have mentioned before we tied the knot, don't you? Isn't that something you should mention before you marry someone? Wouldn't that just naturally come up in conversation? Anyway, I think I'm pregnant. Quintuplets, which is kind of ironic, I think. Sorry, I meant to tell you, but I forgot. It's been so busy! But enough about me. How are things in Chester?"

Mom laughed, just a little nervously. "Well, he sounds nicer than the ninety-five-year-old Nazi prison guard you married last week, sweetheart. Or the Colombian drug lord from the week before. So, I'll see you Sunday, okay? Love you."

Kate put down her phone, looked up the Gandolfi Castle online and found an article about the theft. The castle was bigger than she imagined. It had eight massive towers and seemed to cover a few square miles. There was only one guard? Why didn't they steal anything else? And why would anyone kill for that marble sphinx? It couldn't be worth much, although prices for antiquities had been going up. She had recently read about a Roman marble bust that was thought to have been of Homer, and it sold for over fifty thousand. Still, this was just a sphinx.

She searched the local newspaper. The theft was buried on page fourteen, and there wasn't anything she hadn't heard from Luca. Kate had seen stories about stolen laptops told with more drama in *The Chester Gazette*. Then she looked up Luca on Facebook.

She found eight people named Luca Rosi. Four of them were in Italy, only two of them in Rome. He was easy to spot. He was the one with the romance-novel hair.

There were pictures of a young Luca at a restaurant. Pictures of Luca on a boat, holding a huge fish. Pictures of Luca working out at the gym. Mmm. Pictures of Luca at parties, nightclubs, in fancy cars, many of them with young, smiling women wearing, well, not clothes you'd see in Chester. If she didn't know him, she'd guess that he was probably a real jerk. But then, she didn't know him. Not yet. One post was Luca at a costume party eight years earlier. He was dressed as Indiana Jones. He would have given a young Harrison Ford a run for his money, she thought.

Working in the Art Crime Team was going to be more fun than she thought.

CHAPTER THREE

Paul finished his Manhattan and waved at the waitress for another. "What do you mean, Richard won't be there?" he shouted into the phone. "He has to be there. I'm telling you. I'm commanding you to make sure he is there."

"He's leaving for Philadelphia tomorrow afternoon, Paul," Jennifer said.

"Jennifer, Jennifer, Jennifer. Listen to me, okay? He absolutely must be there. He has to see this. I have an extremely rare piece here." He laid his hand on the box resting on the chair beside him. "I told you it's gold, right? Very valuable. Excuse me, waitress?" The waitress picked up his glass. "Less vermouth, okay?" he hollered at her as she walked away. "That tasted like dog shit." What did he expect from an airport diner called the Corona Beach House?

"Where are you?" she asked.

"In some crap bar in the Miami Airport. Service sucks."

"And you have the cup with you?"

"It's on the seat beside me. You think I'd trust those meatheads in shipping with this?"

"You're carrying an antique gold cup out in the open in an airport?"

"It's insured. Also, it's in a box covered with kids' birthday wrapping paper. Everyone thinks it's just a toy. It's got dinosaurs all over it."

"You're crazy-crazy. Anyway, Richard is leaving tomorrow afternoon. He won't be back for ten days."

"Ten days? That's bullshit. It will be sold long before then." Paul banged his glass on the table, trying to get the waitress's attention. Why was she taking so long? The plane was leaving soon. "I'm about to get on a plane to L.A. To see Richard. You and Richard." His Manhattan finally arrived, and he let go of the cup just long enough to have a quick drink.

"Then I guess you're out of luck."

"You're the one who will be out of luck. You, Jennifer." Paul forced himself to calm down. He spoke slowly, enunciating every word carefully. "And Richard, and your shit museum. Do you understand what I'm saying? This piece is over two thousand years old. It's. An. Important. Piece. Your museum needs this piece. Get it?"

"I understand. It's not complicated."

"I don't think you do. Two thousand years. That's before the goddamn Incas. The guy they buried it with must have been an emperor or something. It's big, it's pure, and it's solid gold. Heavy. Heavy! I can barely carry the thing. And it's in immaculate, perfect condition." Except for one dent near the base, but this wasn't a good time to mention that. "You think your boss is going to be happy if he finds out he missed out on this?"

"Richard is not my boss. We're colleagues."

"Fine. Colleagues. But you can't authorize this, and Richard can. So, actually—"

"You're being a total jerk, Paul. Look, it's waited two thousand years, what's another ten days?"

"Very funny. Listen, I'm trying to help you. This is big. This piece could *make* you."

"Gee, thanks. But we're already the biggest museum in California, so I think we'll be okay."

"Come on, Jennifer. You know I've got an eye for this stuff." He lowered his voice to a serious whisper. "I think it's Sican. Pretty sure the Lord of Sican is carved into this. You know what that means, right?"

"I do. But we've already got a lot of pre-Columbian artifacts."

"Okay, know what? Fuck you. Fuck you. I'm flying into LAX tonight. I'll be at your office tomorrow morning. I'm sure Richard will get it. Tell that jerk he better be there, because if he's not there, I'm taking it to the Drake. The Drake, okay? They'll buy it in one second." Paul banged his phone on the counter and hung up.

"Excuse me, sir, would you mind if we use that seat?"

Paul turned around. A man and his wife were standing behind him. Young tourists, probably Swedish or something. Long blonde hair, backpacks. Back-to-the-land types. She looked pregnant. The man was pointing at the empty seat beside Paul. Except it wasn't empty. It was holding a two-thousand-year-old gold cup, almost two feet high, covered in birthday wrap decorated with dinosaurs.

"No," Paul said. "I mean yes, I would mind."

"But my wife—"

"Look, it can't be moved. It's extremely fragile. That is a rare cultural artifact."

"But sir . . ." He looked at the dinosaur wrapping and a tone of frustration crept into his voice. "We've been flying all night, and my wife is pregnant—"

"Oh, she is, is she? Well, that's too bad. Because this artifact happens to be solid gold, and it's worth about a million times more than you both will ever be. It was here first, and it's not moving."

They stared at him for a few moments, and he stared back. The pregnant wife pulled on her husband's sleeve, and the man gave Paul the evil eye as they wandered off. He finished off two more drinks before his boarding call.

"American Airlines Flight 859 to LAX is starting to board. First-class passengers are invited to start pre-boarding immediately."

Paul picked up the box and carried it onto the plane. One first-class seat for him, one for the gold cup. He put the seat belt around the box first, being careful not to rip the wrapping paper, and leaned back in his seat. He didn't need radiocarbon dating or a team of archeological experts to tell him what this piece was worth. He knew. He had the eye.

He was almost certain that the cup was one of the earliest pieces of hammered gold ever discovered. It was eighteen or nineteen hundred years old, probably closer to nineteen. He would have bet anything that the figure in the middle holding the spears was the Lord of Sican, the icon associated with the sky deity. And the tomb it came from must have held the skeleton of a king. It must have. No one else would have been permitted to lay their eyes on the Lord of Sican. This was a serious piece. And it was in perfect condition. Okay, almost perfect. Still, a thing of beauty. Priceless.

So how much should he ask for it?

Let's see. That Sican mask he read about, a few weeks earlier. That went for—what was it? Half a million? But it wasn't as big as this, and it had a big crack in the side. This cup was bigger, and it only had one little dent. A piece of Peruvian textile from around the same age sold for over a million a few weeks earlier in New York. But textiles were hot now. Still, gold was always gold. And it was the Lord of Sican. Maybe a million? He should hold out for a million. After paying the seller two hundred and fifty grand for it, plus the airline tickets, meals and time, he was still doing okay. A seven-hundred-thousand-dollar markup was very okay.

All he had to do now was get it to Richard. Fast. Crap luck that he was going away. After a couple of months without making a single sale, Paul's credit had never been lower, his bills had never been higher, and his shithead jerk of a landlord had just handed him a third and final notice on overdue rent. He shouldn't have bought these first-class seats, but he thought he'd have a million bucks in the bank by now. So what next? He needed a big sale, and he needed it fast. Richard had to be there. Had to be.

• • •

"I can't believe it. He's really not there?" Paul was sitting in the back of a cab on the way to the Art Gallery of Los Angeles, the cup in its box on the seat beside him. "You've got to be kidding. You said he wasn't leaving until this afternoon."

"He caught an early flight, Paul," Jennifer said. "He's probably in Philadelphia already."

Paul forced himself to take a deep breath. "I told you to—"

"You don't tell me what to do. And stop being such an ass, or I'm hanging up."

"Did you tell him what it was? That it was Sican?" The traffic, already slow, had come to a stop. "Could you have possibly found a worse route?" he shouted at the driver.

"Yes. I told him all that," she said. "But like I told you—"

"I told you they're older than the Incas. The goddamn Incas!"

"And I told you I knew who the Sicans were."

"Did you tell him I was going to sell it to the Drake?"

"Yes. He said he could live with that."

Paul squeezed his hand around the phone, trying not to yell. The cab hadn't moved for several minutes, and he wished he could just get out and walk. "You're lying. I know you're lying. There's no way he would leave—"

"Listen, Paul. You should sell it to the Drake. If you can."

"Of course I can. They've already left me several messages. Practically begging me for it. Listen. The next time you see Richard, can you tell him something for me?" Paul asked, forcing himself to smile. "Can you tell him that he's a lowlife little weasel and I'm never going to deal with his stupid fucking fat ass again? Would you mind? I thank you so much."

Paul hung up. Now what?

He could call the Drake Museum of Art, but he'd heard they were in financial trouble. The New York Museum had already told him never to call them back. Several times. She—Imani, the museum's curator—hated him. Which he couldn't blame her for. The National Museum in London might be worth a call. They had never returned his calls before, but still—he ran his fingers over the warrior holding the spear on the side of the cup—this was a nice piece. Maybe he should call them.

His phone rang. "Jennifer. Change your mind?"

"No. Just—not sure if you're interested, but just in case the Drake doesn't buy it, I heard the Art Gallery of Minneapolis was trying to build up their collection of pre-Columbian art. You might try them."

"How pathetic do you think I am? This is a world-class piece. Do you really think I would sell it to some place in Minnee-fucking-apolis? I was just on the phone with the National Museum in London. They made an offer right away. So did the Drake. There's already a bidding war on."

"You know what, Paul? You used to be a good guy. I liked you. What happened?" She paused, but he didn't answer. "I'm trying to help you, despite the fact that you're being a complete and utter asshole. You're not going to find a lot of museums that will buy pre-Columbian gold, or any ancient art. Everyone is paranoid about buying artifacts these days. They're afraid they'll be accused of stealing somebody's culture or some other kind of politically correct crap."

"Sorry, I have to run. London is calling. Again." He hung up. What a waste of time and money. Idiots! And what was that bullshit about "stealing culture?" As long as he had the provenance that declared the cup was purchased legally, which he did, no one would care where these ancient artifacts came from. Don't ask, don't tell—that's how it worked. Everyone knew that. "We're going back to the airport," he told the driver. At least he could find a good Manhattan in LAX.

• • •

Back at his New York apartment, Paul set the gold cup in the middle of his dining room table. It really was beautiful. Even with that dent, it was perfect. He thought about how much time those artists would have spent hammering that gold by hand, bending it, and shaping it. Months, probably. He loved the way the gold glowed, like there was a fire smoldering inside it. He could feel some invisible power coming from that cup, as if an eternal, universal force were emanating from inside. If he were rich, he'd leave it right there. Right on the table. Stare at it every day.

But a million would be nice.

It didn't even have to be a million. Even eight hundred thousand would do. Enough to pay off his overburdened Amex, stave off eviction, cover the rent for a few months, plus have a nice cushion. But also—maybe even more importantly—if he could get this piece in the Art Gallery of Los Angeles, the National Museum, or even better the New York Museum, he would be an established name. What did they call it? A made guy. The kind of respected dealer that top galleries and collectors called, who got first bids on the best pieces collectors wanted to sell, who did television interviews and had articles written about him in art magazines and got paid to make speeches. He could call the shots.

He was not going to sell this cup to some shit museum in Minneapolis.

The New York Museum. That was the place. His best bet. The biggest, most famous museum in the world. If he could sell it to them . . . But selling to the New York Museum meant selling it to Imani. And she was not going to answer his phone calls. She'd probably have blocked him anyway. The only way he could sell it to her was to see her, and the only way to see her was to go there. Try and charm his way in. Which could mean being arrested, what with the restraining order and everything, but he was willing to take that chance. He didn't think she would call the cops on him.

Paul woke up the next morning, put on the best suit he had, and was standing in the lobby of the museum when they opened at ten o'clock, holding the box with the gold cup tightly in his arms.

"Of course she'll see me," he explained to the receptionist. "We're close friends, more than friends, if you know what I mean. We go way back, back to high school days, believe it or not. We met each other in art class. Just mention my name. Paul."

"I'm sorry, sir, but she's booked solid. I can try and make an appointment for next week," the receptionist said.

"Oh, I hate to have you go to all that trouble. I love your hair, by the way."

Not even a thin smile. She was a tough one. He would have to crank up the charm.

"Listen, I know you're doing what they tell you to do. I understand. But I really am a close friend. Very close. I have a little something I think she'd like to see." He held up the box covered in dinosaurs and raised his eyebrows. Tried to wink, but couldn't.

Once again, the receptionist didn't smile.

"It's almost like a present," he said. "She's going to love it."

"I'm sorry, sir."

The charm offensive was not working. Fine. He had given her a chance. "Look," he said. "I'm going to give you just one more goddamn—"

"Stop. Right there." She held up her hand. "I know who you are. You're Paul Klugman. You're on Ms. Hollis's Do Not Allow Under Any Circumstances list. In fact, you're the only one on the list. So, no. She's not going to love it. She's not going to see it. Or you. I was trying to be nice. But I can see she was right about you. You should leave now. Goodbye."

"But—"

"She knows you're just trying to sell her that piece. She told me who you are. And that she wouldn't buy from you if you walked in here with Tutankhamun's death mask. So, I think it's best if you just—"

"Oh yeah? How'd you like it if I cracked this fucking box right over your thick skull? Now get her—"

She didn't even flinch. "You should get professional help. See somebody before you hurt someone, or yourself. Oh, and also? I've already contacted security. If I were you I'd run out of here as fast as I could. They're not very nice. And they have these big clubs—"

"Shit." He saw two large men turn the corner. He had no choice. He turned around and walked out. Quickly.

But he didn't run. No way was he going to run.

Then he heard the security guards closing in on him, and he ran.

CHAPTER FOUR

Kate kept searching, ignoring all the other files that were piling up, because, really, was the world going to miss another Tiffany lamp? The best place to catch art thieves was in the selling, and the best place to catch them selling these days was online. So that's where she looked, spending hour after hour digging through the dark corners of any online market she could find, including auction houses and private sellers. She found Greek pots and vases, swords and helmets, funerary vessels and sculptures—human and animal, life-like and mythic, miniature and life-size. There were cutlery and plates, coins and jewelry, and lots of other "ancient" artifacts, but nothing that resembled a genuine Greek sphinx. Her eyes glazed, and her sense of hopelessness grew with every new search, but she kept on. She wasn't going to give up.

Until she did. After the fourth straight day of scrolling, a sense of futility overwhelmed her and she had to stop. This search was going nowhere. There had to be a better way. Where else could she look? She could try a few of the local antique galleries and auction houses, ask if they had been approached by anyone selling ancient Greek art or knew of anyone who had. It seemed like a one-in-a-million shot, but it would be better than sitting inside the office looking at ads for fake marble busts of Dionysus.

"You seem a little tense, Kate."

Kate turned around to see Camilla standing behind her. "No, I'm fine."

"Is anything wrong?"

"Not at all! Except, well, I've been working on finding this missing sphinx, and I guess my neck is tight from staring at the computer for the last four days. So I thought I'd check out some galleries."

"I can help with that."

"Oh, great! Do you have any suggestions?"

"I mean I can help with the tension. Have you tried meditation?" Camilla asked.

"I'm sorry?"

"Meditation. I've just started, and it really works. Haven't you noticed how much more relaxed I've been lately?"

"I sure have!" Relaxed? Kate looked up at her. The Robot's smile looked like it had been engineered by computer software. No, Kate hadn't noticed.

"I could show you how to do it." Camilla shut her eyes.

"I'd like that. I really would! But if it's okay, I'm going to take a rain check. I have this file I have to work on." Kate told her where she had been searching for the stolen sphinx and showed her the photograph.

Camilla studied the photo. "I can't imagine why the Carabinieri would be so interested in this particular piece. They must have hundreds of statues like that in museums all over the country." She thought for a moment. "I suppose you could try the galleries, but I don't think the thieves would try to sell this through established channels. How about Customs?"

"Customs?"

"That would be a good place to start. If it's coming into the United States, it has to go through Customs. Call them and ask for Alex. He takes care of most of the art-related shipments."

"I'll do that."

"They'll likely ship it in a container with other art, but really cheap art, or knockoffs, or in a crate filled with gifts and memorabilia so it looks like just another replica. Most Customs agents couldn't tell the difference. A lot of experts couldn't tell the difference." Camilla shook her head and offered a thin smile. "I'm afraid the odds of finding this particular piece are almost nonexistent. Go have a look, but don't forget we have our own files to work on. We can't drop everything for the Carabinieri."

• • •

"You're the one that called, right? That was you? Kate something?"

"Yes. Kate. With the FBI. Hello."

"The FBI's Art Crime Team. I remember. I'm Alex."

Alex sat hunched behind a small desk, peering out from behind stacks of paper. A badge on his shirt read U.S. Customs Border Patrol. He looked fifty or sixty years old and had broad shoulders, a square face and a short brush cut.

Kate held out her hand. He squeezed it, and she winced.

"We don't get a lot of calls for art crimes." Alex stood up and limped towards the door, then stopped and turned around. "Sorry, a bit slow. Breaking in a new hip. You said you're looking for some kinda marble thing?"

"It's a marble sphinx, ancient Greek, with the body of a—"

"Yeah, yeah. Great," he said. "Follow me."

Turning around, he walked out of his office. A row of Segways was lined up around the corner. Alex climbed on one, drove a few feet ahead, stopped and looked back.

"Climb aboard," he said. "The bus is leaving. Let's go."

Kate followed him. Did people still drive Segways? "I've never been on one of these."

"Just climb on, grab the handles, push the button. Lean forward to go, lean back to stop. Ain't nothin' to it."

Kate climbed up and put her finger over the button. "Are you sure?"

"I'm sure."

Kate pushed the button, squeezed her fingers around the handles, and leaned forward. The Segway lurched ahead, startling her, so she leaned back and it stopped so suddenly she almost fell off. She steadied herself, leaned in, and it took off again, still too fast for her, so she leaned back to slow down, and when she turned her head to look for Alex, it veered sideways and almost hit a wall. She then got it going forward again, but this time in the wrong direction.

This is a metaphor for my life, she thought.

"What are you doing?" Alex asked.

Slow down, Kate. Relax. You've got this. "I'm okay! I'm ready!"

Alex shook his head, turned around and took off. Kate followed him, her hair blowing back as she picked up speed, wishing a photographer were here to catch this moment. FBI Agent Kate in action. Check this out, Instagram peeps! Check this out, Chester friends! I'm on an investigation! Your Kate is on a Segway!

They traveled through one warehouse, then another, and then another. Rows and rows of metal shelves reached far over her head, filled with thousands of skids piled with boxes of all sizes built out of cardboard, wood and steel. Yellow forklifts raced up and down the aisles, carrying more square crates and a few odd-shaped, outsized, industrial-looking steel structures that looked vaguely threatening. How could anyone find anything in here? How was she going to find one two-foot marble sphinx in these acres and acres of crates and boxes?

Alex pulled up at the end of a row where six skids sat on the floor, apart from all the others. They were six feet high and wrapped in thick plastic and tape, with labels marking each one.

"This is what you were calling about."

Kate climbed off her Segway and studied the shipping labels on the crates. Three of them read: "Gifts and Memorabilia. Chengdu, China." Two read: "Gourmet Vintage Artifacts. Hyderabad, India." The last one simply read: "Gifts. Stockholm, Sweden."

"You said they might not look like genuine art, or antiquities," he said. "I remember you said that."

"I did. This is exactly what I was asking about."

"And so, you know, they're all in compliance. All the paperwork, declarations, duties, and codes are square. So unless you have some good reason not to, I'm obligated to ship them." He looked around, as if making sure they weren't being watched. "You want to have a look?"

"Let's start here." Kate pointed at the crate from Sweden.

"Okey dokes." Alex limped over and started to unpack the crate. He cut the tape nearest the top with a short blade, then started moving down the sides. "What's your specialty?"

"I'm sorry?" Kate asked.

He pulled the tape off and started cutting the plastic. "What's your period of study? You're an art historian, right? You told me that."

"Oh! Yes. I'm, well, Greek and Roman art."

"Ah. Before my time."

"Your time? What's your time?"

The plastic had been cut and he pulled it downwards, slowly, revealing several smaller boxes inside, each wrapped and labelled. He took those out and laid them carefully on the floor, getting on his hands and knees to make sure they weren't dropped or damaged. She heard his knees crack when he knelt.

"More seventeenth century. I wrote my thesis on the Dutch Golden Age. Bet you wouldna guessed, huh?" He stood up, slowly, wincing. "That's right. Your friend Alex here is also an art history grad. Maricopa Community College, class of 1985. Very big deal, huh? See where my art degree got me?" He looked around the warehouse, a smile on his face. "Ha. Not exactly the National Gallery, is it?"

That hit a little too close. Kate winced. "You mean Rembrandt? Hals?"

Alex pulled a camera out of an orange bag and took photographs of the contents on the floor. "I guess. Yes, Rembrandt, a little. But . . . no. Not really. Everybody talks about Rembrandt, you know? And Hals, Vermeer. And yeah, yeah, I get it. But no, not them. Give me your Lievens, Metsu, Leyster. You ever heard about Leyster?"

"Of course."

"Well, I'm impressed, right there. Almost no one remembers Leyster." Thirty or forty boxes were laid out on the floor in rows of ten, about a foot apart. Alex took more photographs. "I love Judith Leyster. To me, she was twice the painter Hals was. So where do you want to start?"

Kate looked down at the boxes. She knew immediately that none of them were the sphinx. They were too small. She wondered if she should try one of the other crates, but thought again. Maybe the sphinx wasn't here, but there might be some clue in one of those boxes, something that might lead her in the right direction. Another stolen Greek artifact, maybe. Besides, she was in no rush to get back to her computer screen. "Let's start with those," she said, pointing at some smaller boxes.

"Okey dokes." Alex started to unwrap them, taking more photographs as they were unpacked. "Sorry, I need these pictures for evidence in case anything goes missing or is reported broken. For the insurance agents and lawyers." He unwrapped more boxes and photographed them. "Our lives are run by insurance agents and lawyers."

"Can I help?"

"Not unless you want to get in trouble with the union. Which you don't."

Kate watched as he slowly unpacked everything.

"Thing is, with Leyster," he said, "when she was painting, in the early seventeenth century, there were not a lot of famous female artists, you know? Then Judith comes along, and she's brilliant, everyone knew it right from the start. Has a good head for business too, even starts her own studio with apprentices and everything. Huge talent. Even the men had to admit it. Suddenly one day she gets married, stops painting to take care of the household. Gives it all up to wash dishes and feed kids. Disappears from history. She was twenty-seven." He crossed his arms. "You investigate art crimes. How about you investigate that?"

Kate looked down at the pieces he had unwrapped. Cheap trinkets and replicas, and a lot of kids' toys. No sign of any antiquities.

She pointed to a box that had not been opened yet. "How about those ones?"

"You're the boss. Give me a minute."

He unpacked a few more. Still nothing. Trinkets.

"You want, I can just open everything up. But it's going to take a little while."

"Really? You don't mind?"

"Hey, you're FBI. Besides, I'd rather do this than go through another crate of green bananas or wide-screen TVs."

Kate sat on the floor of the warehouse and watched Alex finish unpacking, grunting and cracking as he worked. While she waited, she looked up Judith Leyster on her phone. The first work she found was a self-portrait Kate had studied in school. Leyster was sitting in front of a painting she was working on, several brushes in her hand, gazing at the viewer. She was wearing a smile on her face that looked more like a challenge. Her expression was full of unbridled confidence and her eyes full of attitude, as if she knew exactly how talented she was and dared anyone to suggest otherwise. She was the master in a man's world, and only twenty-four. Alex was right. She deserved better than a life consigned to washing dishes.

"This is brilliant, Alex."

"Huh? What's that?"

"Judith Leyster."

"I know, right?" He took a few more photographs. "All done. There you go."

Alex shuffled over to an empty forklift and sat down while Kate walked around the pieces, now carefully spread out over the warehouse floor. The first crate contained nothing unusual. It was just as the label advertised: gifts, mostly of the dollar store variety. After she was finished, Alex agreed to open one of the crates from China. He spent over an hour unpacking and taking more photos. Again, nothing. He offered to open another, and she quickly accepted. But as he bent over to lay the third crate out, she could tell he was getting tired and sore. He was holding his hip and winced every time he stood up.

The third crate was emptied and every piece carefully laid out on the floor. Kate walked up and down each row, looking closely, her hopes of finding anything even remotely helpful fading quickly. It wasn't until she reached the end of the last row that she saw anything interesting. A scattering of smaller pieces near the far edge of the pile—ten or twelve broken fragments of painted ceramics—glistened in the light of the warehouse.

"Alex?"

"I know, I saw them," he called out. "I took extra pictures of that. Trust me, it was broken when I opened it. Smashed into a dozen pieces. Funny, 'cause they were packed especially carefully, each piece triple-wrapped in Styrofoam and Bubble Wrap. Didn't break on my watch. Better not blame me."

She leaned over them, looking for an identifying mark, something that would help her place what they were, where they came from. Black-figure style, most cut in half, the heads separated from the body. She got on her hands and knees. One of the larger pieces portrayed a woman holding her hands in front of her, as if she were receiving a gift. Other pieces were smaller, mostly feet or hands. Another larger piece featured a woman with a long, full dress, her head covered. It was a wedding scene. Kate had studied similar works at university and was certain these were pieces of an ancient Greek vase. As she inspected them more closely, in the corner of one of the fragments she saw the letter *A*.

An *A*. To Kate, that could only mean one thing. *A*, as in "Amasis made me." If she was right—and she was almost certain she was—this vase had been painted by the Amasis Painter, one of the most accomplished of the black figure painters. Only eight vases in the world had been signed by the Amasis Painter. If that *A* was what she thought it was, this was an exceptionally rare and ancient work of art.

Kate felt a rush of adrenaline. This was something. This was *definitely* something.

But why was it here, and why was it broken up like this? Why were there no other fragments in the crate or any of the others?

She took a dozen photos and stood up.

"Alex, could I ask one more thing?"

"I'm not opening another crate unless you promise to buy me a new hip. I just destroyed this one. Too bad, it was brand new."

"No, that's okay. Just tell me where this one is going."

Alex wiggled off the forklift and stood up. He was bent over and dragged one leg when he walked. "I should be able to do that."

• • •

Kate's mother picked up her glass and disappeared into the kitchen. "You haven't been home for three weeks," she called out. "It's only a two-hour drive, you know. I don't know why you can't come more often."

"It's two hours without traffic, Mom. But there's always traffic." Kate sat down on her couch and picked up a magazine. *Beautiful Homes*. "Besides, we talk on the phone a lot."

A loud grinding noise came out of the kitchen. "What are you doing?" Kate called. No answer. "What is that?" she shouted, louder.

The grinding continued for a few minutes before the house fell silent again.

"Do you want a margarita?" her mother asked.

"What?" As far back as Kate could remember, her mother was a strict two-glasses-of-white-wine-a-week individual. "Since when do you drink margaritas?"

"Since last week. I saw a recipe in a magazine and thought, why not?" She walked out of the kitchen with two large tumblers filled to their yellow brim, set them on the table in front of her, and sat down.

"Don't I get one of those?" Kate asked.

"Oh, did you want one? Sorry, I didn't hear you." Her mom got up and went back to the kitchen. She was back in a minute with a glass for Kate.

"This is good," Kate said after a quick taste. "But margaritas? Mom, I'm shocked. You've always been so . . . I don't know—"

"Boring? Is that what you were going to say?" She picked up a glass, put her feet on the table, and took a drink. "That was because of your father. He was the strict one. Since he died, I can't imagine any reason not to enjoy a drink or two. Or three or four. La dolce vita!"

"Sure, I guess. One or two, now and then."

"Oh, sweetheart, what am I saving it for? I'm almost seventy, for goodness' sake. What am I worried about? Dying young?"

"Right, well . . . you know. Don't turn into a wild woman on me."

"You could use a little la dolce vita yourself." Her mom took a long gulp from her glass and held it in her lap. "You were always studying too hard to get out and have fun."

"Was not! I had lots of fun. That was a long time ago. Can we just—"

"Not that long. I was worried about you, sitting at home every night."

"I didn't go out because there wasn't anything to do. How many times can you drive up and down Chester's Main Street?"

"That all depends who you're driving with."

"Okay, Mom." Kate felt herself getting flushed. She did not want to talk about that. It was a long time ago. Nobody cared. "Moving on. I'm sure we can find something else to talk about."

"Sure." Her mother emptied her glass. "I hope you're getting out now that you're in New York. Are you seeing anyone? Have you made any friends?"

Another subject Kate would prefer to avoid. After three years in New York, she still hadn't formed even a sliver of a social life. It wasn't that she hadn't tried. She had joined a book club, but couldn't keep up with the reading and quit after two months. That was it. Admittedly, she hadn't tried very hard. She'd never felt comfortable with online dating or the bar scene, and it didn't help that she worked in an office with only three people. As it was, her best friend in New York was the elderly man who worked in her grocery store. She felt her mother looking at her, waiting for an answer, desperately hoping her only daughter hadn't become a recluse. Kate felt too much pressure to tell the truth.

"I have met one man. His name is Luca. But it's early, so I'd rather not say anything if you don't mind?" The relieved smile on her mother's face made Kate feel guilty.

"I'm so happy! But I won't say a thing. Promise. Did you want another?" Kate's mother was standing in front of her, two empty glasses in her hands, her eyes glowing. She looked happier than Kate had ever seen her. Maybe being a wild woman wasn't such a bad idea after all.

CHAPTER FIVE

Paul looked at the two men sitting behind the Philadelphia Museum's reception desk. They were leaning over the list of guests, reading the names with a magnifying glass. He thought they looked older than the antiquities in the exhibition. He started to walk past them, but they looked up and shouted at him and he had to stop.

"Your name, sir?"

"Klugman. Paul Klugman."

They went back to the list. "I'm afraid I don't see your name on the list, sir. I'm sorry."

"No, I'm on the list. Absolutely I'm on that list. I came all the way from L.A. today because I am on that list, which is why I am here, to see Richard Demeter's presentation at the opening of the Mesopotamia Exhibit. He invited me personally. Told me, three times no less, how much he wanted me to be here today. Do you understand what I'm saying?"

"Our apologies. Give us another moment." The men at the desk went through the list of names once again.

"Maybe they spelled Klugman with a *C*," Paul added. "Happens all the time."

"That might be it." They picked up another list and started going through that, magnifying glasses in hand.

"Look, if you don't mind, I'm just going to run to the washroom while you're looking."

"Yes sir. Again, our apologies."

He walked into the exhibit room and headed straight to the bar. After spending an hour and a half on the train to get here, and shelling out good money to rent a tux for this faux-elegant affair, did those two old guys really think he's going to stand around waiting while they look for his name on a list? Total bullshit. No one deserved a drink more than he did.

"Manhattan on the rocks, please. Rye. Not bourbon."

The Manhattan was a little dry, but not bad. He looked around. He recognized a few people wandering around the gallery, mostly from magazine articles and newspapers. Sir Nicholas Something-Something, director of the Tate. Marina Abrams, Abromov, Aba-Something, a performance artist who was famous for doing a seventy-six-hour performance piece at MOMA. Dan Loeb, who was famous for having lots of money. Tom Hill. Now there was somebody who really was somebody. One of the few people Paul respected in this business. Knew art, knew business, had money. Good-looking, great suit. He even had all his hair. Guy had everything.

While he was waiting for the presentation to begin, Paul strolled around the room. He had to admit, this was an impressive collection. The Cylinder Seal of Prince Isma-ilum, from about 2450 BC. Beautiful. A bronze statue of King Shulgi, about 2094 BC. Nice. Wonder how much those are worth?

A thin, elderly man with a goatee was standing behind a lectern, holding a microphone. "Excuse me?" he said, but no one paid any attention. He pushed a button on the microphone and said "Excuse me?" again. This time it was loud enough to crack an eardrum. Everyone stopped talking and looked around. "Oh, my. Ha, ha. Well, I suppose that's better.

"I'm Jeffrey Saunders, as most of you know, and I'd like to introduce our special guest for the evening. Richard Demeter has a degree in classical archeology from the New York Institute of Fine Arts and trained at the Ancient and Classical Art Department of the Museum of Fine Arts, Boston. He is a globally respected scholar on Greek art, gems and jewelry, and has published authoritative papers on Greek vase painting and the history of antiquities collecting. Richard has been co-curator of the Art Gallery of Los Angeles for the last three years. He's here today to introduce the Art of Mesopotamia, an exhibition that covers over three millennia, from 3200 BC to Alexander the Great's conquest, currently on loan to the Philadelphia Museum . . ." He went on. And on. And on.

Paul went back to the bar and ordered another Manhattan. These speeches always seemed to last longer than the civilizations they were droning on about.

Richard walked to the lectern and picked up the microphone. He still looked exactly like the Richard that Paul had gone to school with—hadn't aged a bit. Like one of those handsome actors in a second-rate war movie, the guy that always joked around but got the job done. Paul would bet money he used Botox and hair plugs.

"First of all, I'd like to thank the Philadelphia Museum for hosting me today," Richard said. "I hope I can live up to that flattering introduction."

While Richard went on in his irritating Boston accent about the wonders of Mesopotamia and how important they were to the world (we know, we went to high school too, you pompous ass), Paul searched around the room. Everyone stared in rapt attention as Richard held court, as if some kind of art angel had descended from the heavens. They nodded vigorously at everything he said, laughed at every lame joke. Paul forced himself to smile just in case Richard looked over and saw him.

After the speech, the polite applause, and another round of thanking everybody for everything, Richard finally gave up the microphone. Paul finished his drink, stood up, and walked toward Richard. He had his own speech ready in his head: "What a fantastic presentation, Richard! It's so great to see you! How is Jennifer? She is such a sweetheart. I just happened to be in town, wouldn't miss your exhibit for the world. Oh, did you hear about the Sican gold cup? Did Jennifer mention that? Yes, it's in perfect condition, such an amazing piece. You're going to fall in love with it. It would be a coup for your museum, a real prestigious . . ." But by the time he got near him, Richard was already surrounded. He was deep in conversation with ten or eleven men and women who seemed to share the same genetic makeup he had—all high foreheads and jutting chins. They were standing beside the statue of King Shulgi.

Paul pushed and elbowed his way through the crowd until he was right in front of him.

"Richard! How are you? What a pleasant surprise."

Richard turned his gaze toward Paul, a flash of annoyance crossing his face before he recovered with a big fake smile and two-handed shake.

"Paul. So great to see you."

"I wouldn't miss this for anything. Jennifer mentioned you'd be here."

"She did?" He acted surprised.

"She didn't tell you I'd called?"

"No, I don't think so. No, I would have . . . I would have called you."

Paul could tell he was lying. "That's okay! How have you been?"

"Great! Great. Listen, Paul, I'd love to chat, but I've got a few people here," he said, nodding to the crowd standing around, silently waiting their turn. "Can we catch up later?"

"Absolutely," Paul said. "Maybe we can grab dinner or something while you're here."

"That's a great idea. But I'm heading back to California tomorrow."

What? Jennifer said he was going to be here for ten days.

Richard said, "I'll see you there, alright? In L.A.? If you're in town?" He looked like he was about to run away.

"Great, yeah, sure," Paul said. "I was going to say, I've got this piece you would definitely be interested in. It's Sican. Gold cup, perfect condition."

Richard just turned around to the crowd behind him and started speaking with them.

Just like that, it was over.

What a waste. What an entirely soul-sucking, shitty waste of time and money and fake smiles. Paul had flown to L.A., flown back, taken a train and rented a tux, for nothing. He stood behind Richard, staring at his back, and felt his fingers tightening into a fist. All he wanted to do, at that moment, was land one solid punch to the side of that arrogant bastard's head. Right on his ear. Just hard enough to knock the ignorant shit on his ass.

After coming all the way here, after the century-long speeches he had sat through, he'd earned that. Just one solid punch. He could hear his heart pounding so loudly he guessed people nearby could also hear it, but didn't care. Figured he would be arrested, charged, maybe go to jail and get sued and lose everything, destroy his career. He didn't care. Demeter had insulted him for the last time. He'd never liked this waste of human flesh, wanted to do this since university, and now was his chance. He took a step closer, then two. Clenched his fist tighter. Now all he had to do was get the right angle. Right there, on the side of his head. That should do it. Knock him out cold.

Someone on the other side of the room called Richard and he walked away, leaving Paul standing alone by the statue of King Shulgi.

He looked at the statue and took a few deep breaths. His fingers unclenched.

"Hey, king. Whatcha up to?"

The king just stared back, apparently as uninterested in Paul as everyone else.

"Listen. I've got a favor to ask," Paul said. "There's someone I'd like you to sacrifice to the gods for me. Do you think you could arrange that? That guy over there." Paul nodded toward Richard. "If you don't mind, could you just kill him, cut him up into small pieces, throw his heart to the birds and bones in some volcano or whatever it is you guys do? I think the gods would really like it if you sacrificed that guy. 'Cause he's a real fucking jerk."

The king didn't respond. Just kept staring ahead, looking imperiously bored. After a few moments, Paul walked back to the bar.

"Another Manhattan."

He had to think of a way to sell that damn cup. It had been five days, and he had nothing and no one.

"He was, apparently, not a *very* good king."

Paul turned and looked at the man standing beside him. "Sorry?"

"He was not a very good king, or so they say. King Shulgi, the statue you were asking to commit a human sacrifice for you."

The man smiled and lifted his glass. He looked older than Paul, maybe sixty. Had the air of an independently wealthy academic—perfectly fitted suit, long and stylish white hair, and the soft, calm eyes of a man who had never had to worry about money. Or anything, for that matter. British accent, but not the irritating kind.

"You heard that?" Paul asked.

The man lifted an eyebrow and smiled. "Happened to be walking by."

"I was just kidding around," Paul said. "He made a pretty good speech."

"Of course. A stellar speech, if a bit long. My name is Harry." The gentleman offered his hand and Paul took it.

"Paul."

"You know, I once heard an interesting story about old King Shulgi. It's said that he once ran one hundred miles in one day, from Nippur to Ur."

"Why would anybody run a hundred miles?"

Harry swirled his wine around in his glass and sniffed, but didn't touch it.

"Apparently, he was getting back at his father. You see, he was envious of the success his father had had, old King Ur-Nammu, who really was a great king. His people worshipped him. He had protected his kingdom from invaders, built grand temples, gardens and orchards, supported art and culture, invigorated the economy.

"When he died and his son Shulgi took over, well, the young buck couldn't live up to the legend of his old man. So junior Shulgi spent his life trying to prove he was better than his father by accomplishing ever more amazing feats—or more precisely, claiming to have done so.

He wrote great hymns about himself, declared himself a god, and announced to his people that he had run a hundred miles, all in one shot. Which, of course, he hadn't."

"Good for him. I can relate."

"You can run a hundred miles?"

"Ha," Paul laughed. "To being in the shadow of his father."

Harry sipped his wine. "Your father is an accomplished man?"

"I guess you could say that. He owns a big chain of retail stores. Klugmans."

"Successful men do leave large shadows," Harry said. "My father was an architect. Sir Denis. Built the Royal National Theatre, amongst others. He has been knighted and has his own Wikipedia page, so I suppose he is considered accomplished."

Paul looked around the room and noticed that almost everyone had left. Richard was nowhere to be seen.

"What is it you do, Paul?"

"I'm an art dealer."

"Isn't that interesting." Harry stood up and placed his business card on the bar. "Perhaps we can have dinner sometime. I'm a collector."

A collector? Paul felt a flush of adrenaline course through his veins. Had his luck changed? "Of course. Dinner would be nice," Paul said. "I'd like that. Funny, I just acquired this new solid-gold cup you might be interested in. It's Sican—"

Harry held up a finger and smiled. "Specializing in Greek and Roman. I'm looking forward to that dinner, Paul. I'll be in touch." He stood up and walked out.

Dammit. Of course. Why couldn't he be a specialist in Peruvian artifacts? Paul crumpled up his card and threw it on the floor.

• • •

"Ghenette?" Paul asked.

"Ghenette. With an *F* sound. Ghenette Teitelbaum."

"Well! Finet. It's nice to meet you."

Paul had arrived early for his appointment with Ghenette (Finette? Fette? It sounded like "Feet" when she said it, but was that just her accent?) at the Art Gallery of Minneapolis. It had been six days since he'd flown into Miami Airport with the Sican cup, and he hadn't had a single offer. He'd called every museum and gallery, at least the top fifteen, and not had a solitary nibble. Which is how he ended up here. He couldn't wait forever, and there were credit card bills to be paid. So he called the Art Gallery of Minneapolis and asked to speak to the curator. He half expected them to say they didn't have one, but they did. Ghenette-Finette-whatever. She had agreed to see him right away.

"Have you been here before?" she asked.

"I have not, unfortunately. It's very impressive." Paul tried to look impressed by raising his eyebrows.

"Why don't I take you on a short tour?" she asked.

"Absolutely!" All he really wanted to do was hand over the Sican cup, collect his money and leave. But he had to be polite. "I'd love to look around."

He followed her to the museum's first hall, a collection of contemporary art. "We're often overlooked on the grand scale of museums, Mr. Klugman. I think it's simply because we're not in New York or California. But this museum has over ninety thousand artworks. We have an Egyptian mummy, a Monet, and we have five thousand years of some of the most prized artworks and artifacts in the world. The Africa and Americas Department has over three thousand objects alone. We have a reasonable collection of Renaissance art, and as you can see, we have an impressive collection of contemporary art from all over the world."

You have one mummy, Paul thought. Big deal. There are at least thirteen in the New York Museum. Still, he had to admit, the museum was more impressive than he had expected. They walked into a room filled with dozens of ornately carved miniature bottles made of ivory, gold, and precious stones. "What are these?"

"Chinese snuff bottles. They used to stuff them with powdered tobacco and inhale it up their noses. Seems disgusting, I suppose, but they are incredible little works of art." She stopped in front of a deep-red circular piece small enough to fit into the palm of a person's hand. "This is carved out of a rhinoceros horn. It depicts the Eight Treasures of Buddhism that lead to a virtuous life. Rather like an eighteenth-century Stephen Covey."

"The Eight Habits of Successful Buddhists."

She laughed. "Exactly."

They left the hall and went up the stairs. Ancient Egypt. She walked over to a small ivory carving.

"This is one of my personal favorites. The goddess Sekhmet, from around 1000 BC. The head of a lion, the body of a woman. She was the goddess of war and protector of the throne. Girl power was alive and well in ancient Egypt."

"Impressive." Then he saw the look she was giving him. "I'm not just saying that. This piece. Everything, everything you have. This museum is really great."

"Did you think we were just some small-town museum when you called?"

"No!"

She smiled and waited.

"Well, yes. Honestly, I did. But I was wrong. You really have something here. This is an outstanding collection."

"Thank you so much. We are smaller, so we must be more creative. We're trying. Come with me." She grabbed Paul by the elbow and guided him down the hall, back down the stairs and into her office. "Shall we have a look at your Sican cup?"

Paul nodded and carefully opened the crate, pulled the piece out, and placed it on the table in her office. The thrill of carrying it around in a cardboard box had dimmed, so now he packaged it up in a proper wooden crate when he moved it. For a few moments, they both stood there and looked at it.

"It is stunning," she said.

"I've had a lot of offers, of course, but I couldn't help thinking it really belonged here. In Minneapolis, a home that would appreciate it for what it is. Somewhere that understood everything it meant, that understands the important contributions Sicans have made to civilization."

"You don't need to patronize me, Mr. Klugman. I'm aware that we're not your first choice."

Did Jennifer tell her that? Bitch.

"It's yours if you want it. I'm willing to make it very reasonable."

"I do hope so." Ghenette slid on a pair of white gloves. "We're not the New York Museum or the Drake. We don't have their millions."

"Understood. What do you have, if you don't mind me asking?"

"That's not up to me, Mr. Klugman," she said, running a finger over the dent in the side. "It's not exactly in perfect condition, is it?"

"There is a slight aberration. I believe it occurred during the original burial ceremony, so it's part of its history. So, yeah, it's pretty perfect."

"I'm afraid it isn't. The damage is new. If it was original, you could tell by the coloring. I assume you have provenance?"

"Absolutely." Paul pulled a file of papers out of his pocket. "Everything's all above board. One hundred percent."

"Of course we'd need an appraiser to look at it. And I'd have to run it by the board. But my guess, assuming everything is what you say it is . . ." Ghenette walked around it, occasionally running a finger over its surface. Lifted it, feeling its weight. Mumbling quietly to herself.

It wasn't going to be a million. He knew that. Not here. The best he could hope for was five or six hundred thousand. No way was he going lower than that. This was a beautiful piece, she even said so. "I think this could be a real statement piece for your museum. Something that could really get you noticed. People would realize this museum—"

"My guess is the board would be comfortable with something in the range of three hundred thousand."

Three hundred thousand? What? *What?* No.

"I don't know if we can even do that," she said. "But is that in the area of what you were expecting?"

No. Not even close. Why did he even bother coming to this two-bit little town? Why? "Well," Paul began, trying to maintain a dignified, scholarly voice. "Based on similar pieces, and what I have heard from other curators, I had estimated more than that. Perhaps more in the range of—"

"Mr. Klugman. I like your piece. We'd be proud to have it. But I can almost guarantee that's as high as they'll go. Would you like to leave it with us? If not, we'll have to pass."

"No. No, I mean that's okay." He was out of time, options and, most of all, credit. "I'll leave it with you. Thanks."

Paul stood up. Three hundred thousand for this? What a waste. He was barely coming out even.

"It was nice to meet you," she said. "And I appreciate the offer. Really."

He handed her the papers and walked out.

That cup was supposed to be his golden ticket. Put some money in the bank, give a boost to his reputation, open some doors. He would be lucky if it paid off his credit cards.

And what was even worse? Now he had to go visit his father.

CHAPTER SIX

Luca stared at Kate over the Zoom camera. He was sitting in another outdoor café, a glass of white wine on the table. Behind him, a row of brightly colored buildings sat on the edge of a coastline dotted with fishing boats. Above them, what looked like a castle, or a church, rose halfway to the sky. "There's no sign of it anywhere?" he asked. "Have you looked through eBay? Facebook?"

"Until my eyes bled. I also looked through Kijiji, and every other corner of the internet, including the dark web. Which is really disgusting, by the way. Did you know there are sites dedicated to the best ways to do drugs? For hiring contract killers? They have sites that post lessons on the best ways to torture people. How sick is that?" She stopped and peered at him. "Where are you exactly?"

"I'm in Porto Venere. Can you see? It's nice, isn't it?" He leaned back and adjusted the screen so she had a better view of the ocean. It looked like a travel poster. A large, blue-feathered bird with a red beak landed on the concrete wall behind him and stared out at the coast.

"It must have been retouched," she said. "Nothing can actually look like that. What are you doing there?"

"Working. Research." Luca adjusted his screen and came back into view. "You should come and visit sometime."

Was that an invitation? That was definitely an invitation. She should probably start packing right away. "I'd love to. What are you researching? The best place to drink wine before lunch?"

Luca grinned. "You know, all I do is work. Investigating art crime is a 24/7 job."

"Be honest. Are you actually investigating art crimes, or is that just a cover for a luxury Italian vacation?"

"Travel is part of the job. You must build relationships, get to know the artists, collectors, agents, dealers, curators, local officials, and the bad guys. Especially the bad guys. The better they know you, the more they tell you. This is a people business."

"You should tell my boss. The only travel we do is to the coffee machine and back. The only people I meet are . . ." She looked at Geri, hunched over his computer. "Here, I'll take you on a tour." Kate picked up her laptop and turned it around so the screen displayed what was in front of her. She walked to the office kitchenette, which consisted of a dirty counter, a sink full of dishes and a stained coffee pot. "This is where we travel for our cappuccino, or as we call it, watered-down coffee that tastes like rotting fish from the Hudson River. Nice, isn't it?"

"Very nice," Luca answered. "I love it. Bellissimo. It's beautiful."

"Plus, we take a lot of trips to extremely exotic locations. Like, say, Geri's cubicle." She walked across the office and pointed her screen at Geri. "Say hi to Luca, Geri!"

Geri looked up from his computer and glanced at Kate's screen. He managed a slight nod and a pig-like grunt before turning back to his desk.

"As you can see"—Kate turned the laptop around again and walked back towards her desk—"my job is very glamorous, everyone here is warm and friendly, and the views are spectacular. I feel sorry for you, being stuck in Porto Venere like that. Bet you wish you were here."

"I do," Luca said. "I will come and visit, for sure. It's so hard to find good rotting-fish coffee in this country. Do you live in New York?"

"1500 Academy Street, apartment 578, Jersey City, New Jersey. Come by any time."

"I'd love to."

She sat down. Two invitations already. Maybe she wasn't lying to her mother after all. "Honestly, I searched everywhere and couldn't find anything like the sphinx you're looking for. Nothing. But there was one thing I thought might be interesting."

"What was that?"

"When I went to Customs to look for the sphinx, I found something else." Kate told Luca about the broken ceramics, and what she thought must have been the fragments of a black-figure painting. That it may be a work by the Amasis Painter.

"But it was broken? Where?"

"Where? Well, through the middle, mostly. Around their waists. And from top to bottom, between the figures."

"Not through the faces? Or heads?"

Kate thought for a moment. "No. Not once."

Luca leaned back in his chair, put his hands behind his head and shut his eyes for a few moments. His lips moved, as if he were talking to himself. He took a deep breath and leaned back. "I have no idea what that could have been."

She paused, waiting, but he didn't ask her to follow up, try to get the ceramics back, or check where they were being shipped. Nothing. "You don't?"

"No."

"But it was a black figure vase. I'm almost certain it's by Amasis."

Luca shook his head. "No, I don't think so. Well, maybe. But you don't need to spend any time looking into that."

She took a deep breath before speaking. "Luca, can I ask you something?

"Of course."

"I want to ask you about the sphinx. And listen, don't take this the wrong way. I understand what it represents—but not really. The part

I don't understand is why you're so invested in finding it. Why do you care so much?"

"What? What do you mean, why?" He looked at her as if she must be mad. "We should all care. This is our history," he said. "This is who we are. It's our culture."

"I know, and I get it. I do. Don't misunderstand me. I want to stop this as much as you. But—and this is sad and heartbreaking and everything—but Italy is like one big open museum. You know that. Parts of your history go missing every day, and it's been like that for hundreds of years. It's a tragedy and I know we have to do everything we can to stop it, but that sphinx is just another one of hundreds of pieces that go missing every year, and you know you can't find them all. So why is it? Why is that sphinx so much more important than everything else?"

Luca replied quickly. "They are all important. Every single piece."

"I know that. But so is that black figure vase, and you just told me not to spend any time on that."

He picked up his wineglass, emptied it, and put it down again. "I know."

"But why? You said yourself you're overwhelmed. Yet you're investing all your time on one marble sphinx. Why?"

Luca looked back over his shoulder, taking in the view of the ocean. He took his feet off the table and leaned into his computer screen. "You're right. It isn't just another piece of our history."

"Then tell me what it is."

Luca took a few slow breaths. For once, he looked dead serious. When he spoke, it was quietly, as if he were concerned someone might be listening in. "It's not just another sphinx."

"I'm getting that."

"It's something that . . . umm . . . it is, what would you call it? Extremely significant."

"Yes, yes. Still a bit vague. Can you be a little more specific?"

Luca nodded at the waiter, and a minute later another glass of wine landed on his table. In the background, a yacht sailed by. It looked big enough to land a plane on. He adjusted his chair so he was facing the ocean and put his feet up on the short concrete wall. Then he put his feet down and leaned into the camera again.

"No."

"No what?"

"No. I'm sorry, but I can't."

Kate adjusted her laptop, put her feet on the desk and grabbed her rotting-fish coffee. "Why?"

"It's not . . . I just can't. I can't tell you."

Kate put her coffee cup down and crossed her arms. "Maybe you need to try harder."

Luca winced and closed his eyes.

Kate waited for more, but nothing came. "That's going to be a problem. I want to work on this, I really do, but I'm afraid you're going to have to do better than 'it's not just a sphinx,'" she said. "We're overwhelmed too. I've got hundreds of missing artworks I could be searching for. I've got a boss who is wondering what I'm doing all day, complaints piling up, my anxiety level is near breaking and I'm already working twelve hours a day. And you can't even tell me what it is I'm looking for? I can't just keep working on this and ignoring everything else unless there's a reason. Eventually, I'm going to need to explain to Camilla why I should make this my priority."

Luca flinched.

"So you won't?"

"Non è possibile. I can't."

"Why? You don't trust me?"

"It's not that."

"So what is it?"

Luca was silent. For a few moments, they just stared at each other.

Again, Kate waited for more, and when it didn't come, she shook her head. What was he hiding? She wanted to work on this case more than anything, but if he didn't trust her, wasn't even willing to share the most basic information about what they were looking for, it felt like he was wasting her time. Like he was taking advantage of her.

"So, anyway, this has been great! But sorry, I've got to go. There are other files I have to focus on for now. If you ever want to tell me what's going on, let me know, okay? Thanks, talk soon." Kate closed the app and went back to her coffee. After a few minutes, she opened her email. Two new Zoom invitations from Luca. She ignored them.

• • •

"Push your thumb against your nose." Camilla raised her hand to demonstrate, putting her thumb on her nose and finger against her forehead. "Like this." Shutting her eyes, she started breathing slowly, heavily. "Go ahead. You'll be amazed at how it helps you relax. And focus."

The last thing Kate wanted to do was meditate. However, other than running out of Camilla's office, she didn't see any way out of this. She pushed her thumb against her nose, put her finger against her forehead, and took a deep breath. Then two.

"How do you feel, Kate? Relaxed?"

"Yes, so relaxed." She didn't feel relaxed. She felt like an idiot.

"Isn't it amazing?" Camilla took another slow, loud breath. "This will turn your life around. Let's start with twenty minutes."

Twenty? *Twenty?* She must be kidding. "Great!" Kate said.

"Don't think. Just focus on your breathing. Calm. Peace. Love."

"Just breathing. No thinking. Calm. Peace. Love. Got it." Kate shut her eyes and thought: Luca is being an ass, expecting her to work on his file without telling her anything about it. Maybe she should try to find out more about the vase fragments she saw at Customs, despite what Luca said. It's almost like he didn't even know who Amasis was.

"Are you focusing on your breathing?"

"Yes! I sure am." If they were being smuggled, they could be part of a larger smuggling ring. It wasn't likely that anyone would ship just one vase, right? But why would they smuggle something that was broken into pieces? She should check with other galleries, and stores, and museums—someone must know something. That was an idea.

She started to make a mental list of who she needed to contact as soon as she got out of there. *Good thinking, Kate.* Maybe this meditating thing wasn't a complete waste of time after all.

"And that's twenty minutes," Camilla announced.

Kate opened her eyes.

"How do you feel, Kate? Do you feel relaxed? Peaceful?"

"I do," Kate nodded, emphatically. "Very peaceful. I feel at one with myself. Thanks so much for that."

"When you're relaxed and at peace, all the hurdles that life throws at you become like small pebbles."

"Right! I totally understand what you're saying." From now on, Kate decided, Camilla's name would be Maharishi Robot. "Not to change the subject or anything, but can I ask you a question about something else?"

"Of course."

Kate told her about the broken ceramics she had found in Customs.

"Smugglers," Camilla replied. "That was a stolen antiquity. That's what they do. They take the vase, vessel, krater, whatever it is they've stolen, and break it into smaller pieces, and often pack it in different crates, to avoid detection. If they're human or animal figures they don't break it over the face so the cracks aren't as noticeable after it gets put back together. Then they sell it."

Luca must have known. But he didn't say a thing. "And it's never seen again?"

"Precisely. You'll have to file a report on it. Let Customs know, and your contact at the Carabinieri. I'm sure they'll be interested."

She was right. They should be. So why weren't they?

Kate knew that broken vase was being smuggled. Which meant the gallery they were being shipped to was, possibly, part of a smuggling network. An international network, maybe. She didn't know, but it wouldn't hurt to go there and have a look around, see if she could find out anything.

Kate got up to leave and was at the door when Camilla stopped her.

"By the way, how is that file you're working on with the Carabinieri? The missing sphinx?"

Kate pursed her lips and looked at the floor. "It hasn't gone anywhere."

"Unless they have a good reason for us to keep working on this, I think you've spent enough time looking for their missing sphinx. We need to take care of our own matters first. Let's park that file and move on." Camilla went back to work on her computer. "I have another case I'd like you to look into. A couple in Manhattan reported a stolen painting yesterday."

• • •

The couple were sitting on a black leather couch in their two-room Manhattan apartment. Seniors, or close to it. She was wearing a faded dress two sizes too big, and he wore a sleeveless white T-shirt tucked into gray polyester slacks that bunched up around his crotch.

"It's a very rare, valuable piece. Priceless, if you ask me. By Frederico Montefeltro. You know him? *Kapow*," the woman said, wiping her eyes and smearing her mascara. "I can't believe it's gone!"

"Kapow?" Kate asked.

"*Kapow*."

"What is Kapow?"

"That's the name of the work. You know it? I'm sure you must know it. It's famous."

"No," Kate replied. "I don't think I recognize the name Frederico—"

"He's famous," the husband said. "I bet you do know him. Everybody that's cultured does. He's such a grand talent. Absolutely grand. Hungarian, you know."

"Spanish!" his wife interrupted. "Or Italian."

"She's right. Spanish or Italian. My mistake. What an artist! And it's such a beautiful piece." The man pointed to an empty space above the couch. "*Was* a beautiful piece."

"And it's gone!" the woman wailed. "Gone!"

"It's worth forty thousand dollars, you know," he said.

"Forty-five!" she exclaimed. "It's insured for forty-five thousand."

"It was near and dear to our hearts, you know," the man continued. "A real keeper." He got up, walked to the window and looked out, rubbing his neck. "We live in a crime-infested neighborhood, that's for certain." He turned around. "No disrespect to our boys in blue, but this place is going to the dogs."

"Where did you buy it?"

"A private dealer in Newark," the woman answered.

"I'm sorry about all this." Kate pulled out a notepad. "I'll need your names, and photographs if you have any. Appraisals, insurance, invoices, and any provenance you have. I assume you have proof of the insurance?"

"Sure do!" she said, jumping up. "I'll get the papers."

Kate looked around the apartment. It didn't look like the home of anyone who would own a painting worth forty-five thousand dollars. The furniture looked like it was made before the last world war, and the only art on the wall was a landscape print that could have been purchased at a grocery store.

"What do you think, agent?" the man asked. "Can you get it back?"

"Very few missing artworks are returned, unfortunately," Kate told him. She had an overwhelming hunch that the couple wasn't interested in getting the piece back, if it had ever been theirs. What they wanted was forty-five thousand dollars from the insurance company.

"Shame," he said, wiping his face with a blanket. "Shame."

His wife returned with a series of photographs of the painting. It was a faded, scratchy illustration of a comic superhero, his fist punching the air, with the word *kapow* in large yellow letters across the top. Like a Lichtenstein, but different. More distressed, somehow. Like it had been left out in the rain.

"It's very textural," the woman said.

"Yes," her husband chimed in. "That's what first attracted us to it. The texturalness."

Kate gathered the photographs. "And the appraisal?"

She handed Kate an appraisal from a company called NorthRidge.

"Thanks," Kate said. "We'll look into it."

As she walked out, she couldn't help wondering: Was it stolen? Was a scratchy painting of a cartoon worth forty-five thousand dollars? She tried to muster up a sense of interest in the case, but she couldn't. Nothing. It was an insurance scam. Let the insurance company worry about it. But those broken ceramics? That was an ancient Greek vase. And what if it was by the Amasis Painter? That would be history. And so was Luca's missing sphinx, if only he wasn't being such an ass. That was the stuff that mattered. International smugglers, rich private collectors, ancient cultures, rescuing important art and bringing it back to the country it belonged to. That's the kind of case she wanted to work on. Not Stanley Cup rings. And definitely not *Kapow*.

CHAPTER SEVEN

Paul's father was in his backyard, going through a series of warm-ups and stretches that made Paul wince. He was swinging his right leg straight up and straight back, then his left leg, as if he were in some old Russian military parade. His red Adidas track suit looked like it was made in the 1970s. Knowing him, he probably bought it used. For a multi-millionaire, he was the cheapest bastard Paul had ever met.

"Should you be doing that?"

"Of course I should," his father said, panting. "I'm training for a marathon."

"That's a horrible idea. You should not be running marathons."

"Why not? Because I'm seventy-three?"

"Yes, because you're seventy-three. Marathons aren't good for you. They're not good for anyone. The first guy who ran a marathon died right after it was over. That should have been a lesson for eternity, not an inspiration."

"You look like you need a good run as well. Putting on a bit of weight there, kiddo. Why don't you join me?"

"I don't feel like running. I feel like having a drink and going to bed."

"Suit yourself." His father dropped down on the ground and did ten push-ups. "But I'm not sitting around here chatting. I've gotta run."

"You know I just drove eight hours to see you," Paul said.

"Come on, you need the exercise. You're getting fat."

"I'm wearing a suit."

"So what? I'll run slow."

"I can't."

"Why not?"

"I just can't, okay? Let's just not."

"What's the matter with you?"

"It's because I'm wearing Testoni shoes, okay? Testonis. These shoes cost me three thousand dollars."

"Ha! I should have known. What kind of a jerk spends three thousand dollars on shoes? C'mon, let's go." Paul's father turned around and started jogging down the driveway. "You want to talk to me, you better hurry," he shouted.

Paul waited until his father was on the sidewalk and had almost passed the house next door before giving in. He ran to catch him.

"How's the dollar store business?" Paul asked.

"Can't complain. The worse things get for everyone else, the better they get for us."

"So they must be pretty good."

His old man was already getting ahead. "Closing in on nine hundred stores. Even when you sell crap for a buck apiece, at nine hundred stores it adds up."

Paul tried to catch up to him, but his feet were already hurting and his breath was becoming ragged. It had only been one block. He really did need to get back in shape.

"And you? What's happening with your . . . what is that you do? Antiquities?"

"Antiquities. Ancient art."

"Right. Ancient art. How's that going?"

"I just sold a gold cup to the Art Gallery of Minneapolis."

"What'd you get?"

"Three hundred grand."

He stopped and looked back at Paul. "Three hundred grand, hey? What did you pay for it?"

"Two hundred and fifty."

"That's a decent mark-up."

It sure was, thought Paul. Just seven hundred thousand dollars less than he should have got.

"How many of those things have you sold this year?"

"One."

"One?" His father groaned and started running again. "So your total annual income this year is fifty thousand dollars."

"Minus other costs, more like forty."

"Let me guess. That means you need money."

"A little, yeah. I guess I could use a little." Like a few hundred thousand .

The old man sped up, and Paul was almost out of breath.

"Listen, Paul, I know you like what you do," he shouted back. "But I think you need to start getting serious about your life. Why don't you join me in the business? It's time. And I could use a hand."

The idea made Paul shudder. He would rather shoot himself in the face than work at his father's business.

There were times, growing up, when he thought he might shoot himself. His family had enough money to send him to a private school—in fact, they probably had more money than most of the other kids' parents at the school—but when you tell kids in that social bracket that your father runs a chain of dollar stores, you get nothing but smirks and insults. The other kids all had parents who were politicians, lawyers, doctors, tech tycoons, bankers. Their wealth came from old money, respectable money, not from stores that sold cans of tuna for ninety-nine cents. Which made Paul little more than a punch line throughout his school years.

"You could still do what you're doing, you know, that art stuff, whatever, part-time. Be a great hobby for you, right? But come and join me. You learn the ropes, work your way up, and one day you take over the place. Pretty good deal, huh?"

Paul remembered the summer he spent working in the office. He was nineteen. For four months, he sat in his cubicle day after day, pretending to work and listening to his old man shout into the phone. It was always about money: getting a better price from suppliers, employees, real estate agents. Talking them down, bargaining for an extra nickel here, a dime there. "Why you sticking it to me?" "Know what? Eff you. I can get a better price in five minutes." "I'm going to walk." He'd slam the phone on the desk, repeatedly. "Hear that? That's me walking." It seemed like every other call ended with a phone being thrown across the room.

Paul's life had been planned out for him long before. Even when he was a child, hiding in his room reading books by Robert Louis Stevenson, Roald Dahl and Lewis Carroll, he knew what was expected of him. He would study business at university, then work with his father. Spend a few months in one of the stores, on the front lines, then onto head office where he would work his way through different departments—marketing, finance, sales—and when he was ready, into the corner office with the old man. Take over when his father was ready to move on. Paul didn't remember ever being asked, or even discussing any of this. It was just understood.

But something went wrong.

You could blame it all on Giotto. Or perhaps Donatello. Yes, better to blame him. And Gentileschi, that poor, brave, brilliant soul; she was also responsible. Also Parrhasius, Arellius, Velázquez, Bernini, Caravaggio; blame them all, and dozens more. But if you were forced to choose just one person to blame, that person would be the professor of Paul's art history class, Hayden Maginnis. It was Professor Maginnis who opened the doors to the strange and beautiful world of art, a world as far removed from ninety-nine cent cans of tuna as was humanly possible. That was the world Paul fell in love with. Somewhere between the first art history class and the final exam, Paul decided this was what he would do for the rest of his life. A world not of cheap plastic toys but priceless, beautiful art. And if he couldn't be an artist (he didn't have that kind of talent), well, he did have a business degree. He could be a dealer.

At least he'd thought he could. Now, after eight years of trying, he wasn't so sure.

"Think about it." His father was running backwards, shouting at Paul. "You're going to need more than a little money if you're going to buy shoes like those. And I can't just keep giving you money."

Who was he kidding? Of course he could. If he wasn't such a cheap bastard, that is. What was a hundred thousand dollars to him? "I will. Just let me give it one more try. Let me give it a real chance." Paul stopped running, bending over to catch his breath. "Hold up. Wait."

His father stopped. He wasn't even breathing heavily. "You've been at it for eight years. I'd say that was a real chance."

"There are a lot of things happening. I can feel it."

"My bullshit meter is hitting eleven right now. I made my offer. You want money, you take the job. Now get your ass moving. We've got another four miles to go." He turned around and ran.

Paul wished he could start running and keep running and never stop. Maybe that's why King Shulgi wanted to run a hundred miles: not to one-up his father, but to escape. To disappear from the world and never come back. In his heart Paul knew his old man was right—eight years was a long time. He'd had his chance and had nothing to show for it. Which just made everything that much worse. He couldn't work at the dollar store. He had promised himself he would never, ever sink that low again.

• • •

But the sad fact is, overdue rent and past-due bills are more powerful than even the most heartfelt promises. After his father offered Paul a "signing bonus," which felt more like extortion, he caved in to the inevitable and agreed to work in the store. Just for now, he told himself. Until he saved up a few bucks. He could quit anytime.

He started work the next morning. It felt like walking into prison.

"If you want to work in the business you got to start with the basics. And you do that here, in the store, on the floor. The front lines."

But I don't want to work here. You're forcing me to do this. He walked down the aisle, past the ninety-nine-cent garden tools, kitchen utensils and tinned foods. The store smelled like plastic and air freshener, and his shoes kept sticking to the floor as if someone had spilled soda on it.

His father walked ahead of him, pointing out the items that sold the most and which ones didn't. "See this? Kids' plastic baseball set. Hugely popular. We sell it for three dollars. Guess what it costs me?"

Paul didn't want to play this game. "I don't know."

"Guess. Take one guess."

"I don't . . ." But what he wanted didn't matter. It never had. It was always about what the old man wanted. "Two bucks?"

"Wrong! Cost me a buck fifty. Got them from some company in Mexico, or China, doesn't matter. So I make a buck fifty. What's a buck fifty, you're thinking, am I right? And that's where you're wrong. I sell about four, maybe five hundred per store every year. Ninety stores. What's that add up to?"

His father was looking at him with his eyebrows raised, and it took Paul a minute to realize the old man was expecting him to do the math.

"Sorry, how many?" Paul asked.

"Four hundred. Ninety stores."

"I don't know. Eight or nine thousand?"

"Not even close. It's six hundred bucks per store. Ninety stores, that's . . ." The old man was looking at him with raised eyebrows again.

"I don't know. Forty-five thousand? Something like that?" Paul was already bored out of his mind, and he hadn't been there for more than ten minutes.

His dad grabbed the bat, pulled the plastic ball out of the package and threw it up in the air. "God help us. It's simple math, kid. Fifty-four thousand. Fifty-four thousand! For this piece of junk." The ball came down and he took a big swing at it, missing by a few feet. He picked it up and threw it in the air again for another swing. "Since you're obviously mathematically challenged, I'll explain. That's more than you made in an entire year. This cheap bat made more money than your fancy gold cup." He swung, and this time he made contact. The ball went rolling down the aisle. A solid single.

"I get it," Paul said. "You have hundreds, thousands of items in here. And you multiply the buck fifty by all the items, and all the nine-hundred-something stores. I get the drift."

They walked around the corner, where a woman with pink streaks in her hair was stocking shelves with plastic drying racks. She turned around and offered a quick nod and a tight sliver of a smile.

"Hi, Mr. Klugman."

"Yeah. Hi."

"I'm Tabatha."

"Of course. Hi, Tabatha."

Tabatha looked around thirty years old, with anxious eyes and a sea of freckles dotting her face. Paul was about to say hi when a customer walked in, picked up something near the front aisle and rang the bell on the counter. Tabatha hurried back, took care of the customer, and returned to the drying racks.

"Tabatha? The dish-drying racks go on the bottom shelf. Dish soap on the top shelf. We've talked about this."

"Sorry, Mr. Klugman. I'll change them now."

Paul's father rolled his eyes. "Everybody says sorry."

"I am sorry," she said. She didn't look sorry. She looked like she wished she could punch him.

"The higher-margin stuff goes at eye level. How many times do I have to say that?"

"I know, I said I'm sor—"

"Sorry isn't going to pay the rent. So, rather than being sorry, how about just get it right the first time?"

She stared back for a few moments and Paul was sure she was going to tell him to go to hell. Instead, she turned around and started moving the drying racks to the bottom shelf.

"And don't fuck it up," his father said.

They stood and watched. Paul almost felt sorry for her.

"Finally. Okay, that's better. Tabatha, this is my son, Paul."

"Hi, Paul." Tabatha turned around and looked at him. Her face was an unnatural shade of red, and she looked at him with her head down, sneering and breathing hard. Like a bull getting ready to charge.

"Paul has a PhD in art history."

"Isn't that sweet," she said with a delicate curl of her lips.

"Tabatha, I'd like you to show my son the ropes around here. Show him how it's done."

She forced a smile, but the effort almost broke her jaw.

Paul wanted to turn around and walk away. But he couldn't. Not now. Not after he had agreed with his father to "just give it a shot," knowing he wasn't getting any money from the old bastard until he did. The idea of running a chain of dollar stores made Paul want to throw up, but he had an American Express card that wasn't going to take no for an answer.

"I'll leave you two alone. Tabatha, you're in charge."

His father disappeared.

"I have some new shipments that have to be unpacked," she said, turning and walking away, sneer held firmly in place. Paul followed her to the back of the store.

"How long have you worked here?" he asked.

"Ten years," she answered, without looking back. "Why?"

Why? I don't know. Why not? Why anything? Why work here? Why put up with bullshit from my old man? Why ask questions, why try, why think, why live? Why work hard all your life just to end up working at a shitty place like a dollar store? Why go to school, why have dreams about making a career in the art market, if you're just going to end up stocking shelves with dish soap and drying racks? Why anything? "Just wondering," he answered.

She opened the door to the back room and held it for Paul. "You can start in here."

The door swung shut. A pile of sixty or more cardboard boxes sat in the corner.

"Did you know your dad once called me a lazy, stupid, dog-ass-face?"

"I didn't know that. We don't talk much about work." But Paul wasn't surprised. His father was a bastard to anyone not in his family. Actually, he was a bastard to everyone in his family as well. "I know he acts like a bit of a jerk sometimes. But that's just because he *is* a jerk."

She half smiled. "See those boxes over there?"

"I do."

"Unpack them and put them on the shelves. Think you can figure that out, with your degree in art history?"

"I think I can figure it out."

"There are fifty-seven boxes there. They have to be unpacked and put away by early afternoon. There's another truckload coming in at three o'clock, so . . ."

Paul walked over and picked up one of the boxes. He just about threw his back out.

"Oh, and Paul?"

He looked over at Tabatha, who was standing at the door with her arms crossed.

"Don't fuck it up, okay?" She walked out.

Within twenty minutes, Paul had already learned an important lesson in working at a dollar store: Never wear a three-hundred-dollar shirt to work. Forty-five minutes later, Paul had unpacked exactly one crate of Cheetos and one box of Instant Noodle soup. There were fifty-five boxes to go. And he was supposed to have these done by early afternoon?

Tabatha's voice screeched over the PA system. "Paul Klugman? Customer checkout in number two."

He walked into the store and towards the checkout counters. Tabatha was in aisle number one, reading a copy of *Us* magazine.

"I don't know how to work this thing," he whispered to her.

"But you have a degree in art history," she said. "Surely you can work a cash register."

"You have to show me how."

"No, I don't. I'm in charge, remember? I decided that you can figure it out." She held up her magazine. "Besides, I'm busy."

"What the hell? Why are you doing this?"

"So you can personally experience how your father has treated me for the last ten years—and everyone else working in his stupid-ass stores."

"It wasn't me! I didn't do that!"

"No. And maybe after this, when you become the big boss, you never will."

"This isn't a one-man job! I've still got all those boxes to unpack."

"No? Isn't that funny, because apparently it's a one-woman job. See, I've been doing this all by myself for ten years, and I didn't take a single class in art history."

"Look, I need your—"

"I'm sorry, but look. I'm not asking you to do anything I haven't done ten thousand times. So quit whining and get to work." She went back to reading her magazine. "I have to catch up on what the hottest stars are wearing this season."

Twelve more customers and four hours later, Paul still had at least forty boxes to go. He was sweating, tired, and so bored that his skull felt like it would crack. It seemed like he had been working here for a hundred years.

Tabatha appeared at the back door. "It's three o'clock. That new shipment is coming soon and you're not even close. Is something wrong?"

"I keep getting interrupted!"

"Thought it was easy, huh? You're kind of pathetic, to be honest."

"Fuck off."

"I'm in charge. So I get to decide who fucks off."

She walked away. Paul lay down on the boxes and stared at the ceiling.

He was still lying there when the truck rolled into the parking lot. And when the driver opened the delivery door and walked into the warehouse. The driver asked Paul when he was going to unload the truck, and Paul didn't answer.

He was still there when the driver gave up, slammed the truck door shut and drove off.

He was still there when Tabatha walked into the room, laughed and said, "Your father's going to disown you for this."

Paul knew he couldn't do it. Couldn't unpack boxes, ring in customers, or stock shelves. Strike me dead, someone. Put me out of my misery. I can't do this, I can't do anything. I can't make it in the art world, I can't even make it in the dollar store world. Please, take me out and shoot me, hang me by the neck and disembowel me, let horses drag my body parts through the streets. Anything would be better than this.

He was still lying there when, an hour later, his phone rang.

"Hello?"

"Hello, Paul. It's Harry. How are you?"

Harry? Harry . . . what Harry? Oh, right. Harry from Philadelphia. The King Shulgi guy, from the museum. Why was he calling him? "Harry? Right, Harry. I'm fine—no, I'm not fine. Honestly? It's been a horrible, awful, nightmare of a day."

"I'm so sorry to hear that. Is there anything I can do to help?"

Paul sat up. He couldn't remember the last time he had heard a friendly voice. "No, I'm afraid not, Harry. I wish you could. This nightmare is my own doing. But thank you for offering."

"Listen, Paul. Perhaps there is something I can do to make it a little better."

"You couldn't make it worse."

"Would you care to join me in London for dinner tomorrow? I have something I think you'd like to see."

And Paul, staring up at rows of fluorescent lights flickering above him like a universe of dying stars, drowning in an infinite void of bone-crushing hopelessness, tried to resist the irresistible temptation to believe a lifeline had just been thrown his way.

CHAPTER EIGHT

A "Stone Elbow Pipe," pre-Columbian, limestone, that looked like it had been found in an abandoned construction site. *Leda and the Swan*, a bronze sculpture by Christian Miller, that would have been X-rated if there were a rating system for stolen art. *Tempest Temptress*, a painting by Christopher Rote, which looked somewhat interesting in a postmodern kind of way. Three New England Patriot Super Bowl rings, inscribed with "Kato." Occasionally, one of the cases Kate worked on was interesting: A few months earlier, she'd recovered a stolen 1735 Stradivarius. Most—like the case on her desk, a missing map of Lima Post Office routes from 1850—were not. She posted them on the website and had forgotten them before she took her finger off the submit button.

For the third time that morning, her phone buzzed and Luca's name appeared on her screen. This time, desperate for any distraction, she decided not to ignore it. She grabbed her phone and stepped into the hall.

"Hi, Luca."

"This will just take a minute," Luca said. "I have something important to tell you."

Of course he would think what he had to say was important. But so was what she had to say. "Did you look at the information I sent you on the broken ceramics?"

"Not yet," he said. "I will, one day. But right now, we must focus on the sphinx."

Unbelievable. She had discovered a rare, smuggled, ancient Greek vase, and all he had to say was "I will one day"? "I'd like to, Luca, but I'm very busy right now."

"I need your help on this case. I'm asking you to please—"

"And I would like to help you. But I can't keep putting our own files on hold for this. Unless you can tell me why it's so important, there's no way—"

"I have zero authorization to do that. But there's something I can tell you."

Kate was about to tell him that Camilla had told her to park the file, but Luca spoke first.

"There's been another murder."

"What?"

"A car drove off a cliff on the highway near Balze, in the north. The driver was killed. It was reported as an accident. But later we discovered the driver, a man named Gamal Saleh, used to own the marble sphinx. He ran a small art gallery in Cairo. He's the one who sold the sphinx to the woman who donated it to the Gandolfi Museum. Remember her? Angelina Bernardi."

"Yes, I remember. But you're sure it wasn't an accident?"

"Certo. We are positive."

A dead guard and ticket agent at the Gandolfi, and now a dead art dealer. It had to be more than just another marble sphinx. But what? "You have to tell me what it is. Why it's so important."

"I'm sorry, I can't."

"Maybe it's a coincidence."

"It's not."

"So tell me what's going on!"

"Kate. I want to tell you. I would love to. But I've told you everything I can. This is not Luca's decision. This is the Italian government's decision. They take this stuff very seriously. If I told you, I would be the one in jail."

"I'm already behind on about a hundred files. We have more coming in every day. I don't have time to just—"

"This is different."

"How? Just give me a clue."

"I told you, I have zero authority to do that. That doesn't mean it's not important. You'll have to trust me."

"I have to trust you. But you won't trust me."

"It's not that. I do. It's just that, this case, it goes beyond Italy's borders. There are people in New York involved. We have to work together, or else. We need your help. It's our only chance."

There was a note of desperation in his voice. She thought about Camilla telling her to drop the file, and how she would react if she found out Kate was still working on it. Which reminded her of the files Camilla did want her to work on. *Kapow?* Lamps? A route map from the Lima Post Office? Come *on*. And maybe, maybe, Luca did have a good reason for not telling her.

In the end, she decided it wasn't about whether he trusted her or not, or what Camilla wanted, or what Luca thought she should do. It was what she wanted. She wanted to work on important files, and she thought the sphinx was important, more important than any of the other files piling up on her desk. So that's what it came down to. She wanted to, so she did.

"Okay, okay, okay. Fine," she said.

"Fine?"

"I'll help you."

She heard a breath of relief. "Grazie mille. I'm glad. I missed you."

She was about to tell him that she was not authorized to work on his file anymore, but decided against it. She'd just have to find a way to tell him, and Camilla, later.

"The woman. Bernardi. How did she die?"

"Natural causes. She was ninety-eight years old. Nothing suspicious."

"So what should we do now?" she asked.

"I wish I knew. I'd have done it."

"Well . . ." If he didn't know, with all his experience, how would she? "Have you posted a reward?"

"Remember, no one can know this is missing."

"How about posing as a buyer?"

"That's a good idea. But we believe that whoever stole the sphinx already had a buyer. Someone who has a thing for ancient Greece, perhaps, or whatever this piece represented to them. And, of course, lots of money. All the thieves had to do was deliver it to them and collect their payment."

"That makes sense," Kate said. She heard the sound of cutlery, voices, and a loud whistle in the background. "Where are you?"

"On a train. Heading to Cinque Terre."

"Can you do me a favor? The next time I ask where you are, can you just say you're sitting in a little office cubicle? Just once?"

"By the way, we must move quickly," Luca said. His voice was cutting in and out. "Once it's . . . the buyers, it will . . . impossible to find. I'm excited to work with you again. I'm . . . the train is going into a tunnel, so if . . ." The line went dead.

I better go to Cinque Terre, Kate thought. Right now. Just to make sure he's okay. If he is in trouble, I'll have to save him, even though it would be dangerous and I'd have to risk my life. After I did that he would probably fall in love with me, because I was so brave and beautiful, and we'd end up traveling the world on a huge yacht, having a lot of crazy misadventures while we chased down art thieves with a glass of champagne in one hand and a gun in the other.

Focus, Kate. Focus.

• • •

Without any better ideas, Kate went back to searching online. After three days, all she had learned was that she was wasting her time. She was no closer to finding the sphinx than when she started. There had to be another way, but what? There were no phones to tap, no computers to trace, and no one to follow, because there were no suspects, no leads, no anything. Even the theory that the sphinx was in the United States was based more on probabilities than facts.

Kate wasn't even supposed to be working on the case, which made everything more difficult. She had gone rogue, sneaking around and searching in her spare time when no one was watching her. Even then she was making zero progress. It felt hopeless. There had to be a better way.

She walked to the window, pulled it open and stared outside. Watched the endless stream of vehicles and pedestrians, breathed in the car fumes and smelled the cooking hot dogs. What was it Luca had said? The Carabinieri sometimes posed as buyers to catch art thieves, except in the case of the sphinx they couldn't do that because the thieves probably had a buyer already. But wait.

If the thieves had a buyer, that buyer had to be someone with piles of money and an interest—not just an interest, an obsession—with ancient Greek artifacts. An obsession deep enough that they would risk arrest and prison to get their hands on it. There couldn't be many people who fit that description. So if we can't catch the criminals who stole the sphinx by posing as buyers, she thought, what if we posed as sellers? If we put the word out that we had some other Greek artifact for sale—something this buyer just had to have—he might contact us. That could work. Couldn't it?

Of course it could. She called Luca.

"Kate, it's nice to hear from you. How is everything?"

"I've been staring at a computer screen for three days. My eyes are burning and my brain has requested an organ transplant. But otherwise, great!"

"I'm glad you're having fun. Have you found anything?"

"Nothing." She told him how she had looked everywhere and had gotten nowhere. Explained how it was virtually impossible to find the piece, or the buyer, by searching online, or any other traditional approach. They had to try something different. "So, I had this thought. If we can't find the art collectors, why don't we get them to find *us*?"

Silence.

"Luca?" Kate asked. She checked her phone. "Luca, are you there?"

"I'm here." Another pause. "I don't know what you mean. They can find us anytime. We're not the ones hiding."

"Yes but, well, not us . . . I mean, we're not going to tell them who we are," Kate explained. "Listen. We know, whoever it is, that they're interested in ancient Greek artifacts, right? So we get the word out that we have something they want, something we're willing to sell that is so rare and valuable they would just have to have it in their collection. And they will find us."

More silence.

"Luca?"

"Scusa. Just thinking. We usually pose as buyers. You're suggesting the opposite. That we pose as sellers."

"That's the idea." She waited, anxiously drumming her fingers on the desk.

"It's like using bait to catch them."

"Yes. Exactly."

He paused. "It's a good plan," he finally said. "I like it. Very much."

"I know, right?" Yes, she was right! It was a good plan. Kate was the best rogue agent anywhere.

Another pause. "There wouldn't be many people with the interest and means to buy something like that. It could work. But—"

"But what?"

"The problem, if I have this right, is that you're posing as the seller, which means exposing yourself to serious criminals. Criminals who have already killed three people. That's three that we know of, there could be more. That is a concern."

Kate put her feet on her desk. Geri was out of the office, and Camilla's door was closed. She looked around the dusty, worn-out room and took a deep breath. She had left Chester three years earlier to escape the endless boredom and wound up here. Staring at computers, talking on phones, filing papers. *Yes, please. Give me something that puts me in danger. If someone doesn't put a gun to my head, I might do it myself.*

"So the thing is," Kate added, "I'm going to need something to sell. It should be from somewhere around the same time and place as the sphinx. And it has to be worth enough to get them to take a chance and contact us, you know? Something big enough to really shake the trees."

"I don't know what that means."

"I need something big to attract them," she explained. "If you want to catch a big fish, you need big bait. Big, precious, priceless bait."

"I agree. But where are you going to get something like that?"

Where did he think she was going to get it? "From you!"

"From me?" Luca thought about it. "Yes, but no, I don't think I can do that. I mean I wish I could, I like your plan, but there are too many risks. For you. And for us. You're asking us to risk losing another invaluable piece of art. I don't think anyone would accept that. And also, I don't have access to—"

"Come on, Luca. You live in Italy. You have hundreds, thousands, of galleries, museums, private collectors. There must be something." Kate realized it was unreasonable to ask them to send a valuable artifact to her. But then again, if this sphinx was as important as he said it was, why wouldn't they?

"Don't get me wrong. I wish I could. But you can't honestly think we will send a rare, priceless artifact to be used as bait?"

"Yes! That's exactly what I was thinking. You even said it was a good plan."

"It doesn't matter what I think." Luca shook his head. "They won't do it, Kate. Mai. Never. We may have a lot of them, as you said, but they are invaluable. They can't be replaced. No one is going to take a chance on losing another priceless piece of art. The insurance alone would be too much."

"Luca. It's not like you won't get it back." Kate did her best to sound confident, as if she had thought this whole plan through. But even now, as she explained it to Luca, she could see dozens of questions coming up that she hadn't answered yet. What if he agreed, and her plan didn't work? And what about Camilla? What would she think?

"Look, Luca. I get it. It's risky. For both of us. But if this sphinx is such a big deal, we need a better plan than searching online and asking Interpol for help."

"So ask your FBI Art Crime Team to provide something. There are a lot of Greek and Roman treasures in the United States."

"This is the Carabinieri's case. The piece was stolen from Italy. You asked us to help you find it. Remember?"

For a long time, Luca was quiet. It made Kate uncomfortable. She forced herself to stay calm, to wait, to not say anything. Maybe it was a crazy idea. But right now, it was all she had. And they hadn't come up with anything better.

"No. No, I can't do it."

"But Luca, listen—"

"We'll have to think of something else."

"You've already had two, almost three weeks, to think of something else."

"It's not just the 'bait' I'm worried about. It's you. These people, they're . . . they're not very nice. Do you know what you're getting into?"

A gray future of searching for lost lamps and hockey rings stretched out before Kate. "Just think about it, okay?"

CHAPTER NINE

The Savoy was one of those restaurants where you'd expect to see prime ministers, members of the royal family, and hedge fund billionaires cutting into plates of roast beef and Yorkshire pudding. You would, shortly after entering it for the first time, assume it was a place where loyalties were tested, borders shifted, wars started or were averted, and contracts were awarded over multiple glasses of gin and tonic. You would be right. Deep, wood-paneled walls, white tablecloths, and chandeliers the size of small cars whispered to everyone that this was an important place.

This was a restaurant that had earned its place in history. It was almost two hundred years old, and most of the staff appeared to be roughly the same age. So was the menu, which had yet to bow to the trifles of such trendy fashions as vegetables. The entrées were "simple and classic," which meant you could choose between roast beef and lamb.

"We're sitting at William Gladstone's favorite table," Harry announced.

Paul smiled and nodded. "Nice." As if he knew, or cared, who William Gladstone was.

"How is business with you?" Harry asked.

"Business is horrible, thanks for asking. It seems like everything is being sold directly through eBay or Facebook and bought by Russian and Chinese billionaires these days. The museums can't compete anymore. And dealers? Why go through us when you can buy online and avoid paying commission?"

"I'm afraid the internet has made intelligent dealers a dying breed."

A waiter appeared silently beside them, and Harry greeted him with a smile.

"Hello, Rupert."

"Good to see you again, sir. May I offer you something from the bar?"

"Might I suggest the Simpson's Old Tom?" Harry asked Paul. "They are a legend here, you know. Have been since the eighteenth century."

"Thanks, but I'm a Manhattan man. On the rocks. Whisky, not bourbon."

"Indeed. And I'll have the usual, Rupert. Thank you kindly."

The waiter disappeared as silently as he had appeared.

Paul's phone buzzed. His father. The third time he'd called today. He ignored the call and blocked the number.

"The internet is dumb. No one knows anything." Paul leaned back in the chair, his hands behind his head. "For example, there are dozens of original Greek vases painted by Exekias for sale online right now. I counted thirty-eight. Which is quite the trick, considering he only made fourteen."

"Oh, I agree," Harry said. "Of course, it's difficult to tell what's authentic these days. Some of the fakes are better than the originals."

"They're probably all fakes."

"How can anyone tell anymore? Proof of authenticity has always been more of an art than a science. A rather dark art, at that."

Paul looked around the crowded restaurant. Every customer looked like old money. Gentle manners, quiet voices, impeccably tailored suits, and elegant cocktail dresses. He was wearing a tailored Garrison suit and still felt underdressed.

The drinks arrived, and Harry picked up his Old Tom and toasted Paul.

"I'm a Eurydemos man myself."

"Sorry?" Paul asked.

"You mentioned Exekias. A brilliant artist, and master of the black-figure technique. But I prefer Eurydemos."

"Yeah, he's great too." Paul sipped his Manhattan. It was almost perfect, just a little light on the ice. "I bet a genuine Exekias vase would sell for a million bucks."

"Of course. You can find a decent replica on eBay for a couple of hundred dollars, if you want to put a price on it."

"I put a price on everything," Paul said. "I'm a dealer."

"Of course. Someone has to pay for the champagne and truffles, correct?"

"Correct."

For the next hour and a half, dinner passed in art talk. The latest rumors, gossip, and scandals, who paid how much for what, what was hot and what was not. They ordered roast beef. A waiter returned with a silver-domed trolley, lifted the lid, and pulled a knife with a long, thin blade from his belt. He carved the meat as if he were performing surgery on the Queen of England.

"Carving is its own art form," Harry whispered, as if he were afraid of disturbing the man with the knife. "Mukesh here is one of the best in the world."

For the hundredth time that evening, Paul wondered when Harry was going to get to it. What was it that Harry had said Paul would want to see? He'd hinted, on the phone, that he had a piece to sell. Hadn't he? Paul had gone there out of a sense of desperation, knowing he was out of options. He'd used most of the "hiring bonus" his father had given him to purchase airline tickets and book a hotel, all for some hazy idea that Harry had a great treasure he was going to offer Paul. Now, it looked like he had come all this way just to listen to this upper-class twit impress him with how much he knew about carving roast beef.

"Are you married, Paul? Children?"

"I was. Love, marriage, house, mortgage, the whole catastrophe. It didn't last. Thank God we didn't have children. It got messy."

"And your ex-wife?"

"She's now curator at the New York Museum."

Harry winced. "I imagine that could get awkward."

"It does." Paul quickly changed the subject. "And you? Married?"

"Oh, goodness no. Art is my wife, my children, and my mistress."

"Good plan," Paul said. "No painting ever asked me why I drink so much." The two men shared a quiet, hollow laugh.

Rupert had snuck up beside them again. "A bottle of your '82 Latour, please," Harry said.

Paul was tired, bored, and increasingly irritated. What if he had come all this way for nothing? He realized, now, that he had absolutely no reason to think that Harry was going to offer him some way to make a lot of money. It was just a desperate hope that someone would swoop in and save him. All Harry had said was that he had "something he'd like to see" that would make his day better. The rest was just Paul's intuition. Which, he admitted, hadn't been very intuitive lately.

What if Harry was just a lonely old man, looking for someone to drink with? What if he was gay, and this was supposed to be a date? What if he asked Paul to pick up the check? Was this just a con to get Paul to pay for a nice dinner? He felt like he'd walked into a trap, but he couldn't see where the trap was.

The Latour arrived, and in a painstakingly slow ceremony, the wine was drizzled into a long crystal decanter and poured into their glasses. Paul was tempted to grab the decanter from the waiter's hands and drink from it, if only so he could get out of there faster.

"A toast," Harry offered. "To art."

"To art." Paul clinked glasses.

They drank silently for a few minutes. Harry swirled the wine in his glass, sniffing and sipping, and Paul emptied his glass in three gulps.

"You are familiar with Eurydemos's work?" Harry asked.

"Eurydemos? Of course. Considered the best of the red-figure-style painters."

"I'm impressed," Harry noted. "Not everyone knows that."

"Don't be. It's not a state secret."

"You're too modest. Did you know his masterpiece—the one that is now in the St. Petersburg Museum—was found in Kerch?"

Oh, please don't go on, Paul thought, but he tried to act interested. "Everyone knows that. In Kerch, which is in the Crimea."

"It's known as the Crimea today, but it was an ancient Greek colony two or three thousand-odd years ago." Harry picked up his glass and took a tiny sip. He lowered his voice and looked around the room as if someone might be eavesdropping. "That masterpiece in St. Petersburg? It isn't the only one."

Even through the jet lag, the lack of sleep, a Manhattan and a glass of wine, Paul could read the not-so-subtle message Harry was sending. He was wide awake now. "There's another one?"

"Oh, yes. There is." Harry had a sphinx-like smile on his face. "And it's just as beautiful, perhaps more so. It is a breathtakingly gorgeous, stunning work of art."

Paul's heart skipped three beats. If what Harry just said was true . . . Was it possible? Everyone knew the Eurydemos Vase. It was one of the most famous vases in the world. Could there really be another?

That would be like discovering a second *Mona Lisa.*

"Are you serious? And you've seen it?"

"Yes, I have seen it."

"Wow. That's . . . interesting. No, it's more than that. It's unbelievable. Where is it?"

"It's in my apartment." Harry flashed a Cheshire cat smile at Paul and turned his attention to his roast beef.

If Harry really had what he said he did, it would be a piece that agents, dealers, and curators would whisper about over linen-covered tables and single malts from L.A. to Berlin. And if he did—was he hinting that he might sell it to Paul? Was that why Harry had invited him here? Paul tried not to think too far ahead, but he couldn't help it. A headline flashed in his mind: "Met Acquires Second Eurydemos Vase from Dealer Klugman." It would be the piece that established his name, that made him a recognized brand, that earned him access to grand events and invitations to dinners at the homes of Very Important People. This was only the third time in his career that he thought he had maybe, just maybe, landed the big one. He knew the feeling well, recognized every symptom: the shortened breath, slightly increased pulse and dry tongue, like he was having a mini-seizure. He told himself to slow down and took a deep breath.

"Would you like to see it?" Harry asked.

"Yes, I would." Of course he would. More than anything.

"Splendid. Let's go have a look after dinner."

Having been given the choice, Paul would have happily gotten up and left the table right then and there. Would have skipped the remaining courses, forgot the bottle of wine, and rushed out to see the Eurydemos. But Harry seemed content to sit and chat, so Paul sat and acted interested.

Harry ordered another bottle of wine and rambled on and on. Paul tried to listen, but couldn't stay focused; in the back of his mind, he kept hearing Lewis Carroll's walrus repeating "The time has come to talk of many things / Of shoes and ships and sealing wax and cabbages and kings," although he had no idea why. It just did, as if part of his brain needed something to do while Harry talked. Now that he had a reason to be there, Paul didn't mind. A lot of Harry's stories were lengthy but curiously entertaining, reminding him of reading one of those kids' novels, like *Gulliver's Travels*, that ran a hundred pages too long. You had to skip ahead sometimes, but couldn't stop reading until you were finished. His deep, melodic voice lulled Paul into a kind of dull stupor. And when Harry started delving too deeply into the minutiae of some small and irrelevant piece of antiquity folklore, well, the walrus was always there to distract Paul.

Finally, Rupert dropped off the bill (which Harry quickly picked up, reducing Paul's blood pressure by about half) and they made their way to the exit. An old, white Rolls-Royce was waiting on the street, two men standing primly beside its open doors. A chilly breeze was blowing and light rain had started to fall as they hurried to the car. Paul and Harry climbed in, the doors were softly shut and they drove off.

"Nice car," Paul said. It felt like sitting in a five-star hotel suite.

"Thank you," Harry answered. "It was one of my father's."

Paul could see all the familiar London landmarks as they drove: Buckingham Palace, Big Ben, what he thought was either Westminster Abbey or St. Paul's.

"You've been to London?" Harry asked.

"Only on business. Never saw much but the inside of airports, boardrooms, and museums."

"If you can stay for a few days, I'd be happy to take you on a tour."

As long as you're paying for it, I can stay for a few years, Paul thought. I just quit my job. "I might be able to manage that," he said. "Let me make a few calls."

• • •

Harry parked the car in front of his building on Denbigh Street. It was an old and elegant structure, a white, four-story walk-up with balconies accented by full gardens and elaborately framed windows.

"I apologize in advance for the appearance of my apartment," Harry said as they climbed up the stairs. "I haven't had it cleaned in absolutely forever."

"Everybody says that."

"But I really do mean it. You'll see why in a moment."

Paul was breathing heavily by the time they got to the top floor. Harry, who had been walking ahead, slowed down to let him catch up. By the time they reached his apartment, Paul had almost lost what little breath he had left in him. Harry opened the door.

At first, it seemed as if neither one of them would be able to walk inside. It was full, jammed tight to the edges of the walls and to the ceiling, almost every square foot of visible floor space taken up with, well, stuff. Old stuff. Random stuff. Big stuff and little stuff. It reminded Paul of walking into his dad's garage when he was starting his dollar store business and being overwhelmed with his collection of cheap, plastic household goods. Only these weren't cheap, or plastic, or even regular household goods. Even though most of the pieces were broken and covered with dust, mud and barnacles, Paul could see this was an invaluable collection of rare antiquities and ancient art.

Hundreds of pieces, almost a full museum's worth, were crammed into no more than a thousand square feet. Paul saw marble statues of athletes and animals, friezes capturing wars and military parades, and a vast array of ivory cups and glittering cutlery. There were piles of jewelry, swords and figurines, paintings, and vases. Everything looked like it had just been pulled out of the ground, still covered in centuries-old dirt, and almost everything was cracked or broken. The statues were missing noses, heads and arms, the ceramics were in pieces, and there were chunks missing from just about everything. It looked like an ancient warehouse that had been abandoned three thousand years earlier.

Paul had been inside the homes of some of the most well-known art collectors in the world. Industrialists, celebrities, a member of the royal family: billionaires and multi-millionaires who stockpiled famous art as if it were an amusing hobby. None of their collections looked anything like this. Theirs were elaborately framed or protected in thick glass and displayed for maximum effect, like prize deer antlers on a hunter's mantel. Harry's collection looked like a forgotten trailer in an episode of *Storage Wars*. It was, quite possibly, the most valuable junkpile in history. What was the point of collecting all these magnificent, rare works of art, Paul wondered, if you were just going to leave them lying around like this?

"Apologies again for the mess," Harry said. "I'm afraid cleaning isn't my specialty." He walked through a path Paul hadn't noticed, a thin strip of floor space that allowed him to navigate his way around the room. "Now, what were we looking for?"

"This is incredible! It's like your own museum! Where did you get all this?"

"Oh my, that's a question. I suppose the answer is most of the ancient world if you mean geographically. From one thousand to ten thousand years ago if you mean chronologically."

Harry was picking his way through the piles, brushing dust off the occasional piece and gently rearranging others. Searching for something. He picked up a piece resting on an old wooden table. It appeared to be made of gold.

"This is a death mask discovered in 1876 by Heinrich Schliemann. He claimed he had found the body of King Agamemnon, the king who commanded the Greek forces in the Trojan War."

Schliemann? How could Harry acquire a death mask discovered by Schliemann? "That's awesome."

"He was lying, of course. But it was a good story while it lasted."

Harry handed the mask over to Paul, who held it carefully, afraid he would drop it. It was stunning. The royal face looked peaceful, a smiling, bearded king with his eyes shut, his ancient power still emanating from inside the gold sheet.

"So it's not authentic?"

"Schliemann was known for salting his digs with his own creations. They say this is the second-oldest business in the world, but to me it often appears a lot like the first."

Paul continued to follow the dusty path cutting through the crowded room's many objects: A four-foot sphinx on the floor, nose missing. A rounded goddess, possibly pregnant, wearing what appeared to be three large crowns full of jewels and little else. Boxes full of jewelry, haphazardly strewn across tables and chairs. More death masks. In Philadelphia, Harry had told him he only collected Greek and Roman, but this was clearly not true. This collection came from all over the world. What was he up to? Was he really just a collector? Paul glanced over at him, saw him picking his way through a pile of sculptures, and just got an indecipherable smile in return.

"This is a stunning collection. You must have pieces from every civilization in the world."

"Last time I counted, there were twelve civilizations. But that was years ago."

"This must be worth millions. A lot of millions."

"I suppose you're correct. I don't have any idea. I've never thought to have it appraised."

"But you have provenance?"

Harry wandered over to an old desk, pulled a pile of paper out of a drawer and held it up. "Sales receipts, official statements, provenance for every single one. You can't purchase anything these days without a truckload full of paperwork. Boring but necessary."

Paul picked up a statue of a man with a worried expression on his face.

"Who is this?"

"His name was Imhotep. He oversaw construction of Egypt's first stone pyramid. Doesn't look like he's much enjoying it, does he? I purchased it from a farmer in Cairo. Didn't know what he had. Dug it up in his field one day and sold it to me for a few hundred pounds."

Paul guessed this piece alone could be worth close to a million dollars. "Why don't you sell it?"

"Oh, I couldn't sell any of this. It would be like selling my children. I'm a collector, not a . . . oh, here it is! Here's what I wanted to show you." Harry picked up a vase. "The Eurydemos Vase I mentioned earlier. Come, come here. Have a closer look."

Paul found his way over and leaned in. Unlike everything else in this dust-filled room, the Eurydemos Vase wasn't covered in centuries of grime, wasn't broken, cracked, or chipped. It was glowing, as if it had been recently restored, cleaned and polished.

Harry gazed fondly at the vase. "This is beauty."

On one side were six women in a variety of poses: one washing her hair, one hugging her pregnant belly. On the other side, a group of men, women and a satyr watching Apollo play the flute.

"Think of the passion that went into creating this masterpiece, all those centuries ago," Harry said. "Not for fame, not for money. For the pure love of art."

"Well, maybe for the money," Paul suggested.

"No. No, I don't believe that. A piece like this could only be created out of love. Just imagine all the time they must have spent shaping the clay, coiling, paddling, pinching and reshaping, painting and polishing, until it was . . . until it was this. That's why we love them, still, centuries after the artist himself, herself, has turned to dust." Harry was hugging the vase now, like it was a precious child. His eyes were tearing up. "Sylvan historian, who canst thus express / A flowery tale more sweetly than our rhyme . . . What men or gods are these? What maidens loth? / What mad pursuit?" He stared at it as if it were a long-lost love.

Paul tried not to roll his eyes. "Sure, it's nice."

"When I spoke to you on the phone, you sounded depressed. And I knew instantly what you needed. It was beauty, Paul. You needed to see something beautiful, to balance all the ugliness we see in the world. And here it is. Beauty. It's the only thing that really matters. Don't you agree? Doesn't this make you fall in love with the world again? Doesn't it make you fall in love with *life*?"

Paul didn't know how to answer.

"Now you can see why I could never sell this," Harry whispered.

What? No. He could never sell it? No, Paul could not see why he could never sell it. He could see hundreds, thousands, millions of reasons why he should sell that vase, and everything else here. To him! Why shouldn't he sell it? Otherwise, it was just sitting here. Wasted. Unless money was no object, but since when wasn't money an object? Wasn't that why he had asked Paul to come? To offer him this vase? To make a deal? Otherwise—

"Well," Harry asked, wiping a moist eye. "I hope you feel better. I know you do. True art lovers like us are such rare birds."

"We sure are." Paul stared at the vase and sighed. "And you're definitely not going to sell it?"

"Of course not," Harry answered. "How could I? Would you?"

For a moment, Paul considered killing Harry. Thought about how easy it would be. There were swords and knives everywhere. It would be simple enough to ram an ancient steel blade into this old codger's neck, grab a few pieces—or even just that vase—and run. After all the time and money he had spent getting here, that endless dinner, and getting his hopes up so high, murder would be justified. And after all, no one knew he was there, no one would know he did it. He could easily carry a few million dollars' worth of antiquities out of there and get away with it. Simple.

"I've got an old bottle of Rothschild that's getting near its best-before date," Harry said. "Shall we?"

But Paul knew he couldn't kill Harry. Not because he was worried about being caught, or because he didn't think he could kill anyone. Not because he didn't think he had earned the right to steal some of these treasures. He couldn't kill him because, despite everything—despite the fact that he believed Harry was at least half insane, that he had brought him all the way here for no reason, had pulled the rug of fame and fortune out from under Paul's feet, and tortured him like a cruel boy teasing a cat—no, Paul couldn't kill him for one simple, stupid reason.

He liked him.

CHAPTER TEN

When Kate walked into the office, Camilla was standing behind a vacant desk with a square wooden box, about a foot and a half high and wide, sitting on top.

Camilla pointed at the box. "A package came for you today. From Italy."

A jolt of excitement ran down Kate's spine. After five days without hearing from Luca, she'd given up. She'd assumed he had decided it was a crazy idea after all, too high a risk with too little chance of return. Kate had come to believe he was right. After going over the plan in her head one hundred times, thinking about everything that could wrong, she had convinced herself it could never work. But now, looking at that box, all those doubts disappeared.

The excitement didn't last. As her eyes traveled from the box to Camilla, she was reminded of another problem. Having convinced herself that Luca wasn't going to go ahead with her idea, Kate had never told Camilla about her plan, or that she had resumed working on the sphinx file.

"I believe we discussed the Carabinieri file," Camilla said. She crossed her arms and frowned, narrowing her eyes so that they bore into Kate's. "I believe we both agreed there were too many pressing matters of our own to be taken care of, and that this case had to be dropped. Did we not discuss that?"

"Yes, we did."

"And did you?"

"No. Not exactly."

"Not exactly? What does that mean?"

Kate felt sick. She had overstepped her boundaries, ignored orders, broken rules, and worst of all, she'd been caught. "I was going to tell you. But—"

"But you didn't," Camilla interjected, like a strict teacher speaking to an unruly ten-year-old.

"I didn't completely drop the file. I'm sorry, I know you told me to and I said I would, but I didn't. I should have told you, but Luca talked me into it, I mean, he just, well . . ." Camilla was staring at her, eyes blank and cold. This was not coming out the way Kate had hoped. She struggled to find some plausible excuse and failed. Tried to invent a story that would make this defensible but came up with nothing. So she gave up and went straight to full-on confession.

"He didn't talk me into it. It was me. I wanted to work on it, so I did. And I am sorry, but also, I really believe this case is important and I didn't think we should stop working on it. So I didn't."

"Against my direct orders?"

It sounded worse the way Camilla said it, but also accurate. "Yes," she said.

The Robot lifted her chin and her eyes grew wider and colder. Kate half expected her to scream, "I'll get you, my pretty, and your little dog too!" But instead, Camilla took a few deep breaths and shook her head. "Tell me something, Kate. Why shouldn't I fire you?"

She should have seen this coming, but now it was too late. Kate braced herself, getting ready for what was next. A depressing vision of herself packing up a box, walking to her car, and driving to Chester flashed through her mind. Let's just get it over with, she thought.

"You should have told me," Camilla said.

"I know." Kate stared at the floor.

"This is the FBI. You can't just ignore orders here." A few seconds of awkward silence passed. "Do you understand that?"

Kate lifted her eyes. "Yes."

Camilla's voice turned softer. "Just promise you'll tell me next time, okay? No more secrets."

Kate sucked in a deep breath and felt the muscles in her body uncoil.

Camilla said, "You're lucky Luca called me first."

Kate should have known he would do that. Of course he would. He had to—he couldn't just send over a valuable artifact without authorizations from the highest levels. It would have been nice if he had told her first so she could have told Camilla herself, but why would he? He hadn't known she wasn't supposed to be working on this file.

"He told me about your idea." Camilla smiled and looked at her with an expression of surprise, as if she couldn't believe Kate had come up with it. "It's not bad."

Kate felt a rush of relief and excitement. *Yes.* The world's best rogue agent had done it again. "Thanks."

"I suggested he work with Geri, but he wanted to work with you."

"Are you okay with that?"

Camilla shrugged and waved a hand in the air, as if it were out of her control. "Geri is already jammed, and so am I. So yes."

Kate nodded in response.

"Do you know what's in this box?"

"No idea." Kate picked it up, weighing it in her hands, trying to guess what it was. It was too light to be anything like a vase, statue or sculpture. Maybe coins? "Let's find out."

There were eight screws on each end. They had to search around the office to find a screwdriver. Kate's fingers trembled slightly as she turned the screws, half afraid to open the box. Her anxiety increased every time one of the screws popped out and rolled around on the table. The last screw finally came loose, and Kate pulled the lid off, looked inside—and saw another box.

The second box was also fastened with eight screws. After the last screw came out, she pulled the lid off and found a container made of hard foam. She pulled the top off the foam box and found a layer of bubble wrap. Something sparkled inside. She pulled the bubble wrap out and laid it on the table, pulled it open, and there they were.

The most beautiful pair of earrings she had ever seen.

They gazed at the earrings, then at each other.

"My God," they both said at the same time.

Kate reached out, but Camilla held up a hand. "The gloves."

Kate retrieved the white gloves from the cupboard and put them on. She gently picked up the earrings and stared at them in silence. At the top of the earrings was a circle of gold with finely carved flowers within, surrounded by a pair of golden horses pulling a carriage. Under that were two rows of jewels set in silver frames, glistening under the office's fluorescent lights, and five pendants hanging from thin lines of chain in the shape of snakes. Her hands were still trembling slightly as she turned them around, feeling their weight. A small paper sheet covered in plastic lay on the bottom of the box, like one of those plaques museums place beside artifacts on display. Camilla picked it up and read aloud.

"Gold earrings with disk and pendant. Circa 350 BC. A figure of Nike, the personification of victory, driving two horses is set amidst carriage-shaped forms on these extraordinarily elegant earrings. In all probability they were worn by Olympias, the eldest daughter of Neoptolemus I, king of the Molossians. She changed her name to Myrtale prior to her marriage to Philip II of Macedon as part of her initiation into an unknown mystery cult. In the summer of 356 BC, she gave birth to her first child, Alexander."

Kate was holding the earrings of Alexander the Great's mother.

She swallowed, a rising anxiety in her stomach. What was he thinking? They were too much. She wasn't expecting anything like these. No, they were perfect. They were exactly what she had asked for, the perfect bait, just what she had imagined. No, they weren't—they were far, far more than she had asked for. She set the earrings down, quickly, as if she shouldn't even be touching them. Why would he send something so rare? So priceless? She was expecting something along the lines of an old sword, a bowl, a few coins. Something valuable and rare, yes, but not anything like this. Not Olympias's earrings.

Their eyes locked as they both thought the same thing: What *was* that sphinx?

For a few moments, neither one of them spoke.

"Lock them in the vault," Camilla said.

"Of course. I didn't know . . . I didn't expect—"

"No. Neither did I. Lock them up. Make sure you let me know when you need them."

• • •

Kate called Cassie & Stone Art the next day. It was a "Fine Ancient Arts Gallery," according to their website. They sold antiquities from all over the world, and they were not cheap: Some of the pieces were priced at over a hundred thousand dollars. They had helmets, vases, bronze figurines, statues. Why wouldn't they be interested in a pair of gold earrings worn by the Queen of Macedonia?

"I'm afraid that's out of our price range," the lady on the phone said after Kate described what she was selling. "But they sound beautiful."

"I understand. If you change your mind, you can call me, although I don't think they will be available for long. My name is Judith. You can reach me here." Kate gave her the number Camilla had told her to use.

The response was essentially the same from Barnett's Ancient Art, the Richmond Marin Gallery, Braxton's, and every other gallery she called. She described the earrings to each of them, and they either didn't believe her or said they couldn't afford them. Kate hadn't even mentioned a price. If they had asked, she was going to quote two million, but she didn't actually know if that made sense, and thankfully they never got that far. She called eight galleries and thought, that should be enough. It was a small, close-knit industry. If eight galleries knew, it wouldn't take more than a few days before everyone knew. The trap had been set. If there was an interested buyer, they would call her soon.

She didn't have to wait long. The next evening, just after nine, the call came. Kate was already in her pyjamas, watching the news and wondering whether it was too early to go to bed.

"I understand you have a pair of earrings," the man said.

The voice on the other end of the line had an accent she couldn't place. It was part Eastern European, part New York, part humanities professor. "That's correct," Kate replied.

"I see. Can you prove they are genuine? Do you have all the papers?"

"I can, and of course I do. Are you interested?"

"Perhaps. Describe them to me, please."

Kate read the summary that came with the earrings.

"That is fine. We will meet in the lobby of the Four Seasons Hotel tonight at eleven. Bring them with you. And the relevant papers, of course."

She couldn't do that. The earrings were locked in the vault at the office.

"I can't do that. Not tonight. I'll send you a photograph, if you give me your email, or we can meet another time."

There was a pause on the other end of the line. Kate could hear the man breathing, struggling a little, as if he had asthma. "As you wish." He hung up.

Fine! Kate thought. That was not a legitimate buyer. Legitimate buyers don't ask you to meet them late at night at the Four Seasons. Or do they? Maybe they did. How would she know? She hadn't worked on anything like this before. She thought about calling Luca, but it was too late. She could call Camilla, but whoever it was had already hung up, so what was the point?

Ten minutes later, the phone rang again.

"I can't give you my email. But I am an interested buyer, and if you wish to sell your earrings, I'll have to see them in person tonight. If it's any comfort to you, the crime rate in the lobby of the Four Seasons is extremely low. You and your earrings will be safe."

He was right. He had to see them. And he sounded legitimate. This was exactly how the plan was supposed to work. So why did she feel like a hive of angry bees were swarming in her belly? She took a few deep breaths and calmed herself down.

Kate rang Camilla to tell her about the call and arrange to meet her or Geri at the Four Seasons. But she could only get Camilla's voicemail. Where was she? It was almost ten. If Kate was going to get the earrings to the Four Seasons by eleven, she had to leave soon. He said it had to be tonight. If she didn't do anything now, the whole plan could be lost. She called Camilla again—still voicemail.

It was time to leave. Kate jumped in an Uber, went to the office, signed the earrings out and left. She called Camilla one more time on the way to the hotel, to no avail. She would have to do this on her own. Okay, all she had to do was find out who the buyer was, get his name and contact information, establish a relationship. They could figure out some plan to catch him later. She made it to the Four Seasons at two minutes to eleven and rushed inside.

The hotel lobby was quiet. A few well-dressed customers huddled around the dark wood tables, holding champagne flutes or wineglasses and quietly laughing. Kate felt nervous and out of place. She had never been there before. Everything was hushed. It seemed as if the air itself was holding its breath. The straight-backed hotel staff glided noiselessly around, calm and under control. Kate walked up the stairs to the entrance of the restaurant.

A waiter greeted her with "Right this way, madam," then bent half an inch forward. "The gentleman at table eight is waiting to see you."

Kate tightened her grip on her purse and followed him, trying to figure out which table was table eight. A few moments later she saw a man nod at her. He reminded her of James Joyce, or maybe Joseph Goebbels: pale face, small moustache, round, black-framed glasses, and a well-tailored black suit on a thin frame.

The waiter made a short introduction and left.

"Hi, I'm Judith."

He stood up, bowed slightly, and offered his hand. "Hello, Judith. I am Jacob. Please. Sit down."

They both sat, smiling awkwardly at each other.

"May I offer you a drink?"

"I'll just have orange juice, thanks."

"Please. Have a drink. I'm having one." He smiled a thin smile.

"That's nice, but really, I can't. I'm on medication," she lied.

"I see."

Another awkward pause.

"Are you from Manhattan?" he asked.

"Yes," Kate answered. Yes, tonight she was Undercover Judith from Manhattan, the mysterious dealer in smuggled rare artifacts. Talented, confident, composed, just like Judith Leyster. Except she didn't feel that. She felt like a fake, and that everyone in the restaurant, including Jacob—especially Jacob—couldn't help but know that. "And you?"

"Oh, I'm from Europe," he said, which was about as vague an answer as was possible.

Kate tried to look calm and relaxed, but was certain she was failing. Her face felt frozen into a fake smile. How could she relax? She was in a strange place, making small talk with a strange man, trying to get information out of him while holding a piece of priceless ancient jewelry in her purse and wishing that Camilla would return her call and get over there. "What business?"

Jacob shook his head and chuckled, as if the subject of his business were too trivial to bother answering. "Oh, you know. Boring stuff. Numbers."

Again, not helpful. She needed to get him to identify himself, to give her contact information. Something. Anything. "How long have you been in New York?" she asked.

"It feels like forever."

Come on, thought Kate. Throw me a bone. "Have you been collecting for long?"

"No." Seeing her confused look, he clarified. "These are not for me. I'm acting as an agent for my clients."

This was not going well. She knew what questions to ask, how to act, what she was there to find out—who he was, where he was from, whether or not anyone else was involved. Any information that would be helpful in finding the sphinx. But so far, all she had found out was that he had a talent for evasive answers and wasn't even the one buying the earrings. How was she going to get him talking? One last check on her phone. No one had called.

Fine. She calmed herself down, forced herself to focus. Her looming anxiety attack would just have to wait until after this was over.

Kate called for the waiter.

"Know what? It's my birthday. I feel like celebrating," she told Jacob. "Do you like champagne?"

For the first time since she arrived, Jacob really smiled. "But your medication?"

"Oh, a few can't hurt. What am I saving it for? Right?"

"Of course. You are absolutely right."

"After he pours the champagne, I'll show you the earrings," she whispered, as if sharing a secret. "If you're interested."

"Oh, yes. I'm interested. We're interested."

The champagne was poured, toasts were toasted, drinks downed, and birthday greetings shared. They were deep into their second glass when he asked if he could see the earrings.

She took the box from her purse, unlocked and opened it, then pushed it over to his side of the table without letting go. He stared for a moment.

"May I?"

She didn't want to let go. What if he tried to run with them? What if he refused to give them back? She hesitated, but there was no way around it. She held her breath and let go. "Yes. Of course."

He picked them up and spent several minutes looking at them, examining them closely. Pulled a monocular magnifier out of his pocket and studied them for a few more minutes. Finally he nodded and put them back in the box, which Kate put back in her purse.

She started breathing again. *Safe.*

"That is a wonderful, extremely rare piece. Where did you get them?" he asked.

"My grandfather found them in his attic."

Jacob chuckled. He seemed genuinely amused. "Of course he did. And do you have all the papers in order?"

"Naturally."

It took two more glasses of champagne before he really started talking.

Jacob had been sent by two men he didn't know well but were "a couple of strange brothers with lots of money." From New York, he guessed, they didn't say, but he thought they were Swedish. He knew their names but refused to tell her. Jacob was a connoisseur and appraiser of Greek and Roman artifacts, and the brothers had paid him to verify the authenticity of the earrings. They'd promised they would make an offer if he confirmed the piece was legitimate.

They ordered dinner—he had steak, she had fish—and glasses of wine. Kate told him about the summers she spent working in museums and living in a small town. He told her stories about growing up in his own small town, but he never said which town and avoided any details that could be checked later.

It was long after midnight before they finished, and the restaurant was almost empty. The waiter brought the bill, which Jacob paid, and they stood up to leave. Kate, a little drunk and still nervous, immediately dropped her purse. The contents spilled across the marble floor. For a second, she froze. In a panic, she crouched down, feeling around under the table for the box. When she found it, she opened it to check the earrings were safe. They were. Jacob helped her pick up everything else. They shook hands, and he promised to send an offer to her the next day.

Kate had planned on taking the earrings back to the office and locking them in the vault, but it was late, she was exhausted, and she'd drunk too much champagne. The office was almost an hour away. It would be easier, and probably safer, if she locked the earrings up in the cash box in her apartment and returned them to the vault in the morning.

When she got to her building, she discovered her keys were missing. She must have dropped them when her purse fell. Damn. She might be a brilliant rogue agent, but she was also a klutz. She buzzed the concierge, who let her in and unlocked the door to her apartment. She'd have to figure out where her keys were later. Right now, it was more important for her to write down everything she remembered while it was fresh: what Jacob said, what he looked like. She wrote her notes and filed them away.

It had gone well, she thought. The risk of using bait had paid off. She had made contact, and an offer was coming. Her plan was working perfectly. She felt like celebrating, so she poured a glass of wine and stared at the earrings. She had to fight the urge to put them on, just to see what she would look like wearing these gorgeous works of art. That's not what they were there for, not why the Italians had trusted her with these invaluable pieces. These were truly rare, absolutely priceless artifacts. Just think—the Queen of Macedonia wore these. It seemed almost sacrilegious to even think about putting them on.

She poured another glass of wine and put them on anyway. And took about twenty selfies.

Before long, she realized she was wobbling when she walked and bumping into furniture. It was time to call it a night. She carefully locked the earrings in the cash box. Now she just had to wait for the offer and they could set the trap. *Yay, Kate*. What a perfect plan she had come up with.

She went to bed and was asleep in seconds.

CHAPTER ELEVEN

Paul stared out of the hotel window at London's dark, foggy, dreary city skyline. It was three o'clock in the afternoon, the day after he met Harry, and he hadn't gotten out of bed yet. Big Ben struck again, and it sounded like a death knell. It was time to face reality. He had nowhere left to go. No more hopes, no more dreams he could imagine without an ironic, bitter, soul-scorching laugh. Couldn't make it in the art world: His last chance had just evaporated with the tears falling from Harry's eyes. Couldn't even make it in his old man's dollar store business. His future stretched out in front of him like a black hole, an infinite void of indescribable mass that was capable only of sucking in light, incapable of giving any back. He shut the curtain and went back to bed.

So when Harry called the next morning and asked if he'd like to join him for lunch, he said yes. And when Harry asked him if he'd like to "pop into a museum beforehand," he also said yes. Any distraction from the dark emptiness of his life was welcome. He would have said yes to a Monday night mixed-league bowling tournament in Toledo. It wasn't like he had anything else to do, except try not to think.

They met the next morning on the steps of the British Museum. Visited only one exhibit: *Crouching Venus*, a Roman marble sculpture from the second century AD. Paul had no idea why Harry wanted to see it. She wasn't particularly beautiful. Her ass was flat, she was sagging everywhere, and, besides, she was a copy of a Greek bronze that had been lost, so not even an original. But Harry seemed infatuated with her, and talked on and on, while Paul grinned and agreed with everything he said.

They had lunch and spent the rest of the day wandering the streets of London and visiting other museums and galleries. Paul thought he knew a lot about antiquities and art, but Harry's knowledge far surpassed his own. He seemed to have memorized every textbook on every age and every piece, to have an intimate knowledge of every king and emperor, every civilization, every great and not-so-great artist and piece of art that had ever graced this gray planet.

Over the next few days, they visited more museums, galleries and restaurants. The constant buzz of Harry's voice had an intoxicating effect on Paul. He found himself forgetting what an abysmal failure he had turned out to be. He felt like he was getting an education, not just in ancient art, but in life, in culture, in manners, in being civilized. It seemed as if he was learning how to become one of those born in the rarefied air of the upper-upper classes, as if he had spent his life on private tennis courts and surrounded by butlers. He imagined he was experiencing his own personal Age of Enlightenment.

He even found himself copying Harry's mannerisms, his speech affectations, his infinite optimism and unending courtesy, his way of finding something interesting and affirming in even the most mediocre pieces of art. Once again, it wasn't just art. In every meal, in buildings they passed, window displays they commented on, people they watched, Harry found something positive to say about everything and everyone. He never spoke with a splinter of sarcasm or negativity. Paul had never heard this kind of optimistic outlook from anyone before, and he absorbed it into his bones, felt its gentle warmth and comfort soaking into his soul. It really was nice to be nice. It was a kind of rebirth.

Paul felt as if he were shedding his hard, bitter skin, the one that had built up over the years of living with a you're-not-as-smart-as-me father and a you're-not-as-fabulous-as-me mother. Over the shouting years, the divorce from hell, the horrors of school, that skin had come to be as tough as armor. Now, it was coming off and a new person was emerging: softer, more flexible, with rounder edges and a warm glow. He wasn't angry at everything. Even found himself walking differently—more upright, chin up, back straight. Saying things he would never have said before, things he had heard Harry say: Indeed. Right, right. Fascinating. The kind of stuff that would probably have earned him a punch in the face at school. One day, a man walked right into Paul and swore at him, and Paul said, "So sorry, excuse me." A week earlier, he would have clobbered him.

Around noon on the third day, they took a seat in an outdoor café after spending the morning at the Eden Art Gallery. With tired legs but as excited as a couple of boys skipping high school, they ordered a light lunch and bottle of white wine. To Paul's never-ending relief, Harry insisted on paying for everything, refusing Paul's occasional and tentative offers to pick up the bill.

Harry poured the wine. "Outstanding collection," he said. "Mister Eden has done well for himself."

"Guy's got everything. That Egyptian jar—what was it? Three thousand BC? Can you imagine what that would have cost?"

"I've got a pretty good idea," Harry answered. "A little over two hundred thousand pounds." He raised his glass. "Here's to the Egyptians."

Paul raised his glass and drank, realizing too late that he had spilled half of it on his shirt.

"Shit!" he swore, earning a few alarmed glances from neighboring tables before catching himself. He winced, embarrassed at his outburst. "Apologies, Harry. That was uncalled for."

"Well, it is a tragic waste of good wine," Harry chuckled.

"Sorry, sorry. I'm such a fu—, I mean, an idiot." Paul tried to mop the wine off his shirt, but it just made it worse. He swore again, but this time to himself.

"Is something bothering you, Paul?" Harry asked. "You seem out of sorts."

"What? Not at all! Everything's great! I'm loving this." He pointed to the stain on his shirt. "Well, maybe not this."

"Yes." Harry smiled. "I understand. However—"

"What? However what?"

Harry leaned forward, lifting his eyebrows and lowering his voice. "Every time you think I'm not looking at you, the mask disappears. Your face falls, like a man who is trying to appear happy, but is in fact depressed."

"No, no, I'm not. Everything's perfect. I'm great."

"I can't help but suspect something is extremely less than perfect."

Paul finished off his glass of wine before responding. Thought for a minute. Then two. Wondered if he should say anything. Big Ben chimed faintly in the distance, three times, as if sending a warning. But he decided to ignore it, that he may as well talk. Harry would probably find out eventually. If they were going to be friends, that is. If they were friends, he'd find out the truth. At least that's what Paul imagined friends did. He didn't honestly know.

"Well, this is perfect." He looked around. "All this. The food, the galleries. Spending time with you. The last few days have been some of the best of my life. But the honest truth is that my life is over. I'm busted, out of a job, out of time, and out of hope. I'm finished. Now I'm the one who is history, just another worthless artifact that should be buried and forgotten."

He told Harry about all the years he had spent trying to make it in the art world. About how his university friends had made it, with grand titles and grander salaries, while Paul had to beg his father for money to pay the rent. About how his so-called friends had rejected him, how his wife had left him. How he wished he had gone to business school, or taken commerce, or even carpentry. Something that might have gotten him a real job. Anything but art—antiquities. Anything to avoid the deep shithole he was in right now. The only thing Paul didn't tell him about was working at the dollar store. He wanted to maintain a little self-respect.

Harry knitted his brow. "But money doesn't matter, Paul. You know that. Art matters. Art is beauty, it's forever, it's the only thing that matters and the only thing that lasts. A thousand years from now, no one will be admiring how much anyone earned, or what their house was worth, or what kind of car they drove. No one will be talking about anyone's chain of retail stores, or how they made millions buying and selling this conglomerate or that light bulb company. You understand, don't you? They will be talking about the art. Art isn't about money. It's about who we are, the best of what we are and what we can be. It's about beauty. And you have a brilliant eye for art. You really do."

"That *sounds* nice." Paul crossed his arms and leaned back. "But eventually the rent comes due."

Harry leaned forward, pointing his finger. "Money is not a measure of personal worth. It's a false god, chased by people with black souls and empty lives. It's—"

"And yet," Paul interrupted, "you knew exactly how much that Egyptian jar was worth."

Harry laughed. "I understand your situation, Paul. And I want to help. In fact, I insist."

"I appreciate your concern, Harry. I do. Unfortunately, it's too late for me. It's fine, though. I have a plan. I'm going to declare bankruptcy and get a job driving a forklift at Walmart."

Harry laughed, louder this time, and shook a finger at Paul. "Oh no, you're not. I'm sure I can come up with a better plan. Let me think."

He crossed his arms, mumbling to himself, looking up and around and scrunching his eyebrows. Grimaced, picked up his wine and put it down again. Started to say something and stopped. After a few more minutes of fidgeting, he snapped his fingers and a smile crossed his face. His eyes locked on Paul's.

"I've got it. Do you recall that Eurydemos Vase? Of course you do. Well, I've decided that I'd like to sell it. To you. I . . . I don't have the room for it. You'd be doing me a favor by taking it off my hands." Harry leaned back and crossed his arms. "How does that sound to you?"

And Paul, uncertain whether he could believe his luck, just nodded.

• • •

"What? You want what?"

"Four hundred thousand dollars," Paul answered. He stood on the other side of the dining room of his father's house, close to the door. His father sat at the far end of the table. The antique walnut table was large enough for twenty, but the old man sat alone except for the large chicken carcass splayed out in front of him.

"The hell with you. You bailed on me. I gave you a job—a chance! If you had stuck around, you could have taken over the company one day." He pulled a leg off the chicken and bit into it. "But now you are getting nothing. Zip. You left poor old—I forget her name, but she's a loyal employee, and you just walked out on her. Didn't tell her, or even me, you were leaving. A week later you come back, and this? You want money? Ha! I want the signing bonus I gave you back. You owe me." He threw the bone on the table and grabbed the other leg. "The hell I'm giving you four hundred thousand dollars. The hell with you!"

"I'll pay it back. You lend me the money to buy the vase, I sell it, and I'll pay you back. Fifteen percent interest. Twenty percent. Plus, I'll return the signing bonus."

His father poured the last half of a bottle of barbecue sauce on his plate and dipped the leg in it. "You must think I'm stupid. No, you won't."

"I will." Paul looked at him. He wasn't even sure if his father was listening, he was so focused on eating that chicken.

"What if you can't sell it?"

"I can sell it."

"Says you." He pulled a piece of meat off the chicken and stuffed it in his mouth. "No. That's it. End of discussion."

"Look, I'm telling you—"

"You're a real piece of shit, you know that? Your mother was right. I was always too easy on you."

"When were you easy on me? You've called me a stupid lazy prick every day since I was eight!" Paul felt a fight brewing and wanted desperately to avoid it. "Sorry. I didn't mean that."

The old man shrugged. "Trying to toughen you up. Have some chicken if you're hungry."

Paul could feel exhaustion sinking into his bones. He had driven straight to the airport from his chat with Harry, caught the overnight flight to New York, rented a car and driven straight to his old man's place. No sleep on the plane, thanks to a combination of excitement, dread, hope and fear, not to mention the snoring, slobbering jerk beside him. He was so tired he was hallucinating while he drove—highway signs going blurry and floating away, dots on the road swerving all over the place, other cars appearing and disappearing.

"Come on. Please. Help me out. I'm begging."

"No. You going to eat some chicken or not?" his father asked, like it was a personal challenge.

"Not hungry, thanks." The room was quiet for a few minutes, except for the sound of his old man's fake teeth gnawing on roasted meat. His father rested his feet on the table.

"So. What is this thing again?"

"It's a vase. A Greek vase. It's called the Eurydemos Vase, and they thought there was only one, but there are two, and . . ." He saw his father's eyes gloss over. "It's made to hold wine. Very rare. Extremely valuable."

The Eurydemos Vase. The one that Harry had been holding onto, the pride of the litter, the best of all the treasures he kept in his apartment. The vase that Harry had kissed, that he said he loved. That he swore he would never sell. He had practically cried while he was holding it. But now he was willing to let it go because he wanted to help Paul, because he knew this would get Paul out of the deep trouble he had found himself in. It was more than a gift. Harry had thrown him a lifeline made out of ancient, fired clay.

Four hundred grand was nothing for a piece like that.

Paul tried to talk him out of it, told Harry he really shouldn't sell it, it meant too much to him, that he couldn't take it from Harry. But he was lying. While he was saying the words, trying to sound sincere, the only thing Paul could think was this: I have been saved. Salvation and redemption are mine. I thank you, Lord.

If Paul could get his hands on that vase and sell it, there wouldn't be a curator in the world who wouldn't see him. Not in California, not in New York, not in London. Jennifer and Richard would have to see him; even Imani would be begging to see the piece. This would be it. They'd be calling him instead of hanging up on him. Inviting him to events, asking his opinion. He'd have his reputation made. Selling that vase would be like winning the green jacket at the Masters. Once you win, you're in for life.

But there was a catch, and it was a big one. A four-hundred-thousand-dollar catch. He needed money to buy that vase, and Paul had to squeeze it out of this cheap, wrinkled old bastard with the mouth full of chicken and the barbecue stain on his track suit.

"A vase to hold wine?" The old man ran his finger over the barbecue stain and stuck it in his mouth. "You can get those at my store for ninety-five cents. I'll sell it to you wholesale." He picked up a glass of wine, put it down again. "Ah, not worth it. Ulcer." Walked over to the fridge and poured himself a glass of milk. "This is what it's come to. Seems like no matter how much you accomplish in life, it ends up sucking."

"The vase is over two thousand years old, Dad. Not only is it an extremely rare piece, it's by one of the greatest artists of ancient Greece—one of the greatest artists in history—but it's . . ." Paul struggled for a way to put this piece into perspective. "If it was a baseball card, it would be a Honus Wagner. If it was a palace, it would be Versailles. If it was a . . . I don't know how to say it. This is one of the most famous pieces of art in the world."

"I could give a shit."

Paul leaned on the wall, exhausted, struggling just to keep standing. He felt a cannonball growing in the pit of his stomach. His blood pressure was rising and his last chance disappearing. He was desperate to find one more argument, one more way to keep his hopes alive. There had to be something. Some way to get this self-centered, money-grubbing dollar store salesman to loan him the money.

"How about this. If I can't sell it, I'll give it to you."

"Ha! Big effin' deal. What am I doing to do with an old wine jug? I can barely drink anymore."

"You don't keep it. You donate it to a museum. Say it's appraised at a million five, although it would sell for more than that. You donate it and write the entire thing off as a charitable donation. That would net you . . . I don't know how that stuff works, but you'd get a helluva tax break."

The old man poured another glass of milk, pulled the dentures out of his mouth and plunked them in a glass of water. "It's appraised at a million five?"

The sight of his father speaking without teeth made Paul wince. He looked away. "Yes. Probably more. Maybe a lot more."

"I'm no tax lawyer, but that would probably net me over seven hundred grand."

"There you go. Easiest seven hundred grand you ever made. And you get to look like an altruistic son of a bitch."

"So if you don't sell it, I net seven hundred."

"Easy."

"Or twenty percent interest if you do."

"Yep."

"That's a pretty good deal."

"So give me the money, you cheap old bastard. You win either way."

For the first time in Paul's memory, his father looked impressed. Even proud. "When you put it like that," the old man said, "I'd love to help you out. Anything for my own son."

CHAPTER TWELVE

Kate woke up with a throbbing head and a wretched stomach. She couldn't remember feeling this awful since the morning after she discovered lemon gin in her second year of high school. Fighting the urge to throw up, she stumbled to the kitchen to make coffee, noting the empty bottle of wine on the floor beside the couch. Maybe she should call in sick. Spend the day under a warm blanket with a bottle of ginger ale and aspirin.

Then she saw the cash box sitting open on the dining room table. The key was in the lock. The keys to her apartment were lying beside it.

She walked over, a cold wave of panic washing over her, and looked inside. It was empty.

No. No! She remembered locking the earrings in the cash box. She did, didn't she? Yes, she did. Of course, she'd had plenty to drink the night before. That was a mistake. She must have been drunk and put them somewhere else. But she wasn't *that* drunk, was she? They had to be here somewhere. But her keys, her keys had been missing, and now they were here. Was that right? She wasn't sure. She had been stupid, drank too much, and now she wasn't sure of anything—except that the earrings were missing.

Where were they?

A few hours later Kate had, by her own estimate, checked every square inch of her apartment at least ten times. She had pulled apart every drawer, emptied every closet, checked every pocket, lifted every cushion. Unpacked boxes she hadn't opened since she moved, just because. Searched the fridge and freezer, even though that made no sense either. Pushed her hand down vents and lifted furniture. Checked the cash box several times, in case the earrings were there and she just hadn't noticed them.

Which was impossible.

How could they have gone missing? Kate sat down and stared at the cash box. She thought about everything she had done last night before she went to bed. Putting the earrings in the cash box. Closing it. Locking it. Placing it back in the closet. She remembered everything. So how could the box be open and the earrings gone?

They must have been stolen. That was the only possible explanation. But how?

It must have been Jacob. She remembered dropping her purse and everything falling out. She was so focused on retrieving the earrings, she wouldn't have noticed him grab her keys. He must have followed her home and used the keys to creep in while she was sleeping off all the wine and champagne. It was the only explanation that made any sense. Or did it?

Why hadn't she just taken the earrings back to the FBI vault after she left the restaurant? Stupid, stupid, stupid. The stupidest thing she'd ever done. She should crawl under the bed and stay there. She should run away, disappear, and never come back. No, she couldn't. She had made a mistake, and it was her fault, so she was going to fix it. She was. No one was going to know about this, not now, not ever. She would find the earrings. Before Camilla and Luca knew they were missing, she'd find them and put them back in the vault. Everything was going to be just fine.

But what if Camilla discovered she had signed them out? She'd called Camilla last night. Three or four times. But she hadn't left a message, hadn't told her she was taking the earrings out of the vault, thankfully. As long as Camilla didn't check, she wouldn't know. If she asked why Kate had called, she would just say they were accidental calls, pocket dials. If Camilla didn't check, didn't ask, and if Luca didn't ask, and if Kate found them first, then everything would work out.

That was a lot of ifs.

Kate sat on the floor in the corner of her apartment, trying not to panic, trying to just formulate a coherent thought, when her phone rang. She wanted to ignore it but couldn't help looking at the screen. No Caller ID. Her mother.

"Hi Mom." Kate wondered if she would be able to carry on her side of the conversation without breaking down.

"Kate? I'm going to Mexico." Her mom's voice was wobbly. A song in the background was playing so loud it was hard to hear.

"Really? That's nice . . ." Kate wasn't prepared for this. "Wait. What's that again?"

"I'm going to Mexico. Can you hear that song? It's about a holiday in Tijuana. Doesn't that sound nice? Why don't you come?"

"Well then. Really? That's very impulsive of you, Mom. You haven't been drinking, have you?"

"No! Well, a little. What say you, missy? Want to come with me?"

Missy? "Maybe we could think about that. But this isn't a good time."

"I'm leaving tomorrow, so you have to decide now. How's that boy, you met? Luca?" She was interrupted by a loud crash. "Uh-oh. I'll call you later."

"Where in Mexico are you—?" But she had hung up. Kate stared at her phone, confused. What was that all about?

She'd think about that later. Now she had to focus on the earrings. They were gone, and she had to calm down and think. She needed a plan.

Think logically, Kate told herself. What are the next steps? Searching through her apartment again was the only thing she could think of, but that was not a logical next step. She moved to the middle of the room, lay down on the floor and stared at the ceiling. Pushed back the panic threatening to swallow her. The theft must have something to do with Jacob. But maybe not. She had called quite a few galleries, so a lot of people knew she had the earrings. Someone else could have followed her. Who could it be?

She should tell Camilla. But if she did that, Camilla would tell Luca, everyone would blame her, and she would probably be fired and her whole plan would be destroyed. Her whole *life* would be destroyed. She could jump out of the window, which would probably be the most sensible and convenient thing to do. But she wasn't a jump-out-of-the-window kind of person.

No. A crime had been committed, and she was going to solve it. That was it. That was her plan. She would find the missing earrings and recover the sphinx. When she was done, she would call Luca and tell him.

Hi Luca, how are things? I found the sphinx. Do you want me to bring it over? Of course, and I'll bring the earrings with me. Got them right here. Great! I'll be on the next plane. See you soon. Afterwards, maybe they could go for dinner on some terrace overlooking the sea, have a glass of Aperol, or champagne, and laugh about the crazy adventures they had had. That's exactly how it was going to work. She knew she could do this.

No, she couldn't.

Then again, she didn't have any choice, so she would have do it anyway. Then Kate's phone rang again. She checked it, expecting it to be her mom calling to say she'd been joking, but it wasn't. It was Luca, and she was not ready to speak to Luca. So she ignored it. He called again. She ignored that. He called three more times before she gave up and answered.

"Kate, how have you been? I was getting worried." His voice was different. Slower, more measured.

"Hi, Luca. I'm fine, everything is absolutely fine. How have you been?"

"I'm not so good today."

Kate's first thought was: What could he possibly be complaining about? What could be worse than what she was going through right now? But he didn't know what she was going through, thankfully, so it wasn't his fault. "What's wrong?"

"There is a lot wrong right now."

Had Luca already found out the earrings were missing? Maybe someone had tipped off the Carabinieri, or someone discovered they'd disappeared from the vault and called Luca first. Kate closed her eyes and held her breath.

"The reason I couldn't tell you about the sphinx is because I, because we, couldn't tell anyone. Only four people in the world, other than the thieves, know what it really is. Our prime minister, the minister of culture, the general of the Carabinieri, and me. That's it. There is a good reason for all the secrecy. If the thieves knew we were looking for them, they would go underground and it—all of it—would disappear forever."

"I guess I understand that. Except . . . sorry, all of it? All of what? Are you—?"

"There could be government officials, police, even our own Carabinieri involved. Italy has a reputation for corruption, and that reputation is well earned. Everyone is a suspect. We have to be careful. Even your own officials can't know. Just you and Camilla. Can you do that?"

"What are you telling me?"

"At first, we thought it was just the one piece, you know, just the sphinx. Which would still be incredibly significant. But now we know it's bigger than that. A lot bigger."

"Luca, slow down. I'm not tracking."

"We thought it was just something Caligula stole from Alexander's tomb. But it's not."

"Caligula? Alexander? Luca, you're not making any sense. Can we just start at the beginning?"

And he did. While Kate sat on her bed, staring at the empty cash box and trying not to scream, she heard Luca take three deep breaths. Then he explained.

"It all started twenty, twenty-five centuries ago. Alexander was thirty-two years old, and he had already conquered most of the known world. On June 11, 323 BC, he died. Maybe he had malaria, maybe he was poisoned, no one really knows. But he was a god to his people when he died, the greatest god they had ever known. They built a great funeral carriage for him. It looked like a temple and was covered in gold. The carriage was pulled by sixty-four elephants, each one carrying a golden crown and bell. The body was supposed to go to Macedonia to be buried, but it didn't get there—"

"They were mules."

"Sorry?"

"They weren't elephants. They were mules."

"Va bene. Mules. Horses. Giraffes. It doesn't matter. The thing is that the funeral carriage was seized on the way by a rich and powerful pharaoh named Ptolemy, who, umm, what do you call it? Not stole . . ."

"Hijacked?"

"Yes. Ptolemy hijacked the entire funeral carriage, along with Alexander's body, and brought it to Egypt. He built an elaborate burial complex there, somewhere near what is now called Alexandria, and loaded it with treasures for Alexander's afterlife. That tomb was a place of worship for generations of Ptolemys, and centuries later, after they died out, the many generations of Romans who followed them."

"Luca, this is interesting, in a history lesson kind of way, but I already know—"

"You asked me to start at the beginning."

She had meant a few weeks earlier, not twenty-five hundred years. Her world was blowing up, and Luca was lecturing on Roman history. "Okay, fine."

"Many emperors, including Caesar, Augustus, Titus, Hadrian, and Caligula, came to pay their respects. That body was like a talisman to them. That burial complex was a holy place, sacred, and untouchable. Then Caligula stole the marble sphinx."

"That I did not know. Why did Caligula steal the sphinx?"

"It was believed to have magical powers." He paused. "And also because Caligula was a crazy bastard."

Kate shook her head. She was not ready to believe him yet. "But you can't know that sphinx was Alexander's."

"We discovered radiocarbon testing records the previous owner had done. We're pretty sure."

"Or that Caligula stole it."

"We do not know that for certain. We originally thought that was the only reason the sphinx survived, because it had been removed from the tomb, which many believed had been lost. But no, we don't know. In fact—do you remember Gamal Saleh?"

She thought back. "The dealer who died in an accident. Who sold the sphinx to the lady who donated it to the museum in her will."

"Exactly. We searched his apartment. Found jewelry, papyrus, ancient jars, and coins bearing the head of Alexander."

"Not surprising. He owned a gallery, and Alexander's head is on a lot of coins."

"Yes. But that wasn't the most important find. One of the jars had seeds in it."

Seeds. That would be something. If they found seeds, they would be able to pinpoint their age to an exact year, even if they were thousands of years old.

"And with accelerator mass spectrometry we can date—"

"Luca, I know what accelerator mass spectrometry can do. Can we skip to the good part?"

"Those seeds dated to 323 B.C."

Kate thought for a few seconds. "The year Alexander died."

"Exactly."

She squeezed her eyes shut. That was important, incredible even. But still, it wasn't definitive proof. "That's not a lot of evidence."

"It's not just a few seeds. We've confirmed dating on at least ten other objects in that apartment. They all came from the same time and place as the sphinx."

"This is insane. You're trying to tell me they, whoever they are, have found Alexander's tomb. But that can't be. It's impossible. The tomb disappeared. It was lost," Kate said.

"A lot of people thought that."

"The tomb *was* lost," Kate insisted. "After the Romans fell, the Christians came and destroyed anything to do with pagan gods. Including Alexander's tomb."

"That's one theory, but there isn't any evidence of that. No one knows for sure they destroyed Alexander's tomb. Many archeologists are convinced it's still out there. They haven't stopped searching."

This could just be a series of wild coincidences, Kate thought.

"Over twenty years ago, an archeologist claimed she had found Alexander's tomb near the Siwa Oasis in Egypt," Luca continued. "Before the tomb could be excavated, the Egyptian government shut it down. They claimed it was due to 'political intervention'—that the Greek government was claiming rights to Alexander's treasures, and Egypt had to protect its contents. The Greeks denied making any such claim. The entire episode was complicated, confusing and suspicious. Guards were posted at the site and no one was allowed entry. Only a few people really knew what was inside.

"Years later, it's still locked down. But what if the archeologist was right? What if it was Alexander's? Someone could have access to the tomb and is smuggling everything inside it out of the country."

Kate tried to keep her voice calm and in control, but her mouth was dry and her hands were shaking. She knew where this was going now and wished she could stop it, but she couldn't. Her voice cracked when she tried to speak, but she stopped and gathered herself. "Maybe it's possible. There's a chance, if you're right . . . any ideas who?"

"Government officials. Customs agents. Police. Thieves. Or all of the above."

"And if it is Alexander's tomb—?"

"They'll pull everything out and sell the entire tomb, piece by piece, to the highest bidders. It would be worth many, many millions."

Kate thought about what that tomb could have looked like. A burial complex built to honor the greatest king from one of the greatest civilizations of all time. It would be filled with gifts and treasures for the afterlife, a treasure trove of priceless antiquities and human stories from long-lost civilizations. What if all those Ptolemys and Roman emperors brought more gifts to honor their idol, hoping to catch a reflection of his greatness? If what Luca was suggesting were true, one of the greatest discoveries in the history of archeology was about to disappear. Forever.

"Now you know why we sent you those earrings," Luca said.

Kate's lips were trembling. "Yes!" she said, forcing her voice to remain steady. "I think they're perfect."

"Excellent. When I explained your plan to the director of the Uffizi Gallery, he refused to give me anything, despite my arguments. He even turned down a personal request from the minister of culture. In the end we had no choice—we had to tell him everything, explain why we needed them. Once he realized we were in a race to find the tomb of Alexander the Great, he agreed right away. Those earrings are among the Uffizi's most valuable artifacts, but he knew it was the right thing to do. Now six people know, including you."

Kate swallowed the sheet of bile climbing up her esophagus.

"We still have found nothing on our end, despite everything we've done. I'm guessing we have maybe two more weeks before it disappears forever. Now you're our best chance, maybe our only chance. How does that feel?"

It feels like I should reconsider jumping out of the window, Kate thought. She was even tempted, for a moment, to confess everything. That the earrings had been stolen, that she had drunk too much and made a mess of the whole thing. She'd be known all over the world as that stupid FBI intern who lost the earrings of Alexander the Great's mother, but it would be better than this. "Luca, I . . ."

"Yes?"

The thought of losing all those treasures, and that she would be responsible, left her numb. It was too horrible to think about. She had to fix this, whatever it took.

"Don't worry, Luca."

"I'm not worried. We have faith in you. Remember, though, we must keep this quiet. You and Camilla are the only people in the entire

United States of America that can know. The worst thing that could happen is for this to go public."

Luca didn't have to worry about that either. Kate wasn't going to tell anyone she didn't have to tell.

After he hung up, Kate went to bed and screamed into her pillow until her neighbors banged on the wall.

CHAPTER THIRTEEN

Paul lay back on his couch, hands behind his head, staring at the vase on his coffee table and thinking about how his life had changed. Just over a week earlier, he was about to be evicted from this apartment, unable to pay the rent. He had no idea where he would have gone. He couldn't go live with his old man after walking out on him at the store, and he had no idea where his mother was. He'd pictured himself living in a homeless shelter and wondered how long he would be able to survive. That was then. Now, with that vase sitting just a few feet away, he'd never have to worry again. Never. After he sold it, he'd be able to call his own shots for a long time. But before he sold it, there was one thing he had to do.

He picked up the phone and called Jennifer.

"And how are you this fine day?" he asked.

"Paul. I'm okay, just really busy, so if you don't mind—"

"Oh, I'm very sorry to interrupt. I was calling to say hi, checking in to see how you're doing. Also, I had a question I wanted to ask you about the Eurydemos Vase, but if you don't have time that's not a problem. I can just call someone else."

"What about the Eurydemos Vase?"

"Oh, it's nothing. You probably don't even know what I'm talking about."

"Of course I do, Paul." Jennifer sounded bored, harried, busy, tired—and curious. "Everyone knows the Eurydemos Vase."

"Well, I'm impressed. Didn't realize you were so smart."

She didn't answer for a few moments. Even from two thousand miles away, he could feel the hate she was sending through the phone. "It's in St. Petersburg now," she said. "Originally found in Kerch, an ancient Greek colony in the Crimea. It's two thousand four hundred-ish years old. It was a wedding gift for some Queen—I forget her name. And what else? Oh, I remember. Why don't you stop being such an ass?"

Paul smiled. "Pretty good. I'd give you a solid B-minus for that."

"Screw you. What about it?"

"Did you know there's more than one?"

She exhaled, a loud and long breath that rang of doubt and exasperation. "No, because there isn't."

Now it was Paul's turn to pause. He was going to drag this out because it was too sweet to rush.

"Really? You're sure about that? How do you know? Were you there? I know you're not young anymore, but still—"

"Stop it, Paul. And shut up. There isn't. At least, not that anyone knows about." She was trying to hide her curiosity but couldn't. "What are you suggesting?"

"As it happens, my dear," Paul said slowly, a bit of Harry's British lilt creeping into his voice, "there are two. And I just happen to have the other one."

If you listened hard enough, you could hear exactly what Jennifer was thinking. Paul didn't have to ask. She was wondering if there really could be two—two!—Eurydemos Vases. If there were, how could that fact have been hidden for so many years? So many centuries? But she also must have realized that if this was true, well, that would be big. Bigger than big. Huge. Paul knew exactly what she was thinking because anyone that knew anything about ancient art would be thinking the same thing.

"Where did you get it?"

"A friend."

"Okay, where did your friend get it?"

"I'll tell you later." Paul had the papers from Harry, but he hadn't looked at them. "It's complicated. But in case you're wondering, it comes with all the provenance, proof, invoices and paperwork you could ever need. The genuine article. A little wear and tear, perhaps, but two or three thousand years will do that to you. I mean, look at you—and that's only after a few decades."

"Is it in good condition?"

"Like new. One hundred percent," Paul answered.

"Let me talk to Richard. I'm certain we'd be interested."

"But you weren't interested in the Sican cup."

"I wasn't interested because, like I told you, we've already got a lot of pre-Columbian. That market is saturated. This is different. We don't have too many Eurydemos Vases. Obviously."

"Of course, I understand. So, talk to Richard," Paul said. He sucked in a quick breath. "Oh, wait . . . well, I was not expecting this!"

"What?"

"I'm so sorry, Jennifer. But the New York Museum is calling. Please hold for a moment."

Paul hung up.

Thirty seconds later, his phone rang. Jennifer. He ignored it. Two minutes after that, it rang again. He ignored it again. Five minutes later it rang yet again, and this time he picked it up. Slowly.

"Hello?"

"Paul, it's me. Jennifer. I think we got cut off."

"Yeah, not sure what happened there."

"Richard and I would like to speak to you. We can make ourselves available anytime."

"I'm happy to hear that. Just trying to find some time in my schedule . . ."

"Do you have anything this week?" Jennifer asked.

"I don't. So busy!" Paul wished he was recording this so he could play it back for himself later. "Let me see, let me see," he said, as if checking through his calendar.

"Richard and I can make it to your home or office, if you prefer."

"How nice. I appreciate that. I really do. Oh, let's see. When's a good time . . . when's a good time to see Jennifer and Richard with this rare, priceless artifact . . ." Paul counted to ten. Slowly. "Oh, here we go. How about never? Is never a good time?"

He hung up.

• • •

Paul walked up the stairs of the New York Museum, pulling his crate behind him on a dolly. He walked slowly, carefully rolling the wheels over the stairs one at a time, making certain his vase wouldn't get damaged. Of course it wouldn't. He had taken so much care packing it that he could drop it off the roof and not hurt it. Still, something about carrying a piece like this made you extra-extra careful. He probably shouldn't be doing this himself. He should have hired the so-called professionals to ship it over, but he could never trust them.

He took the elevator up to the third floor and walked down the hall to the executive offices. No one even looked twice at him. He imagined how they'd react if they knew what was in that wooden crate he was pulling along: "A second Eurydemos? Impossible!" Ha. Possible. He walked into the executive offices and straight to the front desk. Once again, he was standing in front of the woman with a big, hard head of red hair. The woman who hadn't even let him talk to Imani just a few weeks earlier, who had smirked at him as the security guards chased him out of the building.

"Hi Linda, how nice to see you again," Paul said.

Linda looked up at him. "Not you," she said.

"Oh yes! It certainly is me."

"Imani's not going to see you, Paul. We went through this."

"No? Are you sure, Linda? Don't you want to check with her first?" Paul rolled the dolly over to the couch and sat down. "Why don't you give her a buzz?"

"I think you'd better leave."

"I think I won't, but thanks for the advice." Paul pulled his phone out of his pocket and started going through emails. "I think I'll sit right here and wait."

"I'm going to call security."

"You could do that. I guess we know that, don't we? Ha ha. But you may want to check with her first, because you might be surprised."

Linda looked as if she'd rather shoot him than call Imani. But after a few seconds, she shook her head and picked up the phone. "Hi Imani. Listen, I know you told me not to interrupt you if he . . ." A pause. "I know what you said, but he . . . I'm sorry. It's just I thought . . . you're right. I promise I'll never do it again." She hung up the phone.

"You just got me in shit," she said to Paul.

Paul rested his chin in his hands and grinned. "My deepest apologies. Trust me, I know how difficult she can be. How about you join me for dinner, we'll have a few drinks, and we can talk about her?"

She glared at him.

A few moments later, Imani turned the corner and walked into the room.

After all these years and all their troubles, he still felt his heart pound just a little harder whenever he saw her. Even today, when she was there for no other reason than to have him kicked out of the place, he still felt the same way he felt when he first saw her. That long, black curly hair, waving under the office air conditioning. Those full, perfect lips, that soft black skin, those big, dark eyes. She was still as perfect as she ever was. A modern-day Cleopatra.

"What the fuck are you doing here?" Despite the pulsating anger coming out of her eyes, her voice remained flat, in control.

"Oh, hi, Imani. I didn't realize you'd be here. How are you?"

"I'm the curator, you shit. Or maybe you'd forgotten?"

Paul stood up and considered offering her a hug but thought better of it. Figured he might end up with a high-heeled shoe in his groin instead. He stayed back.

"You're not supposed to be here," she said. "If I have to get another restraining order . . ."

"I'm sure that won't be necessary," Paul said. He had adopted Harry's language, cadence and tone: friendly, soft, polite. Civilized. He tried to relax his shoulders, like he imagined Harry would do, and smiled. "I love your shoes."

"Linda, call security." Imani turned to walk out of the lobby, but stopped and turned back. "Tell me Paul. What makes you think you can just come in here and threaten me like this?"

"How did I threaten you? I'm merely . . ."

"*Merely?* What the hell's wrong with you?" She took a few steps forward and half whispered, "You know you're supposed to stay away from me. You know that. You're just here to intimidate me. I know what shit you're up to."

"I wondered if you'd like to have a look at this new piece I . . ."

"Fuck you. Get out and stay out of my life forever. I've called security. I'll also call the cops. I'll have you locked up and put away."

"I'm so sorry you're upset, but I'm simply—"

Three large security guards pushed open the door and came into the lobby. They formed a circle around Paul.

"Hello, gentlemen," he said. "How is the security business these days?"

"Let's go," the guard standing in front of him said. "Move it. Out of here."

Paul didn't move. He laughed and held up his hands.

"Gentlemen, I have a meeting . . ."

The guards behind him grabbed his arms and pulled him backwards.

"Ouch! Please, please," Paul said. "This is extremely inappropriate."

"Shut it," the guard in front of him said. "Or I'll do something inappropriate to your skull. Get him out of here."

The two men tightened their grip on Paul's arms, pulling them back so far he thought they were going to break at the elbows. They pulled and pushed him towards the door. His crate was sitting by itself near the couch.

"Gentlemen, I can't leave without that package."

Imani said, "Take your fucking package and get lost."

"I'm telling you, once again, that this is highly inappropriate!"

One of the men, wearing a blue suit that was too small for his wide shoulders, twisted Paul's arm up higher and sideways. It felt to Paul as if it were about to come out of its socket. The taller man held the door open while the other two started to drag Paul outside. Then a voice called from the hall on the other side of the room.

"Excuse me. What is going on here?"

Everyone stopped and looked back. The room went quiet.

Francis Palma, the director of the New York Museum, was standing beside the lobby desk. He was on the short side, thin, bald, and wore large, round black-rimmed glasses and a black suit over a white shirt. His voice was low and deep. It was as if a living Buddha had appeared out of the mist. For a few moments, no one spoke.

"What is going on here?" he repeated.

"This man was threatening Ms. Hollis," a security guard said.

Francis raised his eyebrows at the guards, and they dropped Paul's arms. He looked over at Paul and smiled. "Hello, Paul."

"Hello, Mr. Palma," Paul smiled. "How nice to see you."

"Please. It's Francis. And it's nice to see you as well." He looked over at Imani. "I personally invited Mr. Klugman to our offices to see an interesting piece he had. A very interesting piece. We should be honored that he accepted that offer. Having our security guards trying to break his arms doesn't send a message that we're honored."

"I'm sorry, Mr. Palma," Imani said. "It's just that—"

"In fact, I'd suggest it's highly inappropriate."

"But—"

"The guard said he threatened you. Did he threaten you?"

"He didn't literally threaten me."

"Did he threaten you figuratively?"

"No."

"Then how? Was it with a metaphor? Did he metaphorically threaten you?"

Imani didn't say anything.

"Then I'm afraid there's been a horrible mistake," the director said. "Mr. Klugman, if these men have assaulted you, I welcome you to press charges. In fact, I'd encourage it. Against them, against our institution, against me. We'll pay whatever damages are deemed satisfactory."

Paul shook his head. "Of course not. We just had a little misunderstanding. Absolutely no harm done."

Francis ran a manicured hand over his shining head and frowned. "Imani? Don't we apologize when we almost break the arms of guests?"

She glared at Francis, then Paul. "Not when our guests are assholes." Imani turned around and stomped out of the room.

"My. Well, then. Paul, I will apologize for Imani, these guards, and everyone else in this institution. Sincerely. I truly hope we can forget this unfortunate incident. Please join me in my office. Linda, ensure that we're not interrupted."

Paul grabbed the handle of his dolly and followed Francis to his office. On his way past Linda, he flipped his middle finger at her. She returned it. Twofold.

A few minutes later, they were in Francis's office. It was large enough to be its own mini-gallery, with ancient and contemporary art scattered throughout and floor-to-ceiling windows looking out on the New York skyline.

"Mr. Klugman, please take a seat. Would you like a drink? Brandy? Scotch?" Francis asked.

"I'd settle for a glass of red wine, if you have any."

"Excellent." Francis poured two glasses and sat down next to him. "I can't apologize enough. I suppose you're wondering how we can be such jackasses."

"Not at all," Paul said. "You must get a lot of troublemakers coming in here."

"No, we don't. Ever."

They sat sipping wine and chatting art gallery chitchat. The latest trends, the biggest finds, the increasing demand for textiles, the decline in ceramics, the stability of bronze and gold. The rising artists, agents, dealers, and collectors. They paused, quietly gazing at the city in front of them.

"Is that it?" Francis said, glancing at the art crate.

"Yes."

"So . . . there really is a second Eurydemos?"

"Indeed," Paul said, reminding himself to smile, keep his shoulders straight and maintain eye contact. Channeling Harry had become almost second nature, but he still had to stay on guard. Baiting his ex was not very Harry-like, on the other hand, but it had been fun.

"Did you just bring that here on your own?"

Paul chuckled. "Walked right up Fifth Avenue."

"That is brilliant. And completely insane." Francis glanced at Paul with admiration, polished off his wine and refilled both their glasses. He sat back down but kept turning around to see the crate. "It really is, isn't it?"

"It really is. And all the provenance, papers, everything you need are also there."

"Thank you. We have to be so careful these days."

Francis stood up and walked over to the crate. "It's almost like I don't even want to look at it!" He started to pace around the room. "I'm going to be honest with you. I feel like a nervous young man on his first date. If that's what you say it is," he said, pointing at the crate, "they'll be talking about this for years. About you. Also, and this is presumptuous of me, but—if we can work something out, of course—I'll be known forever as the director who procured the second Eurydemos Vase."

"Would you like to see it?" Paul asked.

"More than anything in the universe."

CHAPTER FOURTEEN

Kate was the first one in the office that morning. After a long and sleepless night worrying about the missing earrings, she decided she might as well get up and go to work. Tell Camilla what happened first thing, get fired, walk out and slink back to Chester. Move into her mother's basement and spend the rest of her life in a never-ending cycle of depression, self-loathing, and regret.

If only it could be that easy. But it wasn't, and she knew it. She was totally and utterly screwed. They would probably arrest her, charge her with gross dereliction of duty. Did that mean prison? Her face would be on televisions and in newspapers from New York to Rome, and just think of all the horrible things they would say about her. There would be a tsunami of hate on social media, everyone talking about the stupid agent who lost the earrings of Alexander the Great's mother's. And there would be Luca. Or rather, there wouldn't be Luca. Not anymore. She felt like she had fallen into a pit of darkness and despair. There wasn't going to be much of anything anymore.

The cleaners were just leaving the office when she arrived, and it smelled of freshly applied antiseptic cleaner. While her computer chugged to a start, Kate debated making coffee, wondering if the combination of exhaustion, anxiety, and enough sugar would make the coffee fit for human consumption. She decided it would not. Starbucks opened in an hour.

Kate clicked on her email icon. She felt even sicker as she watched row after row of unopened emails appear on her screen. You returned one and more kept coming back, like a Hydra regenerating two heads for every one you cut off. She stared at the screen in a dull stupor, pretending to work until Starbucks opened. Kate put on her coat and headed towards the door. She was halfway there when Camilla walked in.

"You're here early. Is everything okay?" Camilla asked.

Everything except my life, thought Kate. But she smiled. "Everything is great, thanks! How are you?"

"Is Geri here?"

Kate thought about telling Camilla about the missing earrings, just blurt it out and keep walking, never to return. But it was too early. She needed coffee first. "He's not in yet. I was just running out to Starbucks, can I get you anything?"

Camilla shook her head and pulled her phone out of her pocket. "He hasn't answered my texts." She looked at Kate, eyes burrowing in on her. "We have a problem."

Kate felt her heart sink. Had she found out about the earrings?

"Francis Palma from the New York Museum called." In a rushed voice, Camilla told her the museum had caught an employee stealing in the middle of the night, and he was being held in their offices until the police arrived. "But they want us to interview him before the police show up. The item is valued at under a thousand dollars, so the police will likely consider it a misdemeanor and let him go with a fine. But they—the museum that is—think there's more to it and want us to question him first."

Kate nodded and sucked in a deep breath. It had to be now. She couldn't leave without telling Camilla what happened first. "I have something I have to tell you. It's about the earrings—"

"Good. Tell me as soon as you get back. They think he's stolen several items from them, and that he's been selling them."

Slow down, Camilla. Give me a minute. I'm trying to get myself fired. "I was wondering if, first, we could talk about—"

Camilla looked at her with an expression of pained exasperation. She held up a hand. "This is urgent. Francis is the director of the New York Museum. You have to leave now."

Fine. Kate shrugged. She had tried, hadn't she? Maybe not very hard, but she had tried. Now she'd been granted a short reprieve. A little extra time before the inevitable axe fell. With a sense of relief, she put on her coat and walked out the door.

Ten minutes later, hot venti cappuccino in hand, Kate jumped on the 9 train to 86th Street and walked five blocks west to Eighth Avenue. It was a warm spring day, still quiet for New York, and a rainfall the previous night had left everything smelling fresh. The museum was still closed when she arrived, and Kate pushed the outdoor buzzer. A few minutes later, she was standing in front of the elevator with the museum's director.

"It's unfortunate," he said. The elevator arrived and they walked in. "It was a minor piece he—his name is Morgan—attempted to steal, just a small, uninspired Roman wine flask. Not especially rare or valuable, which is why it was in our visible storage room. Still, its value can't be measured in dollars and cents. Every single item on these shelves is priceless. We're holding a sacred trust for humankind. For all of history."

Kate wanted to ask him if he wasn't being overly dramatic, but she held back.

"And what if there are more? He could have been stealing from us for weeks. I hope you're going to find that out. We take this kind of thing very seriously. We can't have anyone thinking they can just waltz out of here with our property."

"What's the visible storage room?"

"Only two or three percent of our total collection is on display in the main gallery. Most of the rest is in storage. The visible storage room is for everything in-between. Not quite main gallery material, but too valuable to be locked up in a warehouse." The elevator doors opened on the third floor and they walked down the hall. "Mostly visited by students and visitors with special interests."

"And these rooms have less security?"

"Exactly. The main galleries have motion detector cameras, infrared sensors, ultrasonic sensors, microwave sensors . . . you couldn't kick up a speck of dust without setting a dozen alarms off. In visible storage we're less vigilant, but we still have ample security. Morgan must have underestimated how ample."

"What do we know about Morgan?"

"A new employee. General maintenance, basic repairs, that kind of thing. Sad, in a way. Seems like a nice young man, just a bit, um, different, I guess you could say. But we all thought maybe he's on a spectrum or something. Which we respect. We encourage diversity in every aspect of our hiring. It's just . . . I'm not a psychiatrist, but there is something else. He seems to think everyone is in on some kind of conspiracy."

"What do you mean?"

"For example, he claims the CIA are controlling him through radio waves sent directly to his brain."

"Maybe the CIA made him steal it."

The director didn't even smile.

The suspect was sitting on a leather chair near the back of the office. Two guards were standing in front of him, so Kate couldn't see much more than bits of legs and arms. His arms were waving wildly and one of his knees was bouncing, as if keeping time. She could hear him talking, in small, excited bursts, and the guards telling him to calm down.

The director cleared his throat, and the security guards stepped aside.

"Morgan, this is Kate. She's with the FBI's Art Crime Team. She is going to ask you a few questions." The director crossed his arms and looked down at Morgan. "I'm so sorry this didn't work out. I really am. I hope you get the help you need." He turned and walked away.

"Sorry for who?" the suspect called out. "Sorry for who?"

The director stopped and smiled to himself. "Good luck," he said to Kate. "Thank you so much for coming in . . . oh, and Kate? We're announcing the acquisition of a new piece at an event here tonight. It's a beautiful, absolutely precious piece of ancient Greek art and we're quite proud of it. If you're interested, please join us."

After he left, the guards moved to the back of the room, leaving Kate with the suspect. She sat down.

"Morgan, I'd like to ask you a few questions."

He appeared to be around forty. His clothes looked like he'd grown out of them years earlier, and a button missing from his shirt exposed a pale and extended belly. His hair looked like it had been cut with garden shears.

"I'd be happy to help any way I can." Morgan leaned forward in his seat, staring at Kate as if trying to peer into her soul. "Kate, do you know why you're here?"

I'm here because I'm avoiding telling my boss that I lost a pair of priceless earrings, she thought. It struck Kate that her crime was far more serious than his. "Yes. It's because you have stolen—sorry, allegedly stolen—something from the museum."

He laughed quietly and scratched his head. "Of course that's what they told you. Did they also tell you I stole a lot of other things?"

"No. They didn't tell me that. But since you mentioned it, did you?"

Morgan lay back in the chair and squeezed his eyes shut. "Are you sure they didn't tell you that, Kate? Are you certain?"

He was quiet for long enough that Kate wondered if he was having a nap. She sucked in a deep breath and waited, hoping he wasn't going to make this last too long.

"Did they also tell you I was crazy?" he asked.

"No, they did not. And crazy is not a word that I would ever use, in that context."

He laughed again. "Do you, Kate," he said, without opening his eyes, "ever wonder why people believe the things they believe?"

Kate turned away and looked at the ceiling. Why? Why did the world conspire to keep her from doing the things she really needed to do? She should be getting the missing earrings back, figuring out where the sphinx was, checking in on her mom. Either that or drinking cheap whisky in some dingy bar, crying into a bowl of pretzels and wondering what happened to her life. Instead she was here, interviewing some petty thief over a two-bit crime.

He leaned forward, eyes wide open now, staring at Kate. "It's because they're told to believe them. That's why. Want to know how I know?"

What color is the sky in your world, Morgan? Are there trees? Does gravity exist? These were the questions Kate wanted to ask. Instead, she tried another approach. "Morgan, did you know stealing from a museum is a federal crime? It doesn't matter what you stole, committing a federal crime means you could go to jail for ten years. Would you like that? Or would you rather answer my question?"

Morgan's eyes flashed and he crossed his arms before leaning back in his chair. Recalibrating. "You're with the FBI's Art Crime Team?" Morgan asked.

"Yes."

"Well." He leaned further back. "Let's talk turkey. Let's make a deal."

"What do you mean?"

"I help you, you help me. I tell you what's really going on in here, you make sure I keep my job, and we all forget this ever happened."

"What is going on?"

Morgan leaned even further back in the chair, becoming practically horizontal. "Do you know how much of the shit in this museum is fake, stolen, or smuggled? Do you have any idea how many pieces are here illegally? There are more false provenances and papers in this place than you could ever imagine. I know what they're doing. I know how. I also know who's in on it. And FYI? It's not just the forgers, thieves, tomb raiders and smugglers. They're just foot soldiers in a very big army. Everybody else—the agents, curators, directors, police, the CIA, the FBI, the politicians—they're all in on it. Jesus H. Christ, I could tell you some things."

Kate looked at Morgan, who had shut his eyes again. She imagined the look on Camilla's face if she tried to explain his offer to her. Ha. It would not go over well.

"Look Morgan, I appreciate your offer. But I have no reason to believe you know anything, and I don't have the time or interest in playing any games. If you have something to tell me, tell me now. Otherwise, I'm just going to get back to my life, okay?"

Morgan folded his hands behind his head and shrugged. "I'm so sorry for troubling you. Have a nice day."

Kate shook her head and picked up her purse. She was at the door when he called out.

"Don't you find it odd, Kate? That an institution like the New York Museum would make such a big deal out of one piece like this? Why do you think the director would be personally involved in this misdemeanor?"

He was right about that. "I don't know why. What do you think?"

"He thinks I know too much. That's why."

"If you want me to help you, tell me where everything you stole is."

"What do you think of my deal?"

Maybe he did know something. It was possible. But it was also possible the CIA was controlling him with some device sending radio waves to his brain. Possible, but unlikely.

Kate shook her head. "These are priceless antiques, not baseball cards. Here's my phone number." She threw her card on the desk. "If you want to talk, talk. If not, well, that's up to you."

Walking out the front door, Kate's mind rolled through everything that had happened. Did Morgan really know anything? Or was he just visiting from another planet? Where were the earrings? Jacob was not the only other person who knew she'd had them, but he was the prime—the only—suspect. Where was he? She remembered the director's invitation to the event at the museum. Is it possible Jacob could be there? Probably not, but he could be. She had no idea where else she could find him, so it might be worth dropping by. Just in case.

"Hi Mom, it's me. Just calling to see how you're doing and everything. Did you really go to Mexico? I've left a few messages but haven't heard anything, so call me, okay? Love you." Her mother usually returned calls within a minute or two of Kate leaving a message. Where was she? Kate didn't know any neighbors to call and ask to go check on her, so she decided that if she didn't hear from her by the morning, she'd drive there and make sure she was alright.

Kate knew she should go back to the office and confess to Camilla. But the idea of going through that right now made her feel nauseous, so instead she decided to take the rest of the day off. So what if she skipped out on work for an afternoon? What difference would it make? It's not like they could fire her twice.

CHAPTER FIFTEEN

Paul walked through the crowd at the New York Museum, smiling and nodding, his chest out and shoulders back. Made sure he was polite to everyone, especially the people who had ignored and insulted him over the last ten or so years. No point in holding grudges anymore, and he couldn't blame them anyway—he had to admit, he hadn't liked the old Paul much either.

Everything was different now. Since he had sold the vase to the museum, just a week earlier, he had made a fresh start. He was thinking positively, smiling more, and taking better care of himself. He'd cut back on alcohol and made a point of eating vegetables every day. He was even thinking about joining a gym. Maybe tomorrow. Tonight, he was focused on the big event.

Harry had even flown in for the occasion. They hadn't seen each other since London, and it was wonderful to see him again. But they only had a few minutes together before Francis signaled Paul from across the room. It was showtime.

They made their way to the microphone. After a few loud shushes, the crowd became quiet. Francis spoke for a few minutes, mostly about how great Paul was and how lucky they were to have him here today. He used to hate these speeches, but he didn't mind them so much when they were about him.

Then it was Paul's turn.

"A second Eurydemos Vase. Here. It's hard to believe, isn't it?" The crowd murmured their approval. "The vase in the State Museum of the Hermitage, in Russia, was considered the best extant example of the late classical red-figure technique in the world. Until, of course, this beautiful work of art was discovered. Now we have two. Of course, I think ours is better." The applause was strong and steady. "The other vase was a wedding gift." Paul paused for effect, smiling at the enthralled audience in front of him. "We don't yet know what this one was"—he pointed at the vase beside him, safely enclosed in thick glass—"but one could presume it was also a wedding gift, and the two pieces were separated in the divorce settlement." Great laughter. Paul looked out at the crowd of reporters, critics, sponsors and art lovers who had gathered for the big event. The only person not laughing was Imani.

He had been on the other side of this kind of presentation dozens of times, bored out of his mind, drinking to make the time go faster. It was something else to be doing the talking. This wasn't boring at all. He had spent hours working on his speech, standing in front of a mirror, trying out different lines, getting his timing just right. All the practice had paid off. The crowd stared at him as if he were some kind of Indiana Jones who had just discovered the golden chalice.

"Where was it discovered?" one of the reporters asked.

"I can't give you details," Paul answered. "Except that it was purchased from a private collector."

Then more questions.

"Where are they from?"

"How much did you pay?"

"Can you tell us anything?"

"I'm afraid not. He has asked to remain anonymous, and we must honor that request. I can tell you that he is a significant collector who has many other important artifacts, and I very much hope to procure more pieces from him. I will not do anything that might jeopardize the relationship." He scanned the room for Harry, made eye contact, and quickly looked away. "That's all I can tell you."

"There must be something you can tell us," a voice called out.

Paul and Francis smiled at each other and shook their heads.

"What color is his hair?"

Paul laughed. He loved this, loved the attention they were giving him. Felt like he should give some love back. "He's Armenian. There. That's your one thing." Paul raised his hands. "Please, let's move on."

After the press conference was over, Paul grabbed a seat at the bar and ordered a glass of wine. As he sipped, he looked out at the crowd milling around the vase and thought about the week he'd had. Seven days earlier, he would have happily killed himself, if only he'd had the strength to go through with it. Then Harry—dear, wonderful, perfect Harry—had sold him that vase for less than a third of what he could have gotten anywhere else. Where had Harry gone, by the way? Paul looked around but he seemed to have disappeared.

Now Paul had just under half a million bucks in the bank, and that was after he paid back the old man, cleared his American Express and paid his outstanding rent. People were calling him for interviews and inviting him to dinners and special events. His calendar was full. Even better, people were calling him with rare, "priceless" artifacts that he just had to see. He was in. And once you're in, you're in for life.

He picked up a baby carrot, pushed it into the dipping sauce and jammed it into his mouth. Maybe he should take up running, like the old man. Or, what was that diet? The Keto diet? He could maybe do that. Eat more protein, cut back on carbs. He was pretty sure you could still drink on that diet. Later he noticed some of the sauce had dropped onto his new suit. His new Brioni, the most expensive suit he had ever purchased. Well, what the hell. He could just get another one. He was wondering if he should also pick up new shoes when the director sat beside him and put a soft hand on Paul's shoulder.

"You're a gifted speaker," he said. "Nicely done."

"Thanks," Paul replied. He sat up straight and smiled. Reminded himself to push his shoulders back, the way Harry always did. Relaxed, comfortable, and sophisticated. "I do hope I didn't go on too long."

"Not too long. Not too short. Just right." Francis nodded at the bartender, and in a moment Paul had another glass of wine. He gazed at it with a tinge of regret. It would be rude not to accept, but on the other hand he had managed to get through an entire week without slipping up, losing his cool or telling anyone to eff off, and cutting back on drinking had helped. He had to keep his guard up, and a second wine wasn't going to help.

"Listen, Paul. It's been wonderful working with you. And you've obviously got some connections out there in the art world. I want you to know, if you happen to acquire any other pieces you're interested in selling, we're interested. I like to think of us as not only America's best museum, but the world's best museum. But to do that, I need to count on people like you."

"You are the world's best museum."

"Thank you. And I'd like to keep it that way. I'm wondering if we can count on you. Will you promise to call us first? I know we don't have as much money as some of those billionaires, but would you at least give us a chance?"

"Yes, of course I will. Of course you can."

"So we have an understanding. I'm glad to hear it." The director raised his glass for a toast, and they clinked glasses.

Paul felt like he had just been admitted into one of the world's most exclusive clubs.

"Before we make it official," Francis said, "can I ask you something?"

"Please do."

"It's probably nothing." Francis shrugged and gently rapped the counter with his knuckles. "But typically, a seller would contact the curator if she or he had a piece to sell. In our case, that would be Imani. But you skipped over her. Which seems to have put her nose firmly out of joint. And that episode with security, I thought that was just some misunderstanding, but now—I have to ask, just to make sure—is there anything I should know? I'm not being nosy, understand. It's simply that we're a high-profile public institution and we must be careful about who we work with."

Paul sipped his drink, slowly, carefully, before answering. "It's an important piece. I knew how busy she was, and I didn't want it to get lost in the shuffle."

The director shook his head. "That's not all it was."

"Honestly, I was just—"

"This isn't the first time someone's gone over her head. Usually, she lets it go. But not this time. Why?"

Paul looked over at the crowd until he found Imani. She was standing near the corner, far away from everyone else, huddled with her red-haired assistant. Imani's eyes drifted over to Paul and the director. He could feel her hostility emanating from across the room.

Francis forgot about his question for a moment. "Oh, look. The FBI is here."

Paul's eyes drifted back to Francis. "Who?"

"Over there. The woman in the blue jacket, standing alone, along the wall, with her arms crossed. She was just staring at you. I forget her name, but she's with the FBI's Art Crime Team."

"Why is she here?"

"She was helping us with a troublesome employee, and I invited her. I was just being nice. But I want to ask about Imani. Tell me, if you don't mind, what's going on?" Francis asked. "That wasn't just a misunderstanding with security, was it?"

He had to give him something. But what? How much did he have to know? "We were engaged."

The director slapped the bar with his hand. "Holy shit. Really? Wow. I wonder why she didn't tell me. But why did she call security?"

Paul would have preferred not to say anything, to keep that part of his life hidden in a dark closet where it belonged. He was lucky she hadn't told him anything yet. But what if she did? He had to protect himself, get ahead of this somehow.

"We were just days away from getting married. It's complicated." Paul waved at the bartender for another drink. He didn't even want it, because he wanted to stay sharp, but he had to find a way to stall for time. How could he spin this? Did the director know anything?

Even if he didn't, Imani was likely to tell him eventually. So the basic story had to be true.

"It's a kind of love story . . . but a love story where everything just went terribly wrong. I'm happy to tell you. But first, I'm going to run to the little boys' room," Paul said. That would buy him a few minutes to come up with a solid, defensible, revisionist history of what happened. A story that would check out if Imani pressed her case, presented the facts, and pushed the director to make a choice—"Are you sure that's the kind of person we want to do business with, Francis?" He knew that voice. He knew what she would say. She could end this new chapter of his life before it even started.

That's what terrified him. That she could reveal Paul for who he was, or—no, not who he was. Who he *used* to be. He wasn't like that now. He didn't do that kind of stuff anymore. Which was part of the problem: Paul didn't even know what he had done. All he knew was that he got drunk, passed out, and when he woke up the place was a mess, with glasses broken on the floor, windows smashed, and Imani gone—including everything she owned. An hour later, the police were knocking on the door and charges were being laid. Dammit. He hated that he even had to think about this right now.

Far too soon, his time was up and he had to go back. The best story he had come up with was that he'd had an anxiety attack, forgotten to take his meds, drank too much, and after that he simply could not remember. Had a total blackout. He would plead ignorance on everything else.

Where had Harry gone? Paul wished he could talk to him and buy a little more time. But Paul couldn't see him anywhere in the crowd.

He turned the corner and saw the director at the bar shaking hands with two men. Ah, sweet god in heaven! A distraction. The men were the same height, same build, same age—mid-50s, Paul guessed—and wore identical suits. Twins. He took a deep breath and walked up to them.

"Paul! I'd like you to meet two dear friends of mine."

"We're pleased to meet you, Mr. Klugman. I'm Jon," said the one closest to him. Short blond hair, chunky features, black tie.

“The pleasure is all mine, Jon,” Paul said.

The other brother stuck out his hand. He was wearing a red tie. It was the only way Paul could tell them apart. “I’m Erik. We’re the Ericksson brothers.”

“They’re private collectors, Paul,” Francis intervened. “The kind of people I was talking about. But remember, you promised me we’d come first.”

Paul had met so many people over the last week, he was having trouble keeping all their names straight. These two would not be a problem. They were a little strange, he thought, nice enough and all that, but they were so similar, in looks and mannerisms, that they seemed like one person that had taken over two bodies. After more chat and compliments, exchanging phone numbers with vague promises to keep in touch and perhaps have lunch, Paul made his excuses and walked away. A sweet, if temporary, escape. He felt like he had been handed a last-minute reprieve by the gods.

But the gods, he knew, were not a reliable bunch.

CHAPTER SIXTEEN

The traffic from New Jersey to Chester was even heavier than usual—three or four hours of stopping, waiting, starting, and stopping again. Normally this would drive Kate wild, but nothing was normal right now. Today it just felt good to get out of the city. It gave her time to think while she checked in on her mother.

It required immense effort to focus. In between regular waves of panic about the missing earrings and feeling anxious and guilty about her mother, there wasn't any emotional or mental room to spare. She should be confessing to Camilla, but what if her mother really were missing? Or worse? Her mom came before any old earrings. She should have driven home to see her mother yesterday, but never mind that. The drive would give her a chance to think.

So, Jacob must have grabbed her keys when her purse fell, followed her home, and slipped in while she slept. Therefore, the obvious first step was to find Jacob. Where to begin? She had gone to the event at the New York Museum the night before, hoping to see him, but there was just a bunch of overeducated art-intellectuals making long speeches. It was a long shot anyway.

She had tried to pry information out of him at the Four Seasons, but all she'd found out for sure was that he liked champagne. He'd claimed to be working for two men, and Jacob could have talked to them the night she met him, giving them both a motive and means. So, they were potential suspects too, right? Willing to buy from the black market, so obviously unafraid to get involved in anything illegal? So maybe. But on the other hand, why would they steal the earrings? If they did have that much money, they could have just bought them. It didn't make sense. Did it?

The traffic thinned. The tall buildings had long since disappeared, and Kate was driving by abandoned farmers' fields and half-empty towns with little to boast about but a few stores and their own minor claims to fame: Home of the Cougars, Home of the Spartans, birthplace of some president Kate had never heard of. She used to think this drive was boring. All these towns reminded her of Chester, where nothing ever happened. Now, she looked at them with envy. Nothing happening seemed like a pleasant option compared to what she was going through now.

Who else? The guy that stole that wine flask in the New York Museum—Morgan something—said everyone was involved in art crimes. Directors. The FBI. Police. Of course, she couldn't believe anything he said, except for that one point at the end about why the director was getting involved when this was such a minor piece. It was like the president of the United States intervening in a parking ticket. Maybe he was right about that.

That didn't make sense, but a lot of things didn't make sense. Why was she even involved to begin with? She was still a junior agent. How did she end up in the middle of a search for an international crime ring? These cases never went to her. She just happened to be in the office when Luca first called, and since Camilla and Geri were busy, she ended up speaking with him. Of course, no one thought it was a major case then. But Luca kept working with her, actually asked to work with her. If she were a young and beautiful ingénue, she might have understood, but she wasn't young, beautiful or an ingénue. She wasn't even sure what an ingénue was.

Welcome to the Town of Chester, the sign read. Historic Chester. Hamlet of Sugar Loaf. Population 12,435. She drove by the park, the pavilion, the performing arts center, and the Denny's where she used to work after school. Hey, maybe she could work there again after she got fired from the Art Crime Team. One Slow-Cooker Meaty Melt coming up, sir! Would you like a drink with that Brisket BBQ Skillet, ma'am? At least there wouldn't be any emails.

She turned right on McIntyre Crescent, pulled into number forty-four, and shut off her car. The lights were out and it didn't look like anyone was home. Kate got out and walked up to the door, knocking three times quickly before pulling out her house key. Thinking about the earrings on the way there had provided a distraction from worrying about her mother, but now she couldn't think about anything else. It had been three days since she had spoken with her, which wasn't a lot, but they usually talked every other day. She had told Kate she was going to Mexico, but she had never been the kind of person who would just run off anywhere. Her mother had once spent three weeks planning a holiday in the Finger Lakes, and they were just a four-hour drive away.

Kate went in and checked the kitchen, the living room, her parents' bedroom and her own. Everything looked just the way it had the last time she was here. Every single dish was put away, clothes folded and beds made, the place tidy as a museum. Kate checked every single room, including downstairs, where no one ever went anymore, just to make sure her mother hadn't passed out or had a heart attack or something. She hadn't. She wasn't home.

Kate used her mobile to call her mother again, but it went straight to voicemail. "Mom? Where are you? I hope you're okay. I'm getting worried, I don't know why you haven't called. Call me as soon as you get this, alright? Love you." There was a message from Camilla, but she ignored it. One disaster at a time was enough.

She tried speaking to the neighbors, but the only one at home just shrugged and said she hadn't seen Kate's mother lately. The woman didn't seem worried. "She's probably gone on a mini vacay. Poor old thing, at home all day, staring at the same walls. No one visiting."

Great. Just keep piling on the guilt, universe.

Not finding her mother's body on the floor of the house did make Kate feel a little better. Her mom *probably* wasn't dead. Kate thought about calling the police, but didn't think a grown woman missing for three days would attract much attention. Instead, she'd check with the airlines to see if she could trace her that way. No reason to go into full-out worry mode yet. Her mother was fine. If she wanted to go away on a last-minute vacation, well, good for her. She was *fine*.

Kate climbed in her car, turned the engine on, thought for a minute, and turned it off. It would be rush hour by the time she got on the highway, and the thought of sitting in traffic for hours made her nauseous. She didn't have to leave today. Why not just spend the night here and go back tomorrow?

She went back inside and sat in the living room, but the empty house's heavy silence weighed down on her and made her restless. She remembered she had been promising to get together with Natalie for months. Why not tonight? Natalie had been her closest friend since university. Hanging out with her would help Kate forget everything, at least for a few hours. And forgetting was exactly what she wanted to do right now. She picked up her phone.

• • •

The Martini Room had been Kate's favorite Chester haunt since her last year of high school. The martinis, labelled Pain Killers on the menu, included Shake Your Money Maker, Whiskey Business, Tequila Bomb, Hot 'n Bothered Cosmo, and a dozen others, all "guaranteed to lift your mood and calm your mind." Every single one was certain to be far more effective than meditation, she believed. The waiters were good-looking, the chairs comfortable, the vibe mellow.

Kate had known Natalie since high school, but they weren't close friends until university, where they discovered they had signed up for the same art history course. After first year they got an apartment together and were rarely out of sight of each other for four years.

After graduating from Columbia, Natalie landed a job at the Victoria & Albert Museum in London. There were many times when Kate, sitting at her desk in the Art Crime Team, wished she could join her. Natalie loved her job and told Kate she wanted to stay there forever. But after a year and a half Natalie's mother became ill, so she came back to Chester to take care of her. It was just a temporary move, she kept saying.

Since then they'd remained good friends, sometimes close and sometimes not seeing each other for months, but always there for each other. When Kate's father died, when she didn't get the jobs she applied for, when relationships didn't work out, it was always Natalie who brought her out of herself and got her moving again. And it worked both ways. They were their own self-contained support group.

Kate sat down at a table near the bar. It wasn't quite five o'clock, and the restaurant was almost empty. She recognized one of the waiters from high school—she didn't remember his name, but he used to drive a Corvette and played on the Chester football team. Back then, that was enough to put him on the top rung of the social ladder. He disappeared through a side door and her phone buzzed. It was Camilla again. Almost certainly wondering about the earrings. Kate ignored it.

"Hey, punk."

Kate turned around and looked up at Natalie. With her long black hair, heavy makeup, and hoodie pulled over her head, she looked like the evil character in a manga cartoon. Then she smiled, and Kate saw the Natalie she remembered: that impish grin, the crazy dark eyes, that little upturned nose. How could anyone look so cute and dangerous at the same time? Kate stood up and they hugged.

"If something's wrong, tell me now," Natalie said as they sat down.

"What? No, nothing's wrong. I mean, well . . . not really."

"Just say it. Do you have cancer? Did you kill anyone?"

"No!"

"Rob a bank? Burn down a seniors' home?"

"No!"

"Did you catch the mob doing something and now they're going to cut you up into little pieces?"

"I'm not going to get chopped up into little pieces."

Natalie's eyes burrowed deep into Kate's. "Truth?"

"Truth."

"Okay, geez." A look of relief flashed across Natalie's face. "Fucking hell. You scared the shit out of me."

"Why?"

"We don't see each other for what, a year? And all of a sudden you want to meet right away? I thought you were having a major crisis."

"Sorry! I just wanted to see you. Nothing's wrong."

"I'm glad you're not going to get cut up into little pieces." She smiled again. "It's so nice to see you."

They ordered drinks and fell into the conversation routine they'd had, with variations according to age and circumstances, for almost ten years. What they'd been doing, relationship status, how much Natalie missed London, whatever happened to whomever. Natalie thought her mom would have to move into a nursing home. Kate explained how her mother might or might not be in Mexico. Natalie broke up with her boyfriend after finding out he was still on dating sites. Kate talked about her life in New York, where she still hadn't had a single real date and her social life consisted of visits to the grocery store.

But Natalie was still skeptical. "There is something else you're not telling me," she said. "I know you better than that, Miss Kate Taylor. So what say we order another drink and you tell me what kind of trouble you've got yourself into. Deal?"

"I'm not in trouble."

Natalie raised her eyebrows and shook her head. "Fine. Have it your way."

They ordered and kept talking about nothing in particular. It was somewhere in the middle of their third cocktail that Kate opened up. She hadn't planned on saying anything, but Natalie asked her how everything was at the office, and Kate started talking and couldn't stop. She knew she shouldn't because she wasn't permitted to talk about active cases. But she suddenly felt like she had to tell someone, just to say it out loud and see if that would help her make any sense of the catastrophe her life had become. She didn't care if she wasn't supposed to. It was Natalie, and she could tell her anything.

Kate told her about the first call with Luca and questioning Morgan at the New York Museum. She told her all about the earrings, showed her the selfies she took wearing them, and how she felt when they went missing. After she was finished, they ordered another drink. Natalie sat quietly for a minute or two before she spoke.

"Tell me again. How did you end up working on this?"

Kate told her how no one else had been available to take Luca's call, how they thought it was just a minor case, and how the whole thing had turned into something else.

"And he never asked for anyone else? Even though he knew what was at stake, and that you were still a junior . . . sorry, I didn't mean that, but—"

"I know what you mean. And you're right."

"You didn't think that was a bit odd?"

"I don't know. I guess he just wanted me to work on it."

Another pause in the conversation. "I'm just saying, I don't know about this Luca. I mean, it's weird that he didn't care about the pieces of the vase you found in Customs. He didn't want you to follow up on that. This might just be my Hot 'n Bothered Cosmo talking, but suppose he's involved? If he's getting a cut, he would definitely prefer to have someone with less experience on the file, right?"

"You don't know him. He wouldn't do anything like that."

"Really?" Natalie sipped her drink.

"Really. I would know if he was."

"How?"

Kate thought for a moment. "Just because."

"What does he look like?"

"That's got nothing to do with anything!"

"Tell me anyway."

Kate finished her drink. "He looks alright, I guess." A pause. "I mean, he's got long, thick hair. And his chin, you know, is one of those big, strong . . . he has these big eyes, you practically fall into them every time he looks at you. And even his eyelashes are—they're unreal. The longest eyelashes I've ever seen on a man." Another, longer pause. "So I guess he looks okay."

Natalie laughed. "*Okay?*"

"Fine, he looks good! So? That doesn't mean he's involved."

"It doesn't mean he's not involved."

Kate frowned at Natalie. "I know what you're thinking. But you're wrong."

"You did give him your address."

"Yes, but I was joking. He probably forgot it right away."

"Or not. Actually, isn't it a bit of a coincidence that this Jacob guy calls you late at night and insists on meeting you with the earrings right away? Like he somehow knew you'd go and get them?"

"I don't see that as a coincidence. That was the plan. It was working perfectly, just the way it was supposed to."

"Forget it. I don't know what I'm talking about. I've had too many drinks. But, if I were you, I'd take another look at this Luca. Just make sure he's not using you, okay? And be careful, before . . . I don't know. Don't listen to me. I'm rambling."

"What are you saying?"

"I'm saying don't worry. They'll turn up. Check that vault at the office again, I bet someone just moved them somewhere by mistake."

"There's no way Luca has anything to do with this."

"Why? Because he has big eyes?

"No!" said Kate.

"Alright, sorry, sorry. Let's talk about something else."

The drinks arrived, the conversation drifted, and it was past midnight before they hugged their goodbyes and went home. Kate went to bed in her old room, but with the floor shifting and the bed spinning underneath her, she couldn't stop thinking about Luca.

If Natalie knew him, she would know he wasn't like that. Although, Kate *had* given Luca her address. Which didn't mean anything. Did it?

Kate thought back. When Luca asked her to work on the case, she thought it was because he liked and trusted her. Was she just flattering herself? Maybe the real reason he asked for her was because he knew she would fail. Not likely, but possibly, he wanted a junior person on the file to make it look like he had asked the FBI to get involved, even if he didn't really want them involved. If that was the case, Kate would be perfect for him because she was still junior, and maybe too dumb, to suspect what was going on.

No, that didn't make sense. He wasn't crooked. But if he was . . . well, when Kate suggested the bait idea, no wonder Luca thought it was such a great plan. He could send her some priceless artifact, like the earrings, and arrange to steal them back and blame the FBI for losing them. Presto, he had possession of this rare treasure, and the FBI would be taken off the file since they were incompetent enough to allow them to be stolen. It was a perfect plan. For him.

And the whole story about Alexander the Great? And Caligula? Maybe that was just some crazy story to send her on the wrong trail. Also, what about asking her to forget the fragments of the Amasis vase she found in Customs? Why else would he ask her to ignore them? Thinking she was so dumb she'd fall for it. He was almost right. But not quite. Remember what Morgan said? That everyone was involved? Maybe Morgan knew what he was talking about.

Maybe Luca was involved. And Jacob, obviously. And also that director at the museum—he seemed kind of suspicious. And who knows, maybe Camilla? They were all suspects, and Kate was going to figure this out, she would outsmart them all—if only this stupid floor would stop spinning around and let her focus.

Then the room went black.

CHAPTER SEVENTEEN

If anyone ever doubted that Earth had been visited by aliens, Paul thought, all they had to do was walk around one of Marguerite Victoire's furniture showrooms. Every couch, chair and lamp, the shapes, colors and textures, even the general atmosphere of the place—all of it was out of this world, unlike anything he had ever seen. The couch Paul was looking at had eight different patterns and varying shapes patched together with no discernible theme, and such a mash-up of colors that it felt like a psychedelic experiment. It sat flat on the ground, as if it were too avant-garde for legs. An oversized turquoise pillow lay on the floor where the ottoman should have been, and what appeared to be a giant light bulb, over four feet high, rested on its side at the far end.

It took him about seven seconds to fall in love with it.

He had to have this couch in his apartment. It had the exact postmodern, fun, hip-rock-star, famous-art-dealer-on-top-of-the-art-world look he was going for.

"It's a Pai Gow," the salesman whispered, as if revealing the secrets of the pyramids.

Paul wondered if that was the name of the designer, the couch's brand, or a metaphor. But he didn't want to ask so he just nodded. "I love it."

What Paul did want to ask was how much it cost, but it seemed too early for that. Harry wouldn't have asked yet. The rules of upper-crust furniture civility dictated that you must chat about other things first, like spaces and colors and textures and how it made you feel—circling gently before getting around to the price of it. Only problem was, he didn't want to talk about any of that. He just wanted to know how much it was.

The salesman, who was probably six foot six and looked like he weighed less than one hundred pounds, said, "Would you like to try it?"

That seemed reasonable. Paul sat down in the middle, smiled up at the salesman who was smiling down at him, and slid back. It didn't feel quite right, so he slid back further. He kept sliding until he reached the cushion, and by then his feet were sticking straight out. It felt awkward, but Paul just went with it, like he'd sat on couches like this hundreds of times. Leaned back, put his hands behind his head and found himself staring at the ceiling.

"Comfortable, isn't it?"

It wasn't, but Paul said "Absolutely!" with what he hoped was a note of confident enthusiasm. After a few moments, he scrambled back up. It required some effort—you practically had to be a gymnast to work this thing—but that just added to the thrill of owning it. He wasn't buying the couch to be comfortable. He was buying it because he wanted to look good on the cover of *ARTetc* magazine.

After an extended stretch of small talk, Paul finally got a chance to ask about the price. The answer—forty-five thousand dollars—sent a cold jolt of anxiety running through his veins. But it was fine, nothing to worry about. He could afford it now that he had the money from the sale of the vase, and promises of more deals coming.

It had been less than a week since he'd sold that vase, and Paul had already discovered he was really good at spending money. He had a closet full of new clothes, including five custom-tailored Adam Lamb suits and two new pairs of Testoni shoes. He had acquired a taste for two-hundred-dollar bottles of wine and Michelin-starred restaurants.

He had already checked out a new apartment, gigantic by New York standards, with a stunning view of the city skyline and a stunning rent to match. And if he wanted to spend forty-five thousand dollars on a couch just because it looked good, he was going to do it.

A few hours later, Paul was in his apartment, sitting in his Krug armchair (a relative bargain at eight thousand dollars) and congratulating himself on his purchase. The couch would be perfect. It was the focal point he needed, the crowning glory of the apartment. The photo shoot was tomorrow, and Paul would be ready for his close-up.

He closed his eyes, put his feet up on the ottoman and tried taking a nap. He couldn't. Ever since the event at the museum, just three days earlier, his brain had been spinning and circling, whirring along at speeds and in directions he couldn't control. It snapped through the lunches, dinners, meetings and events he was scheduled to attend, all the new people he had met or would soon meet—curators, directors, artists, collectors, journalists—famous, rich people, people you read about, people you saw on television. It flipped back and forth, from past to present to future and around again, like a glitter-filled highlight reel.

He couldn't help thinking about what was ahead, what he was going to do with this newfound success. He could hire a few dealers, grow the business that way. Or open his own gallery, maybe, or even a network of them. Branch into contemporary art, which seemed more fun than antiquities. There were so many things he could do! And it wasn't just growing the business he was looking forward to. A lot of women—well, three—had been calling him, talking to him in a way he wasn't used to, making overtures and giving him feelings he hadn't experienced since Imani. He had put them off, buying time, trying to get used to this brand-new world before he jumped in with both feet.

He should call Harry. Paul hadn't spoken to him since the event at the museum, and had barely had a chance even then. He felt a stab of guilt about that. After all, Paul wouldn't be here—might not be anywhere—if it weren't for Harry. He would call him, soon. But not now. Paul had a big event to attend that night, and he had to get ready.

If the event at the New York Museum was Paul's coming-out party, this was his debutante ball. It was his formal entrance into high society, his introduction to prospective buyers in the upper one percent of the upper one percent. The annual party—it even had a name, the Brazil Ball or something—was being held at one of the homes of the Ericksson twins, the brothers he had met at the museum. It was a huge mansion in Manhattan South, where homes sold for sixty to eighty million dollars. Francis would be there, as would every other A-list celebrity in the art world and beyond. Paul spent an inordinate amount of time choosing his suit, tie, shoes. Events like this are why a man needs a nice pair or two of Testoni shoes, Paul thought. Of course, his old man would never understand that.

The furniture movers arrived, set up the couch, and left. Paul couldn't help trying it out, lying down on every section, admiring it from every angle of the apartment, imagining how he would sit and entertain guests, what they would say, all the questions they would ask. Why did you buy this crazy couch? they would ask. He saw it and liked it so he bought it, he would answer, smiling and shrugging his shoulders in a "but what could I do" kind of way. Then he would tell them all about the Pai Gow (for he knew now that Pai Gow was the type of couch, named by the designer, who had imagined it as a "champion of free form and expression of individuality"). It would be a great conversation piece. But now, the limousine was going to be here in a few minutes.

An hour later, he was pulling into the driveway of the Erickssons' home. The oak tree–lined driveway went on forever, as he imagined it would. The cars in the driveway—Rolls, Bentleys, Lamborghinis, several black Mercedes SUVs—were exactly what he expected. In the distance, he could see the house, and it was every bit as big and majestic as he knew it would be. Everything was just as he had imagined.

A three-piece jazz band was playing Duke Ellington songs in the front foyer. That foyer opened into a great hall, painted in soft whites and lined with Corinthian pillars. The walls were decorated with a few large-scale canvases of classic paintings that looked vaguely familiar, like a Delacroix maybe, but he couldn't be sure. Thirty or forty people were milling about. The room smelled like money, all subtle perfumes and expensive silk, rare wines, and champagnes. Paul didn't know anyone and felt that nervous tic that comes from the fear of being a stranger alone in a crowded room.

He had expected to feel like a celebrity there, with all the people he'd met lately. Expected people would be crowding around him, asking about the vase and wondering if he had other treasures lined up for sale. But after ten minutes, no one had even looked at him. The people here were truly famous, uber-rich and outrageously beautiful, and he wasn't on their level yet. He didn't feel like a debutante. More like an awkward kid at his first high school dance. Where was Francis?

Maybe he just needed a drink. That would help. He found the bar and ordered a Manhattan.

"On the rocks?"

"Yes. Rye."

He probably shouldn't drink hard liquor here. But one couldn't hurt. Just until he got settled down. He grabbed his drink, walked around, pretended to be looking at the art when he was really just looking at the people. That woman was some politician, federal, he couldn't remember her name. That man was a gallery owner—Arman, or Aram? Someone big. God, this was awkward. Every other person was in a group, and he was so obviously alone. Was Imani here? She probably wouldn't have made the cut. And that . . . was that Charles Fraser? It was! Wow. An actual, live Hollywood celebrity. Paul had just seen him in a movie the week before. He was with Sharon someone, who he'd seen in another movie. They were not even twenty feet away, and they were walking towards him. He'd have to tell Harry about this. He took a big drink and told himself to slow down, stop drinking. But he was already walking towards the bar. Just one more.

"Paul, I'm glad you could make it!"

A wave of relief. Someone he knew. "Thanks for inviting me, Francis. So very wonderful of you." He picked up a glass of water from a passing waitress and smiled gratefully.

"Let me introduce you to some special friends of mine."

And there it was. For the next two hours, Paul did nothing but shake hands and chitchat with millionaires and billionaires. He pushed his shoulders back and smiled, tried to remember as many names as he could—even entering the most important names on his phone after they'd moved on. Paul ditched the Manhattans and stuck to Perrier. He was warm, charming, affable: He was full-on Harry. It was all "wonderful this" and "wonderful that," "so marvelous of you to say so" and "so absolutely kind of you." Francis provided a running account of who was who: which ones would be interested in buying art, and which ones were just really, really good to know.

"And what about the Ericksons? Where are they?"

"They won't make an appearance until two or three in the morning. And even then, only for a few minutes."

Paul was too busy meeting people to think about that. The coolest person he met was Charles Fraser, who was outrageously good-looking, funny, and absolutely reeked of Hollywood charisma. The most important person he met, according to Francis, was the Egyptian minister of culture, who didn't say much but stared at Paul like he was sizing up a ripe tomato. The most beautiful was an actress named Maya, who caressed Paul's shoulder for a few unforgettable seconds. He mentioned his couch to her and she said she'd love to try it, which made his temperature rise by several degrees. They exchanged phone numbers.

After two hours, it felt like he'd met everyone he could meet and was ready to go. He couldn't keep up the act any longer, couldn't keep smiling and laughing, hadn't a single word of witty banter left in him. Feigning interest in everything and everyone took a lot out of him, and he was exhausted. It was just past midnight and time to make his exit. He thought about trying to find Maya and inviting her back to his place, but decided against it. Better to save his energy for the big shoot the next morning.

CHAPTER EIGHTEEN

Camilla's office door was shut, but Kate could hear her talking on the phone. Her stomach was rebelling and her entire body ached as she tried to input another missing object into the art file. A nasty combination of hangover and high anxiety. She had a flashback to the night before, remembered Natalie asking the waiter to pour more vodka into their martinis. It seemed like such a good idea at the time. If only she could go back home, climb into bed, and put off what she had to do for one more day. But that wasn't going to happen. Kate had checked her phone this morning. Camilla had left three messages, asking for an update on the Carabinieri file and her plan with the earrings. She couldn't avoid it any longer. As soon as Camilla's door opened, Kate would tell her everything.

Another hour passed. The door remained closed. Kate had yet to come up with any way to explain how the earrings had gone missing, other than just blurting it out. There was no way to polish it, or make it seem reasonable, defensible, or anything but the straight-up horrible mess that it was. She would just tell Camilla. Then sit back and wait for the bomb—bombs—to fall. Camilla would look at her with that robot expression, her eyes hard and cold, jaw tight, neck stiff, and she would start ranting. How stupid could you be? This is the worst thing anyone has ever done. You are fired. You are under arrest. You have brought eternal shame on the FBI. This is all your fault.

How long was she going to be on the phone? Kate dreaded telling Camilla, but prolonging the agony only made it worse. It had already been three days since the earrings had disappeared, and Kate should have told her right away. She was lucky Camilla hadn't checked to see if they were in the vault.

Kate had not resolved whether she would mention her doubts about Luca to Camilla. During her long night of drunken sleeplessness, lying in her bed worrying about her mother, the earrings, and her entire life, she kept coming back to what Natalie had said about him. It made sense in so many ways. The more she thought about it, the more convinced she became. She had been used by him, had stupidly fallen right into his little plan, and now she was going to pay the price.

Yet. Telling that side of the story to Camilla, well, that was complicated. No matter how she imagined explaining it, it just sounded like she had screwed up and was trying to blame Luca for her mistakes. There wasn't any way she could see herself convincing Camilla that Luca was involved. She could barely convince herself.

The broken pieces of the Amasis Painter vase. They were a part of all this, somehow. She had no doubt. Alex had told her they were being shipped to the Modus Art Gallery, which was not far away. If only she had followed up then, she might have discovered something that would have helped her avoid this mess. Now it was too late.

It was almost noon and Camilla's door was still shut. Kate thought she better get something to eat, something to settle her stomach before she threw up. She grabbed her coat, ran downstairs and outside towards the sandwich shop down the street. An egg salad sandwich would help, she thought. And a banana. She'd heard they were good for hangovers. Her phone rang just as she walked inside. It was Luca. She ignored it.

Fifteen minutes later, sitting on one of the stools at the counter by the window, watching the city pass by and chewing on the last few bites of her sandwich, Kate felt her strength coming back. As the food settled her stomach, she felt her mind unclouding, her anxiety ebbing. She started to think. Clearly, this time.

There was no reason to go back to the office. She could tell Camilla about the earrings tomorrow. It had already been three days, and she was going to get fired anyway. One more day wasn't going to make a difference. She had something else to do.

It was a long shot, but it was worth a try.

• • •

A soft breeze blew waves of dust and empty plastic bags down the cobblestone streets of Tribeca, the newest hot neighborhood in the New York art world. The Modus Art Gallery looked exactly what Kate thought an art gallery should look like. Wide, black marble pillars framed by two large front windows, a single painting hanging inside each. The gallery's name was set in chrome plate in the bottom corner of the front right window. It was so small you would miss it if you weren't looking for it. The gallery sat quietly in a row of stores selling high-fashion shoes, interior design, luxury vacations and expensive real estate. It had been over a week since Alex had told her this was where the ceramic fragments were being shipped. They had to have arrived by now.

Kate swung open the door and wandered in, trying her best to look nonchalant. On a short stand directly in front of the door was a large piece of what looked like a ceramic cream pie with a candle melting on top. Further in was a desk lamp with a woman's body and a straw basket for a head. It was all the postmodern stuff that Kate had never taken the time to understand or appreciate, although she had always intended to try. She couldn't help but wonder why a shipment of stolen artifacts thousands of years old would be delivered to this self-consciously hip contemporary art gallery, and rechecked the address Alex had given her.

People wandered aimlessly about, standing and staring at the different pieces, whispering to each other. Most of them were young couples dressed like they were on the set of a fashion shoot. Their expressions suggested they were either depressed, bored, or desperately serious. Perhaps all three. A woman wearing bright, oversized, red-framed glasses dotted with fake pearls was explaining the meaning behind the pie with the candle to a couple who gazed at it silently.

Kate overheard a man explaining a painting to his companion. "The artist is depicting the banality of the exterior world, contrasted with the fantastical world of the imagination that lives within all of us." She wanted to throw up. Mansplaining is a thousand times worse in contemporary art than it is anywhere else in the world, Kate thought. If you're going to mansplain, do it about something useful, like how to fix a toaster or change a tire. If you're going to be irritating, you may as well be useful. But mansplaining art should be a federal crime, punishable by death.

Twenty minutes later, the lady with the red glasses—Kate assumed she was the gallery owner—was still speaking to the same couple about the same piece of art. It seemed like she was going to be a while, and other couples were standing nearby as if waiting for an opening.

Her plan was to pose as a buyer of ancient Greek vases. It seemed unlikely that this gallery would stock anything ancient or Greek, but those broken ceramics had been shipped there. There had to be a reason for that. If the vase wasn't there, maybe the owner would know where they were. If Kate could find the vase, she might be able to find a way to connect it to a smuggling operation, which might—and this was a hundred-to-one shot, but that was all she had—give her a clue to the whereabouts of the earrings.

Kate moved closer to the owner, hovering just a few feet behind her. The couple appeared to be losing interest in the long-winded explanation about the meaning of the art, and in the artwork itself. A few minutes later, they made a few vague promises about going home to think about it and Kate moved in.

"Excuse me? I'm sorry, hello?"

The owner, who had started to walk away, stopped and turned around.

"Hi!" Kate said. "I'm wondering if you have any ancient art?"

"I'm sorry." The woman smiled and shook her head. "This is a contemporary art gallery."

"I can see that. I was wondering if you had anything in the storage room?"

"We don't. Now, if you don't mind—"

"I'm interested in ancient Greek vases, preferably black figure. Do you have any?"

The woman crossed her arms and gazed at Kate, the smile fading quickly. "No. If you're interested in anything from this century, feel free to look around." She turned around and walked away.

"Thanks! I will."

Thirty minutes later, Kate had pretended to study every piece of art in detail. Those vase fragments had to be here, she thought, or had been at some point. Walking to the back of the gallery, she wandered down a long hallway, past washrooms, a closet, and two offices with their doors shut. At the far end of the hall was a doorway leading into a back room. The door was open a sliver.

She peered through the crack. It looked like a storage room. Curious, she pushed the door open another sliver. She still couldn't see much: just shelves, boxes, dark shapes and shadows. Kate looked back towards the gallery. No one could see her down this hallway. If those ceramics were anywhere, they'd be in here. She slipped inside, quietly pulling the door closed behind her.

It took several seconds for her eyes to adjust to the light. The room was cool and dry, and smelled of all-purpose cleaner, wood and metal—the official smell of an art gallery storage space. Four long rows of metal shelves were stacked with modern artworks of every shape, size and material. She advanced a few more steps, then hesitated. She knew she shouldn't be there. Her stomach muscles tightened, and for a moment she was tempted to turn around and leave. But if she did, she'd never get another chance. She swallowed her nerves and kept going.

She walked up one aisle and down the next, searching every shelf and along every wall. Maybe she should use her phone's flashlight—but no, someone might see her. She was near the back of the room when she realized what a horribly bad idea this was.

How would she explain herself if she got caught? She couldn't. They would arrest her, charge her with breaking and entering. She looked back at the door, thought about turning around and running out, wondered if it was too late. But then it dawned on her that it didn't matter if they caught her and reported her. The hell with it. She couldn't possibly be in more trouble than she was already.

She took another look around, but found nothing. The crate couldn't be here, she thought, or she would have found it by now. It was time to get out. But just as she was about to run back to the door and make her escape, she saw it.

It wasn't anything like what she came here for. Not even close.

It was better.

It was a business card, tied to a wooden art crate, that read:

Hatchwell Fine Art Restoration
New York City
Since 1987

Fine art conservation, repair of damage,
all types of ancient and contemporary art

325 E 21st, New York, NY, United States

She had found what she wanted. Kate took a photo of the card and walked to the door. She opened it and found herself standing one foot away from the lady with the red glasses.

Kate could see the lady's eyes pop open and flare behind the glasses. "What are you doing here?" she said.

Kate thought she should be frightened, but she wasn't. Maybe it was because she didn't care anymore, like she had nothing left to lose. Or maybe it was the way the lady held that look, the way she kept staring at Kate with her eyebrows raised and chin up. It was so over-the-top melodramatic. Whatever it was, the one thing she did know was that she didn't have time for this.

"Either those glasses have to go," Kate said, "or I do."

The woman didn't respond.

Kate said fine, walked around her and straight out of the gallery.

CHAPTER NINETEEN

"I'm so happy for you, Paul," Harry said. "The New York Museum is an impressive institution. Your vase has found a wonderful new home."

Paul lay back on his new couch, pushing the phone against his ear and staring up at the ceiling. He wished he had bought a pillow. "I still think of it as your vase."

"That's kind of you."

"I'm sorry, we hardly had a chance to speak when you were here. You came all this way, and I—"

"Don't give it a thought! You were busy. How have you been?" Harry asked.

"I've been fine," Paul answered. "Better than fine." He told Harry how much his life had changed since he sold the vase. How he had received three phone calls just the day before from people interested in buying and selling art—important, connected, rich and powerful people. How he had been invited to VIP events, chatted with celebrities from inside and outside the art world, even met Charles Fraser—yes, *that* Charles Fraser—who was very nice and really interested in art. He was even interviewed for *ARTetc* magazine, and had his photo taken by a professional who brought her own hair, makeup, and lighting experts. They were so talented, Paul told Harry, they even made himlook good.

As Paul talked, he realized the changes in his life weren't just external. It wasn't just the money or the lifestyle. It was inside him. He felt like he had become someone else, like his DNA had evolved into a brighter, better, more sophisticated being. He remembered waking up one sunny morning a few days earlier, looking out his window, and realizing he was smiling. That hadn't happened since he was eight years old.

"I've got some other nice pieces coming in," Paul told him. "A dealer called with a silver chalice from Cambodia, believe it or not. Not especially old, nineteenth century, but it's lovely. I wish you could see it. Hey—that's an idea right there. Why don't you come and see it? Would you like to visit? I'd love to see you again."

Paul realized he was stealing more and more of Harry's affectations in his speech. When had he ever used the word "lovely" before? Now, it was part of his vocabulary. In fact, he could hardly remember how he used to talk. Or even the person he used to be.

"There are beautiful antiquities being discovered in Cambodia," Harry said. "Thank you for the invitation. But—"

"Why don't you? Stay for as long as you want. It's my turn to play host."

"You're a wonderful person." He let out a long sigh. "I'm afraid . . ."

Harry's voice sounded slightly off, a little less—what? Comfortable? Confident? Less certain of his God-given place in the universe? Paul couldn't quite put a finger on it. "You sound a little put out, Harry. Not quite yourself. Is there something wrong?"

Harry didn't answer.

"What is it?" Paul asked. "I can tell. Something is not quite right."

"You're very astute. I didn't mean to let on."

"Please. We're friends. Tell me what's happening."

Another pause. "This is a bit of an embarrassment, " Harry said. "But I've gotten myself into a bit of a bind."

Paul had never considered the possibility that Harry's life could be anything but perfect. He seemed to have everything: money, culture, intelligence, connections, hair. It had always seemed to Paul that Harry's charmed life was a fact of nature. Permanent and immutable.

"What happened? Did you . . ." Paul paused. It wasn't his place to ask what happened. "What I meant to say was that if there's anything I can do, tell me. I'm happy to help any way I can." It struck Paul that he meant it. Another first. He actually wanted to help another human being.

"I appreciate the thought. But I'm afraid I'll have to take care of this problem on my own."

"Talk to me, Harry," Paul insisted. "There must be something I can do."

"I wouldn't burden you . . ." Harry spoke slowly, drawing out every word. Released a long, guttural sigh followed by a weak laugh.

"A burden? After everything you've done for me? Don't be silly. If it weren't for you, I'd be living in a homeless shelter. I want to help. I absolutely insist."

The sound of cars honking in the distance, feet shuffling, and ice cubes clinking. Paul knew those sounds, even from three thousand miles away. Harry was in his apartment, the window was open, and he was pouring himself a drink.

"You're awfully persuasive. I'll spare you the sordid details, but I find myself in a certain financial situation that necessitates the selling of a few—well, more than a few—of my works here."

"Oh, Harry, I'm sorry to hear that. I know how much you love that collection of yours. Just tell me what you want sold, and you can consider it done. No commission. This is all on the house."

"Thank you. But . . . it's more complicated than that, I'm afraid. You see, under the present circumstances, these particular pieces can't be sold through the traditional channels. Which means no galleries, museums, not even dealers. No press, nothing official. They will have to be sold privately, and only to the most discreet collectors. Do you understand what I'm saying? It's a deeply personal matter, but I can't have my name anywhere near them. I'm sorry. I didn't intend to tell you any of this. Perhaps—no, almost certainly—it's best for both of us if you don't get involved."

Paul wondered what could have happened. Unpaid tax bills? Paul had been caught in that maelstrom before. Or maybe Harry had another problem, a gambling addiction, or something like that. Maybe he was being blackmailed. But it didn't matter. The man had saved his life, and he owed him. "Not at all. It's not complicated for me. I can sell them any way you want."

"It's nice of you to offer," Harry said, and Paul thought he heard muffled crying.

"It's nothing you wouldn't do for me," Paul replied. "Or haven't already." The old Paul would have backed out of the conversation by now, as soon as he had made his obligatory offer to help. But not this time. This time he was determined to do the right thing.

"You must understand, there are certain risks."

"I'm happy to help. Have you decided which pieces?"

"I'm still coming to terms with that. Every time I decide on which piece to sell, I'm up all night worrying about it, changing my mind and changing it back. I suppose I have some difficult decisions to make."

"As soon as you've decided—"

"Absolutely. I'll let you know." Harry lowered his voice to a whisper. "And, please, do keep this quiet. I'll have to send them to you in a way that won't draw attention. I know it all feels rather cloak-and-daggerish, but I'm afraid there is no other way."

"Put my name on them if it helps."

"I can't ever thank you enough. But—since you offer—do you think you may know anyone?"

Paul thought of the twins. "The Ericksson twins. They're private collectors, mostly Greek and Roman. And they're outrageously wealthy."

"That sounds brilliant," Harry said. "Do you know them?"

"Of course I know them," Paul said. "I've been to their house. Let me find their number."

• • •

Two days later, Paul walked into the lobby of 68One68 carrying his tablet, which had an uploaded photograph of the first piece Harry had decided he could part with. It was a Roman marble bust of the Greek goddess Athena, dated around 400 BC. He approached the concierge, asked for the Ericksons, received a smile in return and walked to the elevator. He pushed the button for the sixty-eighth floor and bolted upwards. As he climbed, past floors thirty, forty, then fifty, he felt the air pressure squeeze in on his ears and keep squeezing until he felt as if he were at the bottom of the ocean. Paul swallowed to relieve the pressure, but it didn't help. By the time he stepped off, his head felt like it was stuck in a vice.

There was no point in knocking on the door yet. He wouldn't be able to hear a word anyone said. He walked down the hall and thought he could feel the building swaying with every footstep. Maybe it was. Why would anyone build anything this high? Finally his ears popped, a little, just enough to hear. He walked back to the door and rang the doorbell. Straightened his shoulders while he waited, relaxed his jaw muscles. Swallowed his fear and practiced his smile. Remembered the warm, effusive, friendly hellos that Harry always had for everybody. That was more like it. A few moments later, a stocky young woman dressed all in white answered the door.

"Hello!" Paul said, with what he thought was just the right amount of effusiveness. She gave no sign of understanding how perfectly effusive he was, or even what he had said. Just offered a slight nod, turned around and led him towards a chair near the window.

No, Paul thought. He did not want to go near that window. He'd never had vertigo before, but he'd never sat by a window on the sixty-eighth floor before. If he sat there, he would have to look down, and he was afraid to look down. But what else was he going to do? Argue with the housekeeper?

He sat down but shifted the chair so that it faced as far away from the window as possible. He looked around the room. Art was everywhere: ancient vases, Greek statues, precious stones and jewelry, a selection of classic, modern, and postmodern art. Was that a Modigliani? And a Vermeer? They couldn't possibly own a Vermeer. And this wasn't even their only residence! They also owned that home in Manhattan, and who knows how many others. Based on what he'd seen so far, Paul calculated these two must be worth several hundred million dollars.

"You are Paul Klugman, I assume?"

Paul turned around to see the twins standing behind him. They reminded him of those rich international kids he'd see around university, the ones who spoke six languages and were usually former Olympic skiers or semi-pro tennis players. He stood up.

"Hello, yes, I'm Paul. And you're Erik?" He extended his hand to one of the men.

The other twin said, "That would be me."

"I'm Erik. This is Jon. We are happy to see you again."

"Well, it's nice to see you both again as well. That's a hell of a—" Dammit, Paul thought. That's not how a proper dealer spoke. Get a hold of yourself. "That's a gorgeous view you have." Paul nodded towards the window without turning his head so he wouldn't have to look down.

"Please, have a seat. Thank you for accepting our invitation. We have heard much about you lately, Mr. Klugman. You've become famous in our little world."

The twins took two seats near the window. He had no choice now: He would have to look towards the window or he'd be facing away from them. Were they doing that on purpose, trying to make him anxious? He twisted in his seat, doing his best to keep his eyes directly on them.

"Thanks, Erik," he said.

"Jon." They chuckled mirthlessly.

"Of course. Thank you both for seeing me today. And also for the invitation to the event at your home last week." They both smiled vaguely. Paul couldn't tell if they knew which event he was talking about.

After Harry had told Paul he was willing to sell some of his collection, Paul had called the Ericksson twins right away. He left a message, uncertain if they would even call back. They called the next day. Now he was here, in the penthouse of the two richest people he had ever known, two of the richest people in New York.

Paul tried to stay calm, to channel Harry's dignity and charm. It wasn't easy. He felt nervous, intimidated by the wealth surrounding him and the distance below him. It felt like he was leaning over the edge of the Earth, and if he looked down he could fall. Sixty-eight floors. There would be almost nothing left, just a few shattered bones and a splatter of blood. He leaned back in the chair, sucked in a deep breath, struggled to regain his sense of self, and smiled. "You both look so good, it's impossible to tell you apart."

They laughed. At the same time. And in uncomfortably close to the same way.

Paul heard a quiet clink on the glass table beside him and looked over to see the woman in white setting a Manhattan on a coaster. She delivered two glasses of white wine to the twins.

"We thought you might want a drink," Jon said.

"To celebrate," Erik added, picking up his glass and air-toasting Paul.

"Sure, thanks." Paul picked up the glass. Three cherries, lots of ice. Just the way he would have made it. How did they know that? He had sworn off hard liquor—at least in public—but he couldn't say that now. It would be impolite. He picked up the glass. "What are we celebrating?"

Erik tipped his glass. "Your company."

"We are excited to see what you've brought for us."

Paul looked at Erik, then Jon. They looked back, indecipherable grins pasted on their faces. Their excitement seemed premature to

Paul, since he hadn't yet told them what he had for sale. Perhaps his reputation had created high expectations. That was good news, he guessed. He hoped Harry's piece would live up to whatever it was they were expecting. But before he got into that, he had a major hurdle to overcome.

"However . . ." Paul wasn't sure how to bring up the condition of anonymity. It would be a red flag. They would instantly suspect that what he was selling was there illegally. He wished he didn't have to do it, but it was going to come up eventually. Better to get it out of the way now, before the discussion started getting serious. "However, this piece does come with one fairly serious asterisk. A big qualifier, as it were. I'm afraid I won't be able to reveal the seller's name. He has insisted on anonymity. The item is legit, of course. Nothing questionable about the work or the provenance. But I'll have to ask you to keep this quiet. Just between us. I apologize, but I'm afraid my hands are tied on this."

Jon looked at Erik, and they both shrugged. "Of course," he said.

And that was that. Not even a raised eyebrow.

Unbelievable.

Paul pulled his tablet out and showed them the photographs of the statue. "It's dated around 430 BC. Marble. Almost eight inches high. It has been attributed to Pheidias, and I don't have to tell you what that means."

The twins leaned over, glanced at the photo for a short moment, and leaned back.

"If you're interested, I'll have it delivered here so you can have a look at it before you make any commitment."

"That won't be necessary."

"No? But . . . really? You must know it's not in perfect condition," Paul added. "I have to be honest—"

"We're not purchasing a dining room table," Erik said. "One doesn't expect perfection."

"What is the price you are asking?" Jon asked.

Harry had suggested a selling price of three hundred thousand, which was more than what Paul would have estimated it was worth. He thought Harry was just being hopeful. But now, sitting here . . . Paul glanced up at the painting behind them. If that really was a Vermeer . . . and they seemed very interested . . . "Five hundred thousand," he said.

"We'll have the money transferred tomorrow," Erik said.

"Oh." Paul scrambled to think of something to say. These two men had just agreed to pay half a million dollars for a piece they hadn't even seen. That didn't even come with provenance. Who did that? Maybe they were crazy. They acted like it. He couldn't help thinking he could have doubled the price and gotten the same result.

He calmed himself down, and the three of them raised their glasses. "Congratulations. You have a beautiful new piece to add to your collection." He smiled, but he didn't feel like celebrating. Something didn't feel right. They hadn't asked where it came from, who the seller was, or about the condition it was in. They had barely looked at the photograph. It almost felt like they knew what it was before he got here. He sipped his drink and wondered how they knew he preferred extra ice. He didn't know why, but he felt like two great white sharks had just swallowed him whole.

CHAPTER TWENTY

Of course the subway had to be delayed. It had to be, because Kate was in a hurry, and therefore, by the universal law of the cosmos, the subway must be delayed. The art restorer's shop was only open for another fifteen minutes, and she absolutely had to get there before he closed for the day. She closed her eyes and prayed that the cosmos would just back right off and give her a break for once.

It did. The subway's wheels started again, reached the stop at Freeman Station, and screeched to a halt. Kate was already at the door. She was the first on the platform, first to the stairs, and first on the sidewalk. With eight minutes left before the store closed, she half ran, half walked down the sidewalk, dodging people, dogs, and baby carriages. She saw the Hatchwell Fine Art Restoration sign across the street. Six minutes.

Cars honked and drivers shouted as she ran across the street, but she ignored them. She tried to pull the door open, but it was locked. No! They couldn't be closed yet—her watch said 5:56 p.m. Kate pulled again, a few times. Locked. She leaned on the glass and looked inside. It was dark, and she couldn't see anything at first. Then she saw a shadow moving behind the counter and disappear into a back room. Someone was there. A few loud knocks on the door didn't get any response, so she knocked louder. Then louder. Then she yelled, kicked, and knocked.

A man appeared near the back door, standing behind the counter. "We are closed!" He sounded angry.

"But your sign says you're open until six," Kate shouted back, pulling on the door again. "Come on. Open up!"

"It is after six."

"It wasn't when I got here. Please! It's really important."

The man stood still, his silhouette outlined by the light in the room behind him. He was tall, almost bald, slim. His shoulders seemed to have a permanent curve, as if he spent his days hunched over. He held a broom in his hands.

"Please. I really need to talk to you."

He walked slowly towards the door, holding the broom. Kate could see him staring at her, wondering if he should open the door. At last, he twisted the lock and pulled the door open about a quarter of an inch. "It's late. I'm tired and I have work to do. Come back tomorrow."

"I can't come back. It won't take a minute, I promise."

He pulled the door open another few inches and walked back behind the counter, shaking his head the entire time. A worn leather apron was tied around his waist, and his T-shirt and jeans were covered in paint. He started sweeping.

"What do you want?"

"I'm looking for a Greek vase. A vase with, well, there's a wedding scene, and—"

"This is not a gift shop. I am an art restorer. You've come to the wrong place."

"I'm not here to buy it. I'm here to find it. It was smuggled into the country illegally." He stopped sweeping for a second or two, then started again, but faster. Kate couldn't see why he was sweeping at all. The floor looked perfectly clean.

"It's by the Amasis Painter. You know who he is, don't you?"

He shook his head and kept sweeping.

"I think it's here," she said. "Or it was here."

"As I said, you have come to the wrong place," he said, without looking up. "If you ever need restoration work done, please come back. Book an appointment next time. Goodbye."

His voice was soft, his accent Eastern European.

"But you know where it is, don't you?"

"No. Now I have to get back to work."

"If you do know, you'd better tell me where it is."

He stopped sweeping and looked her up and down. "Or else? Is that what you are suggesting? Or else what? Are you the police? Are you here to arrest me?"

"I'm not the police. I'm with the FBI's Art Crime Team."

The sweeping started again, but slowed down considerably. For a few minutes he was quiet, concentrating on pushing the broom back and forth. His voice took on a slightly higher pitch. "I don't have what you're looking for. I don't know where anything here came from. That's not what I do. My only work is to restore art, and that is everything." He looked less angry now. "That is everything."

"I think you know exactly what I'm talking about."

He stopped sweeping again, and, for the first time, lifted his head and made eye contact. "Would you like to come into the back and see what I do all day?"

Kate would have preferred to stay where she was, find out if he had the vase, where he got it from, where it was going, and get out. But if he did know, he wasn't ready to tell her yet. She said yes.

Walking towards the back room, he nodded to Kate and she followed him inside. It looked like an oversized garage with enough room for nine or ten cars. Six long, wooden tables were lined up in a row, stacked with cans of paints, brushes, scalpels, bits of half-built antiques, pieces of ceramics and metals. It looked like a combination of art class, archeologists' laboratory, and lawn sale.

"What I get, it looks like this." Twenty or thirty fragments of ceramic lay on the table. He picked up one of them, no more than a few inches across, and held it up to Kate. "Except it's still covered in the ancient dirt it was discovered in, what, twenty or thirty feet under the ground." He brushed off a speck of dirt. "What I am doing, I am creating a work of art, using bits and pieces of materials that are thousands of years old as inspiration. You see—come here, you're standing too far away—this little piece. What do you see?"

Kate stood close enough to smell his breath, which reeked of garlic and coffee. She leaned in. "The head of a snake? And a bit of something else . . . is it a shield?"

"Very good. So you see. A snake head here, a fragment of a shield there, maybe part of a sword, or perhaps a tail. It begins like a jigsaw puzzle, with most of the pieces missing. But that is just the beginning. Then I must go deeper, to understand when it was made, where it came from, what materials the artist used." He put down the fragment and picked up his broom. "But even that, that is not the most important thing. The most important thing is the original artist. What was he thinking? Who was he? What did he want to say? I must live inside his head, imagine what he was imagining. Listen to what these fragments are telling me. If I can do that, then I can get the story right, the composition and balance right. The vision. The whole piece. Do you see that?" He was leaning on his broom now, staring at Kate, his eyes wide.

"Those vases you see in the museum, the ones you quickly glance at as you're walking to the *Mona Lisa*, or the Rosetta Stone, or whatever, all those vases start like this. Dirty, broken, pulled out of the ground after thousands of years. But they all have stories to tell, and I'm the one who tells them. I spend every day in here, you know. Sometimes eighteen hours in a row, bent over these tables, trying to tell those stories. Imagining I'm that artist from two, three thousand years ago." He started sweeping again. "That's what I do all day."

Now Kate knew why he wanted her to know what he did. He wanted her to know he wasn't involved, didn't know or care where the pieces came from or where they went. He was just here, working, and wanted to be left alone.

"What's your name?"

"Alfred."

"Hi, Alfred. I'm Kate."

He didn't respond.

"Alfred, I understand why you're telling me all this. I do. The thing is, you're not the one we're looking for. But you can help us. It's not just a vase we're looking for. There's so much . . . I'm talking about treasures of unimaginable splendor, important and historic discoveries. And they could all go missing if you don't help me, right now. If you know anything, please tell me."

"I cannot help you."

"The vase I mentioned. It's here, or was here."

"That is not true."

"So where do those fragments come from?"

Without looking up, he rubbed his forehead and snorted. "From everywhere. Continents all over the Earth. From hundreds of years ago to thousands of years."

"Who do you get them from? Who buys them? Where do they go?"

He sat down in a chair, holding the broom across his lap. Looked at her with a combination of disappointment and sympathy. "You don't have any idea, do you?"

"Idea about what?" Kate sat down at the next table. "Tell me."

He smiled at her, weakly, showing a row of short teeth. Kate guessed they had been worn down by excessive grinding. Inside that lanky, bent-over frame there seemed to be miles of tightly wound nerve ends.

"This business is not like other businesses. In this business, you do not ask questions because you don't want to know. The fragments you are referring to come from some man, or woman, who goes by the name Larry, Susan, Armen, Marco. It doesn't matter. That's all you know, a first name, and all you want to know. Because if you know more than that, eventually you'll either be killed or arrested. Not knowing is how you stay alive. The sooner you understand that, the better. I'm giving you advice. You should take it."

Up until now, Kate had never considered working on the Art Crime Team to be particularly dangerous. Yes, Luca had warned her that it was, and Camilla had mentioned there were risks. But they seemed more like "don't ride a bike without a helmet" kind of risks. Just be careful, don't do anything stupid, and you'll be fine. Looking into his eyes, she knew—with a certainty she could feel in the pit of her stomach—that he was dead serious.

"Alfred, I appreciate what you're trying to do. But I need this. I need something. A name, an address, I don't know. Something. You say you don't know anything, but maybe there's a little scrap, a piece of information, a possibility you can give me. Because if I don't get something from you here, now, tonight, my life is already over. No one will have to kill me because I'll already be dead. There's no need to bore you with details. I'll never tell anyone where I got the information. I promise. I'll walk out of here, leave you alone, and you can keep doing this beautiful work you're doing. But if you can help, help me now. Otherwise, there is no 'eventually' for me. There's no tomorrow."

He shook his head. "There is nothing."

So that was it. If nothing else, Kate could say she had tried. But now, it was over. "There is nothing." Three words, a lifetime of meaning. She supposed that one day she might look back on this as the moment she bottomed out. Maybe after this, she could start a new life, find something else she wanted to do. At least she'd be able to say she gave this life her best shot. Now, it just felt like her world was ending.

She got up, mumbled a thanks, made an effort at a smile and walked to the door. Alfred followed her. He unlocked the door and let her out first, then followed her for a few steps as she walked up the street.

"I'm sorry, what was your name?"

"Kate. Thanks again, Alfred. Bye."

"I'll walk with you." For twenty or thirty steps, they walked together without saying a word. Then Alfred put up a hand and stopped.

"The gallery you're looking for is the Hodges Gallery," he said quietly. "If anyone knows where this vase is, it's them. And as for tracing any of these smuggled pieces back to where they came from, well, that is almost impossible. No one seems to know for sure. For years, there have been rumors about a dealer who lives in northern Italy who is said to be behind most of the shipping of illegal artifacts out of Europe. But no knows who he is, or can get anywhere near him. Or her. I was once told he lives in a town called Torrento, but I have no way of knowing if that's true. I've been told he's Iranian. I've also been told he's English, Turkish, Armenian and Swedish. Who knows? He may not exist at all."

"Why are you telling me this now?"

"It's not safe in that store. It's not safe anywhere. You could be in the middle of the Gobi Desert and you would not be safe. If they want to find you, they will. Be careful. These people don't ask questions before they shoot. I've told you everything I know. Now do me a favor. Do not ever come back here. Your kind of curiosity will get me killed."

"Alfred, thank you. A million times, thank you."

"Be careful. Have a good life, Kate."

• • •

"I cannot believe this." Camilla scrunched her face up and looked at the ceiling. "If you knew the earrings were stolen three or four days ago, why are you just telling me now?"

"For one thing, I tried to tell you the very next day, but I couldn't because you insisted I go to the New York Museum. Remember how you rushed me out? Then I had to go see my mom, in Chester, and I still don't know where she is, and your door was locked all morning yesterday—"

"I left you messages. You could have called."

Kate tried to think of an answer for that, but couldn't.

"Four days, Kate! Four days! You've withheld information from me before. You promised you'd never do it again. I should have known I couldn't trust you. But this!"

"It was just three and a half days, if you think about it. And there's been a lot of—"

Camilla put up a hand in front of Kate's face. "Stop. Just stop."

Kate stopped.

Camilla closed her eyes, and for almost a minute, Kate listened to her slow, heavy breathing.

To Kate, it felt like a hundred years.

"Okay." Camilla opened her eyes again. "Take me through everything."

Kate told Camilla the entire story, starting with meeting Jacob at the Four Seasons and ending with her visit to Hatchwell Fine Art Restoration. She told her all about Jacob, Alfred, and Luca's story about Alexander the Great's tomb. Camilla's expression wavered from disbelief to hostility to disgust, with lots of head-shaking and lip-curling tossed in, but at least she didn't interrupt. She listened.

"So that's why the Carabinieri is so interested in the sphinx," Camilla said. "They think it could be a link to the remains of Alexander's tomb."

"Yes."

"They should have told me."

"So should I."

"And they didn't, because they're worried about—"

"No one is else is supposed to know."

Camilla thought for a minute. "And you think this Hodges Gallery may have the vase you're looking for?"

"They have, or they did, or they will."

Kate paused and waited. It took everything she had just to remember to breathe.

Camilla's face expressed nothing. There was still a good chance Kate wouldn't have a job in the next minute or two.

"I suppose we'll have to tell the Carabinieri. What's his name again?"

"Luca." Kate's doubts about Luca had only deepened, but this was not the time to express them. She didn't have enough information, and no evidence. She just nodded. "I'll tell him."

Camilla spun her chair sideways and stared out the window. "Don't do that yet. Hold off for a day or two. If he calls, just say we're working on it. Don't tell him anything."

"Okay."

"I've been in the FBI for thirty-odd years, Kate. I've made mistakes too. Some big ones. It's possible everyone has. But your mistake is, in all probability, the biggest, stupidest, most horrendous mistake anyone has ever made. I should just fire you. But I can't." Camilla turned to face her. "Do you know why?"

Kate shook her head.

"I can't fire you because when the shit comes down on these missing earrings, as it no doubt will, everyone's going to be coming after me. Not you. Me. This is too big to blame on you. They'll want my blood. They'll say I should have known they were missing, or I should have checked, or shouldn't have agreed with this entire plan in the first place. And they'll be right. So firing you now isn't going to help me. Do you understand what I'm saying?"

"Yes, and I'm sorry that I've—"

"You say sorry a lot, but you never sound like you mean it. It's more like an 'I'm sorry, but I'm going to do it anyway, too bad for you' kind of sorry."

Kate started to respond but Camilla held up her hand.

"So, instead of both of us getting fired, what we're going to do is fix this big fucking mess we're in. Let's check out this gallery first, before we start an international incident. Do you understand?"

"Absolutely."

"Do you? I'm hearing you say the right things, but have you really internalized the concept?"

"I absolutely have. I understand."

"Then why do I feel as if I'm making another huge mistake?"

Kate didn't have an answer to that either. While Camilla just sat in her chair and shook her head, Kate thanked her, again and again. Camilla didn't respond, so Kate finally got up and walked out. Her life wasn't over. She didn't have to leave the country and disappear. She still had a job. It might not be for long, but she had that. A thimbleful of hope in an ocean of desperation. She texted Natalie.

I told them about the earrings.

Did you get fired?

Nope.

Great! Are they going to cut you up into little pieces?

Don't think so.

K. Let me know if they do.

I will! See you soon.

♥ I still think it's Luca.

Kate didn't answer that. Natalie could be right, but what if she wasn't? She decided, instead, to send Natalie a picture of Luca from his Facebook page.

Is that him?

Yes.

If he's guilty, it's totally OK.

CHAPTER TWENTY-ONE

Paul had been to airports all over the planet and resigned himself to the fact that they all looked the same. The same white tile floors and walls, the same stainless-steel highlights, the same gray chairs, fluorescent lights, stores, and restaurants. Still, he had assumed the Athens airport would be different. He didn't have any reason to think that, except that it was, well, *Greece*. Cradle of western civilization and all that. The airport in the birthplace of democracy should not look the same as the airport in, say, Boise. It shouldn't, but it did. The only difference was the number of men walking around with semi-automatic guns.

He lifted his suitcase onto the moving sidewalk and kept walking, pushed past a family that was standing in his way, mumbling sorry and meaning the opposite. Exhausted from the ten-hour overnight flight, parched from drinking too much wine and not enough water, hungry from not eating the mediocre food, wallowing in the misery of long-distance travel. Then he walked out of the departures gate and saw Harry.

His old friend was standing near the railing, waving and smiling, impeccably dressed in his fitted linen suit, full head of long and styled white hair, looking so alive and full of vigor. What was that old ad? "You're not getting older, you're getting better." Paul had snorted the first time he heard that. Even as a little kid, he thought it was a pile of crap. Now, looking at Harry, he wondered if it could be true. Paul self-consciously straightened his shoulders, smiled, and waved back, shrugging off the hunger and exhaustion. He was here, he was on holiday, and this was going to be a great week.

"Paul, you have arrived! It's so nice to see you." Harry gave him a one-armed hug and a big smile. "As always, you look wonderful. How was the flight? Not too horrible, I hope?"

"So wonderful to see you as well, Harry. And the flight was not horrible, it was quite pleasant. Thanks again for inviting me." Paul wondered what his old man would think if he heard him using the words "quite pleasant" and "so wonderful to see you." Probably whack him in the head and tell him to stop being a pansy.

"You deserve a vacation. You've been working night and day, thanks to me."

It was only a few days earlier that Harry had called Paul and asked him if he'd like to visit. Stay for a week or so at his "residence in Greece." He said it as if he were asking Paul to pop over for a beer, as if everyone had a residence in Greece. It was, of course, impossible to say no. Harry was right. Paul did deserve a vacation. He'd been busting his ass. On the phone, meeting people over lunches and dinners, making sales, meeting lawyers, reviewing contracts. Dealing in antiquities is harder work than people think.

"We'll get you back to my place straight away. You can unpack, shower, nap, have a drink or just lounge in the backyard and enjoy the view," Harry said as they climbed in his car and left the airport. "This is your holiday."

Paul looked out the window. It was a warm Saturday, and beside the busy highway the empty factories and office buildings lounged peacefully under the hot sun. In the distance, mountains and pine trees lined the horizon. The Acropolis looked down on the city from its rocky outcrop, as if waiting patiently for the country to return to its past glory. Byzantine structures sat awkwardly in the middle of crowded streets. "How long have you had a home in Greece?"

"A month or two."

A month? Paul thought for a moment. It was just over a week earlier that Harry had called him, distressed and depressed, claiming he was in a financial crisis and had to sell pieces from his beloved collection. He sounded like he was crying when he said it. Paul had already sold the marble bust to the Ericksons, plus a few other pieces, and had meetings lined up to sell more. They had been shipped incognito, per Harry's request, discreetly packed in crates marked as gifts and memorabilia, and passed through the border as easily as a bag of coffee beans. How could Harry have bought this home a month earlier if he was in such dire straits?

As they drove, the heavy, noisy traffic of the city turned into country, and the country turned into a quiet drive along an ocean road. Paul could smell the salt of the ocean, feel the sun on his face, hear birds singing overhead. The ocean was a deep green, small waves lapping lazily up on the shore, in no rush to get back. Everything was beautiful. The warmth of the sun sunk into his bones. Paul could feel it relax every cell in his body. He would try and figure out the math behind Harry's financial picture later. For now, he would just sit back and enjoy the scenery.

He woke up to a hand squeezing his shoulder. "We're here, my friend."

Paul opened his eyes. He had no idea how long he had slept and it took a moment or two to focus. When he did, he saw a wide expanse of still blue water surrounded by a low concrete wall. Was that a wading pool? It was the size of a small lake. Beyond that, there was a row of evergreen trees, and another of juniper shrubs, all carefully cultivated. Behind all that sat a glowing, pearl-white house. Or mansion. Or palace. Whatever it was, it was impressively humungous. This could not be Harry's "residence."

"Is this yours?" he asked.

"Yes."

Harry parked the car and pulled Paul's new Louis Vuitton suitcase out of the trunk, and they walked inside. Two of the largest couches

Paul had ever seen sat in the middle of a living room. They made his new couch look like an ottoman that got carried away. There were two fireplaces, a circular staircase, and an entire wall of ceiling-to-floor glass doors that opened onto a view of the ocean.

"Nice place," he said.

"Thank you. It's comfortable."

Comfortable. Like the Taj Mahal must be comfortable. Or Buckingham Palace.

"There are eleven bedrooms, you can choose whichever one you prefer. If you'd like to relax, there is a jacuzzi in the back and a sauna upstairs. I've been told there's a steam room somewhere, but I've never found it. Or just sit by the pool and have a drink. You must be exhausted from your travels."

"No, no, I'm fine. A drink would be nice."

"Ideal! I'll meet you out back. Please make yourself at home."

Paul took his suitcase and went upstairs. Paintings hung on every wall, but it wasn't the antique art that he had come to associate with Harry. It was mostly modern and postmodern. A few he recognized—Picasso, Pollock, Richter—and a lot he didn't. He found a bedroom with a panoramic view of the Aegean Sea, dropped off his bag, and couldn't resist the temptation to lie down on the bed. Solid king-size mattress, fresh mulberry silk sheets—everything looked new. He had to fight the urge to fall asleep. He wanted to explore this palace, sit by the pool and soak up the sun, have a drink, and find out how Harry could pay for all this.

He looked up at the painting on the wall in front of him. A cartoon-like image of a round head, big eyes and Mickey Mouse ears smiled back. It was signed by someone named Murakami. No one Paul had ever heard of, but he wasn't up to date on contemporary art. He looked it up on his phone and discovered Murakami's art regularly sold for two million or more.

Paul went downstairs. Through his exhaustion and jet lag it was difficult to think, but one thing was crystal clear. He didn't know anything about Harry.

• • •

Three days later, Paul had settled into the routine of the lazy, rich, and famous. He got out of bed late, usually after ten, and spent the days sitting beside the pool, watching television in the media room, or sleeping. Harry left for work every day—Paul still didn't know what kind of work that was, and Harry had been vague when asked—so he found his own ways to amuse himself. One day he ventured out in a kayak and paddled up and down the beach, checking out the neighbors' palaces. Total relaxation. Pure bliss. Paul even found himself reading in the library. He couldn't remember finishing an entire book since he was at university, and then only because it was required reading. But something about this place made him want to read.

He picked Mary Shelley's *Frankenstein* off the shelf and was surprised at how much it wasn't like the movies he had seen. When the doctor, Victor, said something about how nature will soothe his pain and "elevate me from all littleness of feeling," Paul felt a rush of blood. That struck a chord. He felt the same way. Ever since he had started making money he'd felt different, but it was hard to put into words. Now Mary Shelley had done it for him. "Elevated from all littleness of feeling." Elevated. That was it exactly. He took the book out to the pool and finished it that day.

But he couldn't get the question out of his head: How could Harry afford all this? He had hinted he had old money, that his father had built some theatre or something, but Paul didn't think it was this kind of old money. He thought it was more like the "we can afford to keep the old mansion but not the butler" kind. And those financial difficulties—Paul had sold a few of Harry's pieces, but you could take all the money Harry had received on those sales, multiply it by a hundred, and you still wouldn't come close to paying for this place.

Paul was on the balcony of the second floor at the front of the house when Harry arrived home. It was getting dark as he watched Harry drive up and park outside the garage. He almost shouted a greeting, but what he saw stopped him short. He had never seen

Harry like this before. Harry was wearing a T-shirt and cargo shorts, socks that went up to his knees, and work boots. His socks didn't even match. It was nothing like the upscale designer fashions he was used to seeing him in.

But it wasn't just that. It was the muck and dirt that covered Harry. He looked like a kid who'd been rolling around in mud all day. It was in his hair and on his face, in caked layers thick on his boots, and all over his arms. Harry shut the car door, looked around and disappeared into the house. Half an hour later, he reappeared. Fresh, high-fashion clothes, sparkling clean. The old Harry.

"So what did you do today?" Harry asked.

"Read a book. Attempted to kayak. Mastered the jacuzzi."

"Sounds extremely hectic."

"Just go, go, go." Paul laughed. "There were two other kayaks on the ocean, so, you know, middle of rush hour."

That night, as they were enjoying drinks by the pool, Paul tried to find a way to ask. Subtly. "How about you? What did you do today?"

"Oh, just boring business. You know."

"Art business?"

"You could say that," Harry answered. "More wine?"

"Thanks," Paul said. "At the office?"

"Yes. Meetings. Phone calls. Shaking hands. Paperwork. Lawyers. Insurance agents. Typical day at the office. You know."

"I do," Paul said. But he didn't.

The moon was almost full, falling just a splinter short of a full circle. The stars glimmered, and a warm breeze blew in from the ocean. A few birds sang from the trees and a yacht sailed lazily in front of them. It was too idyllic, too perfect, like one of those boy-meets-girl movies where everything works out so, so beautifully in the end. Paul couldn't resist the urge to mess it up.

"But I don't really," he said. "You were covered in mud when you got home. Didn't look like a typical day at the office to me."

He could see Harry smile, even in the dark. Like he had been expecting this.

For a few minutes, he didn't say anything. Paul wondered if he was going to ignore the comment, change the subject, pretend it wasn't anything. Maybe he would get upset. It was, Paul supposed, bad form to suggest your host was a liar. Paul guessed he should apologize, but he didn't. He waited for Harry to say something.

Instead, Harry stood up. Walked in front of Paul and stood there, still. His head was partially framed by the moon, but it was angled to one side. It looked a halo slipping.

"Quite right, Paul. My office isn't what you'd call typical." Harry scratched his head, and it left his hair standing on end as if an electrical current were running through it. With the moon behind him and his hair sticking out, he looked possessed. Like Victor's monster. Then he smiled, a slightly mad little smile, and the impression was complete. "Would you like to see where I work?"

"Well, I don't know." Harry was being un-Harry-like. Paul noticed a strange tone to his voice that he had never heard before. "Sure, I guess. If you want to. I was just—"

"I think you'd rather enjoy it. It's quite a sight." Harry turned around and started walking through the house, towards the garage. "Come with me." It sounded more like a command than an invitation.

They walked to the garage, the pea gravel crunching under their feet, the wind picking up speed, and Harry marching ahead. Paul saw what looked like the glint of a gun in his belt, and he felt his chest tighten. Harry opened the door and Paul saw a small fleet of ATVs. They sat low and wide, with extra fat tires that stuck out from the side of the frame and oversized exhaust pipes in the back.

"Yamaha Raptors," Harry said. "Highly modified. Run like banshees. You'll have to be careful."

"Should we really be driving?" Paul asked. "We've had a few glasses already."

"It's Greece, Paul. Drinking and driving is part of the culture. They teach it in grade school." Harry climbed on the ATV nearest the door. "Pick whichever one you'd like." He turned the key, pushed a button and the motor jumped to life. It sounded deep, pulsing and angry, like an overexcited monster truck. "Let's go!" he shouted.

Paul climbed on the ATV nearest him. He had never driven one before, it was dark, and he was more than a little drunk. Also, shouldn't they be wearing helmets? It took a moment to find the key and start button, but as soon as he pushed it the engine started and he felt the machine rumbling underneath him. He was tempted to beg off, claim he wasn't feeling well, say he needed to sleep. But if he was half terrified, he was also half curious. Maybe this would answer the question: Who *was* Harry?

"Accelerate with the right handle," Harry shouted. "Rear brakes are also on the right."

"Where are the turning signals?"

"Ha!" Harry laughed. He took off down the driveway. Paul gently twisted the accelerator, and the ATV crawled out of the garage. He twisted the accelerator another half-notch and it raced ahead, too fast, his head snapping back and his front tire coming within inches of smashing into Harry. It took a few more tries before he got settled into a steady speed, and after that he stayed about ten feet behind Harry. A few minutes later, his friend lifted his left hand and pointed right, turned off the driveway between a couple of cypress trees and onto a pathway Paul hadn't noticed before. He turned and followed.

The path was wide but dark, and for most of the time Paul couldn't see much more than Harry's taillights. Every now and then the light of the moon would find a gap in the trees, and Paul could see more of the landscape. Tall trees and wild shrubs covered both sides of their route, and twice they had to drive around a large trunk that had fallen over the path. The pathway was marked with rocks and crevices. After thirty minutes Paul's stomach, still full of food and wine, felt like it was on spin cycle.

Harry, who had started off slowly, picked up speed and Paul had to hurry to keep up. If he got lost now, he would never find his way back. The taillights ahead of him disappeared. Panic flooded his senses until he reached a steep hill leading to a wide, empty field, where he could see Harry's lights in the distance. Once again, Paul had to pick up speed. Harry slowed down, waited for him to catch up, then went down a bank and turned left into a creek. The dark, cold water reached halfway up the tires and soon Paul was soaked up to his waist. Twenty minutes later, they exited the creek, turned right and went up another hill. They had been driving for almost an hour before Harry pulled over and shut his engine off. Paul did the same.

"Having fun?" Harry asked.

"Absolutely," Paul lied. He was soaking wet and felt sick, lost, and anxious. "I kind of wish I knew where we were going."

"My office! It's just over this hill."

Paul thought he could hear the dull roar of heavy machinery for a moment, but the sound of Harry's engine drowned it out. He followed him to the top of the hill, where they stopped again. Paul shut his engine off and stared.

The open plain was lit primarily by the bright moon, uninterrupted by trees. Paul could make out three rectangular areas carved out of the long grass, each a few feet deep, sporadically lined with trenches. The entire area, perhaps the size of two or three football fields, was surrounded by a barbed wire fence. A man with a machine gun slung over his shoulder was standing beside the gate, gazing warily at Paul. A dozen or more people wearing small lamps on their heads or carrying flashlights were working in the field. He saw two backhoes digging up the ground, while other men and women were digging with pickaxes. Others were using metal detectors to sweep the ground. A few of them saw Harry and called out greetings.

"Welcome to my office," Harry said. "Otherwise known as the Lost City of Boura."

Paul looked around the dig. The scene had an ominous feel to it, as if they were opening up an ancient graveyard. He wished he could turn around and run, but there was nowhere to go.

CHAPTER TWENTY-TWO

What do you wear when you're going shopping for rare antiques? Kate hadn't given it much thought when she went to the Modus, and now she realized that was a mistake. Her old denim jacket and discount-store blouse would have raised a warning flag with the owner. She didn't look like she could afford a framed print at a flea market. Kate knew she needed to dress with more style for her visit to the Hodges Gallery. She needed something that looked artsy and expensive.

Unfortunately, she didn't have any clothes that fit that description. The best she could do was a silk blouse, her most expensive jeans, and a bracelet her grandmother had left her. Could she get away with running shoes? They were Brunello Cucinelli running shoes, so they'd be okay. No one would know she got them at a warehouse sale.

It was almost time to leave. Shortly, she would be walking into the Hodges Gallery. Camilla would be somewhere nearby, listening in on the surveillance wire Kate was wearing, ready to provide assistance if she ran into trouble. "It's starting to look like summer" was all Kate had to say, and Camilla promised she'd be there in seconds.

They had been through the plan a dozen times: What questions she would ask, how to act, which names to drop. Working on different ways to convince the owner she was an authentic buyer, like acting as if she'd done this a hundred times before and showing off how well she knew the art market. She also had to convince him she was wealthy enough to spend several hundred thousand dollars on an antique vase.

Her phone rang. No Caller ID. Her mother!

"Mom, hi! How are you? Where have you been?"

"Hi, sweetheart. I'm fine! How are you?"

Kate shut her eyes and felt a wave of relief wash over her.

"I was so worried. Why haven't you called?"

"What? I said I'm fine. Fantastico! Mexico is the best!"

But why did she have to call now?

Kate could tell from the wobble in her voice that her mother had had too much to drink. At least she was alive. And clearly happy. Kate heard laughing and shouting behind her, and a loud pulse of what sounded like a combination of rap, mariachi, and polka music.

"Mom, I'm so happy to hear from you—"

"Sorry, honey, I can't hear. Can you speak up?"

"I'm happy to hear from you!" Kate was practically shouting into the phone.

"That's great, honey, I'm so excited for you. Did you say his name is Hugh?"

"What?"

"What happened to Luca?"

"Mom, can you go somewhere where it's a little quieter?"

"Just a minute honey, I'm having trouble hearing you."

For the next minute, all Kate heard was music and laughter. It got quiet again and her mother came back on the phone.

"Kate?"

"Mom. That's better. So where are you?"

"I'm in the washroom. It's the only place I can hear you."

"No, I mean where are you in Mexico?"

"At a resort called the Pirate's Cove. It's all-inclusive, so you can drink and eat all you want. The tequila is delish!"

"Yes, well . . . that's great, I guess. But why—"

"I needed a change. Sitting around that house watching the squirrels run around gets old. I was going out of my mind. Now I'm here, and it's so much fun. Every afternoon they have Crazy Crazy Time, which it really is. I should have done this years ago, but your dear old dad never wanted to leave his beloved United States. I am having a fucking blast."

Having a what? A *what*? Kate cringed. She hadn't heard her mother swear in—in ever. Not even a damn or a darn. "Why didn't you call me earlier?"

"I'm sorry, I kept meaning to, but my phone ran out of battery, and it took a few days to get an adapter. And, I've been busy. Getting to know people, and swimming, and dancing, and yesterday I went kayaking, and—"

The sense of relief Kate felt was overwhelming. She hadn't realized how much worrying about her mother had been weighing on her. "Don't ever do that again, okay? Call me next time."

"Sorry, honey, I have to go! It's almost Crazy Crazy Time. Oh, and I met the sweetest man. He's funny, good-looking, and very suave. His name is Alejandro, and he's half my age. He's built like Brad Pitt, he adores me. Bye, love you! I'm looking forward to meeting Hugh!" She hung up.

A man? A young, suave man? Brad Pitt? Kate wasn't sure if that was good news or bad news, but she didn't have time to think. Camilla was waiting.

• • •

Kate walked down the wide, cracked sidewalks of Fordham Street in the south Bronx. The street smelled of garbage and car fumes, and was populated by young, lost-looking women and blank-eyed men who looked at her as if she were alien. She felt like she was. Kate counted five sirens coming from three different directions. A man sitting on the sidewalk was holding a cardboard sign reading "Seeking Human

Kindness." He smiled at her. She smiled back and put ten dollars in his tin cup. He reached out to grab her leg and she stepped back just in time. A few minutes later, she found what she was looking for: the Hodges Gallery, squeezed in between Payless Shoes and an Art of War Tattoo Parlor.

The gallery windows were barred. She pulled on the door, but it was locked. She rang the buzzer and heard a loud click. Before she walked in, Kate glanced quicky around to see if Camilla was anywhere in sight. She wasn't.

"Hello, good afternoon," a voice called from the back of the store. "If there's anything I can help you with, just shout."

"Thank you," Kate called back.

The space was jammed with art and antiques in every shape and form. Masks, weapons, and paintings hung on the wall. Small sculptures, jewelry, and vases sat on tables or were displayed in glass cases. A dozen chandeliers hung from the ceiling, and five life-size statues gazed at Kate from various points around the room. None of it was the kind of art one would find at Sotheby's or Christie's. It was second- and third-tier stuff, the kind of antiques that mainstream collectors and hobbyists bought, not museums and the uber-rich. Nothing was over a few thousand dollars. If this gallery had what she was looking for, she wasn't going to find it on these shelves.

She wandered to the back of the store. The man who greeted her was sitting at a large walnut desk, working on his computer. He had long, gray hair hanging past his shoulders and round, black-framed glasses.

"Excuse me?"

He looked up and smiled. "Can I help?"

"I'm interested in buying a vase," Kate said, trying to sound as casual as possible. "An ancient Greek vase?"

"I'm sorry. We don't have anything from ancient Greece. There are a few vases, though." He put his feet on the desk and pointed towards the front of the store. "They're near the window. Feel free to have a look."

"I'm afraid that simply won't do. It's for our foyer, which is rather expansive, and it will be the first thing guests see when they visit. Do you understand?" Kate wondered if her fake rich-person accent sounded as fake to him as it did to her.

He shook his head. "I'm afraid that's not our thing. This ain't the National Gallery, you know."

Kate had planned for this. If he did have any authentic and rare antiques with questionable provenance, he wasn't going to tell a complete stranger. She would have to establish her credibility first.

"Could I place an order?"

"I'm sorry. We don't have what you're looking for."

Camilla had told Kate about setting these kinds of sting operations. The biggest challenge was establishing trust. Typically, an agent posing as a buyer would spend weeks or months building a relationship. All they had was a few hours. So instead of building relationships, they would gamble on a name.

"How unfortunate. Jacob assured me you would."

The man's eyes flickered. "Jacob?"

"Yes. A friend of mine, an art appraiser, recommended you. But he must have been mistaken. I apologize for taking up your time. Thank you so much."

The man took his feet off the desk and leaned forward. "What did Jacob tell you?"

"This is the Hodges Gallery, isn't it? Jacob said if I was looking for anything truly exceptional, such as a black-figure Greek vase, Hodges was the place to start. Is there another Hodges Gallery?"

He took a long look at Kate. "What is your name?"

"Judith."

"Hi Judith. My name is Leon." He punched some keys on his keyboard. "Let me have a look. There is a chance we may have what you're looking for after all."

"How wonderful!"

"Could you be more specific?"

"Well, it's a black-figure vase, as I said. There's a wedding scene on one side. On another, there is a woman holding her hands up in front of her. By someone named Onassis? Or Omasis? I don't recall much else."

Recall much else? That felt like a British upper-class twit, not authentic New York upper-class. She'd really have to work on her accents next time.

Luckily, Leon didn't appear to notice. He just kept typing, humming to himself while he worked. He leaned into his computer, squinting his eyes. "There's nothing here at the moment, but it looks like we may have something like that in the next two or three weeks."

She didn't have a few weeks. Now what was she going to do?

"Is it still in Torrento?" she asked.

Again, she saw his eyes flicker. Another note of recognition, she was certain. But he didn't respond, not directly. He leaned back and folded his hands behind his head. "I will let you know when it comes in."

"Please do."

"Can I get your phone number?"

She wrote down the number Camilla had given her.

He smiled. "Thank you. It's been a pleasure."

Kate got up to leave. She took two steps, stopped, and turned around. "May I ask . . . how is your selection of ancient Greek jewelry?"

"We don't have any here, however—"

"I'm primarily interested in earrings, to be specific."

"I'll keep my ears open, Judith."

Kate walked to the door, pulled it open, and stopped. Should she push her luck? Could she get away with asking one more question without making him suspicious? She turned around again. "I almost forgot. We're also interested in a marble sphinx. Preferably Greek, somewhere in the neighborhood of, say, 300 BC. Do you have anything like that?"

His smile disappeared and a flash of doubt crossed his face. But he recovered instantly, smiled again and raised an eyebrow. "Afraid not. Have a good day."

Kate walked out and down the street. Had that gone perfectly? No, but it had gone almost perfectly. Progress had been made. She had made a connection from the gallery to Jacob, and possibly Torrento. And he had promised to contact her. She regretted asking that last question, but he didn't seem to think anything of it.

At the next street corner, Camilla appeared beside her. She walked silently, head down, without making eye contact. Nothing was said until they crossed the road.

"What did you think?" Kate asked. "Did you hear everything?"

"I did. You got some solid information. You did well."

Camilla didn't sound happy. "But?" Kate said.

"But . . . I don't know. Something felt off. It's possible I'm just imagining things, but I wonder if he suspected something. He was being so careful not to give anything away. What if he knew what you were doing, and he was just playing along?"

And what if you're just jealous because I was so brilliant, Kate thought.

"I'm afraid we may have just poked the bear," Camilla said.

And I'm afraid you don't want to admit how amazing I am. "Why would he suspect anything?"

"I don't know. But he basically told you to go away, and he would call you in a few weeks."

"We couldn't expect much more than that."

Camilla just nodded.

"So where do we go from here?"

"I don't know yet. In a perfect world, we'd watch that gallery 24/7 and follow the owner everywhere he went, but we don't have those resources. We'd also search the store and tap the phones, but there's not nearly enough evidence for a warrant."

They continued walking in silence. The wind was blowing harder, the sky was dark, and it felt like a storm was about to begin. The streets were starting to clear out as people headed for cover.

"We're lucky I didn't need our code word," Kate said. "'It's starting to look like summer' would not have sounded convincing."

Three blocks later they reached the parking lot where they had left their cars.

"I'm going to work from home for the rest of the day," Camilla said. "I'll see you tomorrow."

Kate climbed in her car, checked her emails and was getting ready to drive home when her phone rang. No Caller ID. Her mother again. Good. Maybe Kate could find out where the Pirate's Cove was, and what this suave man was all about. "Hi, Mom," she said.

"It's Luca."

Kate swore under her breath. She knew this call would come, knew she couldn't avoid him forever. But she was not expecting him to block his number so she wouldn't know it was him when he called.

"Kate?"

"Hi, Luca, it's great to hear from you! How are you? I'm sorry I haven't had a chance to call you back. It's been crazy!" There had to a better excuse than "it's been crazy." She had been rushed to the hospital with some life-threatening disease? Her apartment was on fire?

"Is that why you've been ignoring my calls? Because it's been crazy?"

"Ignoring your calls? Oh, no, no, I haven't been ignoring them. Why would I ignore you? I've just been, well, you know how it gets."

She could feel him shaking his head from four thousand miles away. "Apparently it gets crazy."

"Right! You're right about that." Kate tried to change the subject. "So how have you been?"

Complete silence.

"You're probably wondering about the earrings, right? And everything?"

"Naturalmente. Of course I have been wondering."

"Of course you have! And you'll be happy to know everything is going according to plan. It's great. They're locked in the vault now, absolutely they are, and we've got a few leads already, and, well, yes. So everything is great."

"I see. Can you tell me more about the leads?"

"Yes. I will. But wait, I've got a call coming in from Camilla. This is urgent. Luca, I'll call you tomorrow, okay?"

"Kate, don't—"

She hung up, threw her phone in her purse, and started the car. In a few days, she'd be ready to talk to Luca. But not today.

The first thing she did when she got home was open the fridge door. She hadn't eaten anything all day, and she needed something. Anything. Preferably something that was fast and easy to make. A cheese sandwich, chicken, leftovers, who cares. There was nothing. Maybe in the cupboard? Also nothing. She could run out and grab sushi. And wine. She'd earned a glass of wine, and if she was going out anyway—

"Hello, Judith."

She turned around. He was in the far corner of the room, sitting on a stool he had dragged over from the breakfast bar. It was dark enough that she couldn't see his face. All she could see was the silhouette of a man holding a gun.

CHAPTER TWENTY-THREE

Paul watched a backhoe driver scoop a load of dirt into his steel bucket, hit the gas, drive to a pile at the far edge of the pit and dump it, race back to the trench he was working in, scoop up more and do it again. He worked at a manic pace, like he was driving a race car instead of a backhoe. "You found a city?"

"Well, perhaps more of a town by today's standards." Harry chuckled. "But three thousand years ago, it would have been considered a city. People lived here, worked here, slept, drank, ate, kissed their lovers, and disemboweled their enemies. Not so different from today, is it?"

Paul stared out at the dig. His mouth went dry, and he shut his eyes and wished the entire scene would disappear. It was both breathtaking and horrifying. He could see ancient walls sticking up through the dirt, revealing the outlines of the stone buildings that once stood there. It was dark, but he could make out a large vase at least four feet high resting nearby, and several other artifacts on the ground. He imagined what other treasures were buried here, or had been, and looked away. "It's a city. An entire city."

"Not a huge city," Harry replied. "It's not Xanadu."

"And you're digging it up with backhoes?" Paul's stomach, still queasy from the ride on the ATV, felt like it had become a pit of bile.

"Backhoes, shovels, picks. I know what you're thinking, and you're right. We're not exactly following traditional archeological protocols. But we don't have time for all those trowels and toothbrushes." Harry shrugged. "I just hope we don't break anything particularly valuable."

Paul heard the sound of a pickaxe banging against metal and winced. He couldn't help wondering what ancient artifact just got maimed. "How did you find it?"

"Let's go for a walk, and I'll tell you all about it."

They walked between the trenches, looking down at the people working on the site. One man was pulling pieces of a vase out of a shallow trench. Someone else had a row of broken cups and plates lined up beside the trench, like he was setting a table for dinner.

"We found it through a combination of research, technology and luck," Harry explained. "Many years ago, a friend was telling me about ancient texts he'd read that referred to a city called Boura, and they pointed to somewhere around here. We used drones flying Lidar technology. Have you heard of it? It's an airborne scanning technology—quite extraordinary, really—to search the area and find the most likely sites. Then we hired a few locals to begin searching and with their help, a dozen metal detectors, and some good fortune—"

"What have you found?"

"Quite a lot. A couple of days ago we pulled a gold statue of a horse out of the ground. Last week we found two royal tombs. We're almost certain one was an emperor, and the other was, we believe, his queen. The queen's tomb had been raided, but the emperor's tomb, buried a level deeper, was untouched. It was quite incredible, full of jewelry, carvings, paintings, household items, a few vases in almost perfect condition, and almost one hundred coins. I was so excited, I was jumping up and down like a little boy on Christmas morning." He threw his head back and laughed, a high-pitched laugh that didn't sound anything like the Harry Paul thought he knew. "It was unbelievable. Unbelievable."

Paul had become accustomed to dealing in antiquities with questionable provenance. That was how the business worked. He didn't know where they came from, had never wanted to know. To him, it was like ordering steak at a restaurant: The cow was already dead, so why worry about it? But this was different. This was an entire undiscovered city. He heard another crunching sound, and cringed. "What are you doing with it?"

"On its way to buyers in China, Russia, and the good old USA. You bought and sold a few pieces yourself. I believe your friends the Erickssons purchased one."

So this was where they came from. This was the source of the art and antiquities Harry had been sending Paul. They weren't from his collection at all. They had been pulled out of the ground, smuggled out of the country, cleaned up, and sold on the black market. By him.

"I don't know, Harry. I don't know. This is so . . . brutal."

"Don't pretend, Paul. You know this is how the business works." His voice took on the tone of a public schoolteacher. "We dig it out of the ground, clean it, glue it together, polish it up, and ship it to a trusted dealer—such as you—and you sell it. No one asks questions, and everything works like a charm. Everybody pretends to care where it all comes from, and no one really does." Harry picked up a piece of broken ceramic and threw it away. "The same system has worked for centuries. Nothing has changed except the phony posturing of the officials, who huff and puff and cry, 'It simply must stop!' Hypocrites and liars, all of them. The truth gets buried deeper than the artifacts."

"No, no . . . this is over the line. This is way over the line," Paul whispered. "I don't believe this."

Harry gazed at Paul, an expression of disappointment on his face. "Oh dear Paul, don't play naïve. The role doesn't suit you at all. You know how the business works. You just did what everybody else does—every gallery owner, director, curator, auction house, dealer, and middleman—you all do it. You all know and pretend that you don't. You choose not to ask too many questions, because if you did know where it came from you'd have to give it all back. It's so much better not to know."

"So all the provenances you claimed you had, everything you said . . . was any of it true?"

"Not a word. Pure make-believe."

"But I saw them." He must sound childish, he thought. Gullible. Or just dumb. "Sales receipts. Statements from galleries and previous owners. I saw them in your apartment."

"A friend of mine who owns a gallery in the Bronx makes them up for me. He does good work, don't you think? In a way, he's an artist in his own right."

Paul stopped walking to take some deep breaths, holding his stomach. "This is a whole city—and you're just ripping it up."

"Having a little existential crisis, are we? Well, it's a bit late for that. You're deep in it now. You just crossed the line from that thin veneer of respectable deniability to the dark muck of guilty complicity, and you can't go back. There's no way out now."

"No, no," Paul stuttered. "I didn't agree to this." Just a few hours earlier he had idolized Harry. He had wanted to be more like him, tried to live up to him. Now—what? Now he just wanted to turn around and run. "What about the Eurydemos Vase?"

"You must be shockingly naïve or purposely blind. There is no second Eurydemos Vase. It's only because of you that people believe there is."

"But the New York Museum . . . They would not do that."

Harry laughed. "Don't you think Francis knew where that came from? Of course he did. I told him myself."

"Not the New York Museum. No. They wouldn't."

"You're disappointing me. Why, I'd wager that thirty or forty percent of their main collection is either fake or smuggled. Have you ever read the little plaques beside those magnificent displays? 'Goblet. 2000 BC. Greek.' Ha! Didn't you ever wonder why they were so ridiculously vague? It's not because they don't know. It's because they don't want anyone else to know, so they can't be traced."

Paul couldn't look at Harry. He looked back at the site, sickened by what he saw, and wrapped his hands around his stomach.

Harry put his hand on Paul's shoulder and spoke, quietly, deliberately. "You bit the apple, whether you wanted to or not. What are you going to do? Tell on us? Report us to the authorities? Do you really think they'd believe you didn't know the truth, after all the pieces you've moved for me, all the money you've made off them? Of course not. Your name is on all of it. But then, it should be, shouldn't it? You knew. You always knew. The only difference between now and a few hours ago is that you can't pretend anymore."

Paul couldn't think. He couldn't talk. He was trapped.

"You know the story of the Trojan horse, don't you?" Harry said. "I'm surprised you didn't recognize it when it happened to you."

He heard another hard crunch, and to Paul it sounded like his own teeth gnashing. Harry pointed to the backhoe driver, who was climbing out of the cab. "Oh, look. I think they've found something. Let's go have a peek."

Paul stayed where he was. He didn't want to look. While Harry disappeared into the dark, Paul walked to the other side of the site, away from everyone, and sat on the ground. He picked a piece of a broken vase off the ground. The black outline of a Greek warrior with a snake wrapped around his upper body looked back. He had probably been lying around here undisturbed for three thousand years, in perfect peace, until some jackass in a backhoe cut off his legs. Paul put it in his pocket.

Shit, shit, shit, shit. Harry was right. Paul had known. He had chosen to believe the lies and ignore the truth. He had lived in the bliss of ignorance, hovering happily in the same morally ambiguous zone that separated the drug user from the drug dealer: One was just a customer, the other a crook. He had told himself he was on some higher moral plane than tomb raiders, thieves and smugglers. Now he wondered whether he was any different at all.

As he sat there, it occurred to him that he had a decision to make. Should he go to the officials and confess everything? Or should he keep going, pretending, playing the same old game? Did he really have a choice? Either way, he'd probably end up in jail.

Harry appeared out of the dark and sat down beside him. "Typically I'd be digging in those ditches with them. It's fun, searching for treasure. I'm just not dressed for it tonight." Paul didn't respond, just stared at the ground. "You seem so surprised. You shouldn't be. I did tell you I had an expensive lifestyle to maintain."

"Why did you bring me here?"

"Maybe I just needed your moral support. To tell me I'm not a bad person. After all, do you really think what we're doing is all that bad?"

Paul cringed at the word "we," but Harry didn't notice.

"I understand all these archeologists and academics love to whine. 'It's a crime against humanity, all these antique pieces of art should be left here so they can be studied by future generations. They belong to the world! Think of the stories they tell!' That's what they say. It's all a bit self-serving and sanctimonious, don't you think?" Harry smirked. "Be honest. Does the world really need another museum, or more ancient vases?"

"But it's . . . it's a whole city."

Harry kept talking as if he hadn't heard. "They'd do it, too. Build a museum here and take money off all the tourists who come to gape at it. And where does that money go? To the governments and rich sponsors who pretend to be so altruistic. So cultured! But what about these people, Paul?" Harry waved at the workers digging in front of them. "They live here. They need this money to survive. Another museum won't do them any good. But they'll make enough off this dig to eat for a year. This is their land, you know."

"Nice speech," Paul said. "It's complete bullshit, but it's a nice speech."

"Oh, Paul, come on. I thought you were better than those sanctimonious academics and self-serving politicians. I really did."

Paul's shoulders slumped. How had he talked himself into thinking Harry was special, that he was cultivated and smart and civilized? Now he felt embarrassed. Stupid. "That's not why you brought me here."

"You're right. It isn't." Harry pulled a small antique coin out of his pocket and rubbed it with his fingers, as if trying to make it shine. "I suppose you're wondering why. Oh, it may be because it gets a little lonely sometimes. Being the only one willing to admit what's happening here. Everyone else in the business can be so, you know, high and mighty. They act like they're an advanced species of human beings. Like Francis. He is such a pompous ass."

Paul put his hands over his ears. "No. No. There's a difference. Between you and them. And me."

"Stop lying to yourself. Where would you be without me, Paul? You said it yourself. You'd be homeless. And look at you now. How much money have you made from me? How much money have the galleries, the auction houses, made from us? Would you really want to go back?"

"Yes."

"You wouldn't. You're lying."

Paul wasn't sure he was wrong. "So why me?"

"Due to some unfortunate circumstances, my name has become compromised in the industry. I needed someone else to distribute the materials, and you appeared at just the right time. You seemed like such a wonderful person. I really do like you, you know."

"You're so full of bullshit, Harry. Bullshit, bullshit, *bullshit*!" Paul was shouting now and stumbling to his feet, earning a few curious looks from the workers in the pit. "Can you please just stop it and tell me the real reason why I'm here? It's not because you're lonely."

Harry lay back in the dirt and put his hands behind his head. Stared at the stars, shut his eyes, took a deep breath, hummed a few notes. "Alright. You've got me, and now I must confess. So the truth, and nothing but the truth? So help me God? Okay, here it is. The fact is, I need you. This lost city we're digging up is nice. I'll make a lot of money from it, and so will you. But I've recently discovered a bigger treasure, much, much bigger, and for that I need your help. For that I need you fully committed, right in the game, the way I am. Eyes wide open, as it were. But I promise you, this one will be worth it. It is gigantic. Far bigger than this little city we've found."

"What is it? What's the big treasure?"

Harry sat up and grinned at Paul, his teeth flashing in the moonlight. "Have you ever heard of Alexander the Great?"

CHAPTER TWENTY-FOUR

Kate felt frozen in place. A cold tremor ran up and down her body as she stared at him. His dark silhouette was still. Her eyes ran down his arm to the gun pointed at her, the black barrel faintly glimmering. Every one of her muscles tightened.

A few seconds passed in silence. In the dark she couldn't see much of his face, other than it seemed middle-aged, big and round. Like a retired football player. "Who are you?" she managed to say.

"Air conditioning. Here to take a look at the HVAC."

She clenched her jaw. "How did you get in here?"

He made a clucking sound with his tongue. "Your concierge isn't overly inquisitive, is he? I had official identification all made up for him, and he didn't even ask to see it. Walked right up with me and let me in. Friendly type."

Kate remembered all the warnings. Alfred was right. They had all been right. But now, even as she stood staring at the man holding the gun, she didn't fully believe it. It felt unreal, like all she had to do was blink and he'd disappear. How long had he been there? And how much did he know? She tried to keep her voice steady, to make it look like she wasn't afraid.

"What do you want?" she asked.

"You've been visiting a lot of art galleries lately."

"Yes. I go to a lot of galleries." Her eyes adjusted to the light, and she could make out more of his features. A brush cut. Pale white skin. A smirk spread across his face.

"Just window shopping, then?"

He must be connected to Jacob. Someone must have followed her home after her meeting at the Four Seasons. Was this the same person who had stolen the earrings? "Yes. Just shopping. Why are you asking?"

"The real question is, why are *you* asking? Why the sudden interest in our galleries? Why all the questions about vases, and earrings, and a marble sphinx?"

So it wasn't Jacob. It was Leon. Kate remembered the look on Leon's face after she'd asked about the sphinx. That must be what had made him suspicious. That must be why this man was in her apartment. If only she hadn't pushed.

He shook the gun at her, like a teacher shaking a finger at a misbehaving student. "You are treading on sensitive toes. I'd suggest you stop what you're doing before you get yourself in deeper trouble."

Kate looked at the ground, felt her lips trembling and forced them to stop. "I was just looking. One day, I'd . . ." But she knew how dumb it sounded and just let it go.

He looked at her with a knowing smile.

"How did you find out where I lived?" she asked.

"I can find out where anybody lives."

They stared at each other in silence for a few seconds. Kate heard neighbors talking in the hall and thought about shouting out to them, but knew they wouldn't do anything. This was New Jersey, not Chester.

"Some of my colleagues would rather you didn't ask so many questions. They're finding your interest is getting a little too personal, and it's making them uneasy. So I'm here to make you an offer on their behalf. If you promise to stop asking questions, I promise not to put a bullet in the back of your skull. How does that sound?"

It was his casual tone that frightened her most. As if he were negotiating the price of a cantaloupe. "That sounds fine," she said.

"What does that mean?"

"I'll stop."

His face broke into a grin, and she heard him snicker. "So we have an agreement. That's good." He stood up, took a few steps toward the door, and stopped. "By the way, just in case you decide to change your mind after I leave, I should remind you that I know where you live, and that your young concierge isn't providing a particularly good defense system. I can get in here anytime I like."

"Don't worry. I won't. I mean, I will. Stop, that is."

"That's a good girl." He grabbed the door handle, thought for a second, and turned back. "And if you decide to disappear, we'll just track down your family. Or friends. We're very resourceful." He smiled again, opened the door, and walked out.

Kate felt a sharp pain in the bottom of her stomach. She remembered her mom talking about that suave guy. She had wondered why a young man who apparently looked like Brad Pitt would be interested in her mother. Now it made sense. Or did it? Would they go that far? Or were they just trying to scare her?

Fingers shaking, she dialed her mom. The call went to voicemail.

• • •

Camilla walked over to the window and looked outside. Kate joined her. The medley of cars honking, reversing trucks beeping, and police sirens sounded like a street orchestra conducted by a drunken maestro.

"I'm sorry," Camilla said. "We should have . . . *I* should have done something, got you protection, I don't know. I had no idea." She shook her head. "Dammit. I didn't expect anything like this to happen. Stupid of me. Now what? We'll investigate of course, send our agents over, but I doubt they will find out anything. I'm so sorry, Kate. Why didn't you call me last night?"

Because my hands were shaking too much to dial your number? "I didn't want to wake you up. It's not a big deal. I'm fine."

"You're not fine. You are in danger. You are lucky he didn't just shoot you. *We're* lucky." Camilla went back to her desk, sat down, picked up an empty coffee mug and banged it on the table so hard that Kate thought it would break. "You can't go back to your place. Not now. Maybe not ever."

"What about my mom?"

Camilla shook her head. "They don't know where she is. I highly doubt she has anything to worry about."

"But what about that young man, the suave one that—"

"I'm sure your mom is having a great old time. Let her have some fun. Right now, we have to worry about you."

Kate didn't agree, but Camilla wasn't going to change her mind.

Camilla sat down. "I was afraid of this. We poked the bear. They know we're sniffing around now."

"So what do we do?"

Camilla buried her head in her hands. "I need to think . . . Have you spoken with Luca?"

"We've been keeping in touch."

"You haven't told him the earrings have gone missing?"

"No." Kate had debated sharing her concerns about Luca with Camilla. She just couldn't find a way to say anything without making it sound like she was blaming him for losing the earrings. She needed some kind of evidence, something that resembled means, motive and opportunity—even one of the three—before she started pointing fingers at a respected colleague who lived four thousand miles away.

Camilla was tapping her pen against the edge of the desk. "Do you have any place you can stay?"

"I suppose I could stay at my mother's house. In Chester."

"Good. Go there. Today. I'll have someone bring you to your apartment so you can pick up anything you need."

"But I want to be here, I—"

Camilla shook her head. "Just go. Please. I need time to think . . . Oh! What was the name of that city? The one the guy at the gallery mentioned?"

"Torrento?"

"Yes. Thanks. I'll call you in a day or two. Do not tell anyone where you are. Don't go out, don't call or text anyone, don't answer the phone unless it's me. If you see anything suspicious, let me know right away. Be safe." She held Kate's eyes in a steely glaze. "And please, for God's sake, do as you are told this time."

Kate agreed. But as soon as she got home, she called her mother.

Their conversation was short.

"I don't believe this," her mother said, her tone of voice expressing a level of irritation Kate had never heard before. "You're actually suggesting he's only interested in me because of you?"

"I'm trying to tell you that you could be in danger. He could be—"

"This," her mother said, "is not about you. Why would you even think that?"

Kate told her a source had made a threat.

She didn't tell her that the source happened to be pointing a gun at her.

Kate could hear her mother breathing. Even her breath sounded angry.

"Kate, I'm going zip-lining. With my boyfriend. I'm sorry you've decided he's only seeing me to get back at you, but I also know you're wrong. You don't know him. He would not do that. Thanks for the call. Have a good day." She hung up.

• • •

After five days in Chester, Kate had walked from one end of the house to the other approximately one thousand times. Even more times than that she had turned the television on and off, or started and stopped reading various books, or checked her phone for missed calls, or wondered why Camilla hadn't called. She hadn't been this bored since she was grounded for a week when she was fifteen.

The world had forgotten her. Just when life was getting interesting, she had been shipped back to Chester and ordered to sit and wait. Not even Luca had called. Camilla had said she would call in a few days. At the end of the fifth day, after a sleepless night of wondering, Kate felt like she had waited long enough. She picked up her phone and called Camilla.

"I have an idea," Kate explained. "I should go to Torrento."

"What? No. You're not going anywhere."

"I have to do something. We aren't getting anywhere here."

"It's not safe for you. And besides, this even isn't our case! It's the Carabinieri's case. You've got lots of work you could be doing here—as soon as it's safe to come back."

"This isn't just the Carabinieri's case anymore. It's bigger than that. If they're planning on clearing out the tomb of Alexander, it's our case, it's everybody's case. And if we poked that bear, if they do know we're investigating, that's on us. We can't just sit around and wait. We have to do something, and we have to do it now."

Camilla was silent. Kate took that as a good sign.

"What would people think," she continued, "if it came out that we knew Alexander's tomb had been discovered and didn't do anything about it while it was being robbed?"

Another stretch of silence. "But what about you, Kate? I can't just risk sending one of my—"

Kate had had a lot of time to think over the last five days. And she had come to believe that if she was going to solve this case, she had to be in Torrento. She was too far away from where everything was happening. She had to go to the source. And Luca? She still believed he could be involved, probably was involved, but sitting in this suburban bungalow in Chester wasn't going to resolve that either. She could only find out the truth by confronting him.

"I'll have Luca for protection," she said, interrupting Camilla. "It'll be safer than sitting around in this house alone, won't it?"

CHAPTER TWENTY-FIVE

They had woken early, driven to Athens in the morning, and flown to Rome that afternoon. Before they left, Harry had handed Paul a fake passport and credit card and asked him to use them for the ticket and car rental. Paul didn't argue, didn't even ask any questions. Just felt the rope growing tighter around his neck. Little had been said during the trip, nothing but the bare essential information passed along in muttered monosyllables and curt nods. Occasionally Harry had tried to initiate conversations, but Paul had barely made eye contact since leaving the dig the previous day.

The best car available at the airport in Rome was a mid-size Subaru. Harry took the wheel, telling Paul they were driving to Torrento, about six hours away. Paul ignored him. As the city disappeared behind them the multilane highway turned into a single-lane road, cutting through the tree-lined hills of the Italian countryside as they drove north. The Adriatic Sea appeared, then disappeared again. Every now and then Harry made another attempt at conversation. Every entreaty was met with a stony silence.

Paul looked out the window, shutting his eyes behind his sunglasses. He didn't want to think about who he was with, where he was going, or what he was doing. Instead, he tried to focus his thoughts on his life back in New York, the life he had been living until just three days earlier. His life of ignorant bliss and unbridled luxury. Imagined himself lying on his Pai Gow couch, Maya by his side, drinking wine and watching his new sixty-four-inch home theatre television. Then he opened his eyes and saw the scruffy Italian landscape surrounding him. His suddenly perfect life had suddenly become unbearable. He clenched his fists and swore at himself.

"Paul, I know you're having a hard time right now, but you've got to pull yourself together," Harry said. "We've got serious work to do, and we're going to need you on top of your game."

"I've got to pull myself together?" Paul squeezed his eyes shut and tried to remain calm. His voice rose an octave. "*Pull myself together*? You shit. I could go to jail because of you. Go to hell."

"No one's going to prison. We're going to have a little adventure, then we'll be rich, and life will be wonderful. You'll see."

"Do you remember you told me there was no way out?"

Harry nodded. "I do remember saying something like that."

It was the offhand delivery, the smug self-assurance of that statement—Paul thought he detected a smile—that set him off. Harry said "I do remember" as if the subject of trapping Paul in this conspiracy carried no more significance than squashing an irritating flea.

He lost it.

"Do you? Do you remember saying that?" Paul tried to control his voice but couldn't. "Do you also remember that you dragged me out to that fucking dig and basically told me I was screwed for life? Do you remember telling me you trapped me, set me up, and that I wasn't getting out of this?" He took a deep breath and turned away, amazed at his own stupidity. "I believed you, you know. I trusted you. No, okay, I didn't. There are no angels here. I get it. I didn't ask, I should have known. But you played me, right from day one. You sucked me in, you bastard. So yeah, it's nice of you to remember saying something like that. Because now I'm fucked, and you know what?" Paul took his sunglasses off so he could be sure Harry looked him in the eyes. "I'm not going down by myself. You know that? I'm not. Fuck you."

He knew he wasn't being very Harry-like. He no longer cared. From now on, the less Harry-like the better.

The Italian countryside passed by. Paul wished he could just get out of the car and walk away. But first, he'd like to punch Harry in the face, kick him a few times, make him bleed, break his teeth, and bust his skull wide open. Leave his body in the woods, where wild boars could feast on his repugnant hide. But he couldn't do anything. They were stuck in this Subaru, and his tirade just got bottled up along with all the bitter energy he carried inside. He felt too empty, tired and depressed to punch anybody.

They'd gone another mile or two by the time Harry responded. "I completely understand, Paul. I really do. And I apologize. I wish there could have been another way."

"Well, that makes me feel a whole lot better."

They drove a few more miles in silence. A road stop appeared on the side of the highway, where a few cars were parked while the occupants gazed out at the Adriatic Sea. Harry pulled in, shut off the car and admired the view for a few moments. He turned towards Paul and smiled. But something was different this time. This wasn't the smile Paul was used to. Harry's eyes had turned cold, and his lips curled. "I hope you'll excuse me, Paul. But you'll have to stop acting like a child. You're in this now, and you have to accept that. There is no other way. None. Do you understand?"

Paul felt for the handle of the door. "No. I don't. I don't understand any of this. I want out. Just drop me off and let me go."

Harry stared into Paul's eyes without blinking. "Listen to me very carefully." His voice had turned harder, and he spoke slowly. "I'll make this crystal clear. It's simply too late for you to get out. There's too much at stake. If you do try to get out, you will end up dead. If you try to, as you suggested, bring us down with you, you'll end up dead. The only way you will live is if you do everything exactly as we tell you. Does that help clear things up?"

On some level, Paul had expected this moment was going to come. He'd resisted it, blocked out the possibility that his life might be in acute, immediate danger, but he had suspected. From the moment he saw the dig in Greece, he understood that no one was going to let his puny life get in the way of what they were planning. Still, dealing with the reality of the situation required adjusting. He looked into Harry's eyes and knew that if he was going to get out of there alive, he had to go along with everything. At least for now.

"Alright," he said.

"Is it alright?"

"Yes." Paul tried to sound convincing. "It's just perfect."

"Do you have any questions?"

"No."

"So we're good then."

"We're all good."

The cold smile turned into a warm grin, and he snapped back into the old Harry as if they'd never been anything but the best of friends. "Wonderful! I'm so glad you've decided to join the team. Let's get out of the car, soak up this beautiful view, and I'll tell you the whole story."

They stood by the railing, looking out over the sea. It was a clear and brilliant sunny day, and the bright blue and green colors of the Adriatic shimmered like shards of glass.

"Where do I begin?" Harry thought for a moment. "I suppose at the beginning would be the best place.

"It all started five or six years ago. A little-known Egyptian archeologist named Adel announced that she had discovered Alexander the Great's tomb. It wasn't the first time someone had made that claim, and her announcement was greeted with overwhelming ambivalence. But she was persistent, and a few weeks later the officials got around to checking it out. They were there for one day before officially claiming that it belonged to some unknown pharaoh, barely worthy of note and certainly not Alexander. They closed access to the site, citing safety concerns. The archeologist argued, insisting it was the real thing, and spoke of the spectacular treasures buried there. The Egyptian government was adamant, kept the site sealed, and announced the subject closed. A few months later, it was almost forgotten.

"The archeologist kept insisting it was Alexander's burial chamber, but no one cared anymore. Remember, more than a dozen people have claimed to have found that tomb, so it wasn't exactly headline news. Then, a few months ago, a woman named Bernardi died, and in her will was the donation of a marble sphinx to the Gandolfi Museum. The will claimed it was from Alexander the Great's tomb. There wasn't any provenance to support that claim, so of course no one believed that either. It was just a footnote in a trade magazine. No one paid attention. No one, that is, except me."

Paul was trying not to listen. He didn't want to know. All he wanted was to shut out the world that was closing in on him. He started to recite the "The Walrus and the Carpenter" in his head to block the noise coming from Harry's mouth:

The time has come to talk of many things / Of shoes and ships and sealing wax and cabbages and kings.

"I was the only one who made the connection between Adel's announcement and the Bernardi will. The timing, the circumstances—it was all too convenient. But was it really Alexander's? There was only one way to find out. I hunted down the man who had sold the marble sphinx to Signora Bernardi. He told me everything. Under duress, of course. And he had proof, lots of it, just lying around his apartment. No question it was the genuine article. He was working for the Egyptian minister of culture, who had known what it was all along. But rather than tell anyone, rather than open another museum, this minister had decided to keep it all for himself. He's the one who ordered Alexander's tomb locked up, claimed it was nothing, threatened or bribed anyone that knew different to keep it to themselves, and hired this dealer to sell everything in there, piece by piece."

And why the sea is boiling hot / And whether pigs have wings.

"I went to the Gandolfi Museum with a few friends. And there it was. Unbelievable. A gorgeous, stunning marble sphinx, once gazed upon by Alexander the Great himself, admired by centuries of kings and emperors, just sitting there. Practically ignored."

"But wait a bit," the Oysters cried / Before we have our chat.

"After all these centuries, the tomb had been discovered! What a momentous occasion. One of the greatest mysteries in history, the whereabouts of Alexander's tomb, had been solved! And this minister was just going to parcel its treasures out, one at a time, to the highest bidder. Are you following, Paul?"

Paul was doing his best not to follow. Reluctantly, he turned to look at Harry.

When he saw that he had Paul's attention, Harry continued. "I couldn't let that happen, could I? So I stole the sphinx from the museum. Not as difficult as you might think! We just walked in, packed it up and took it home. I had to shoot the guard and the nice young woman at the front desk, but there weren't any serious complications. And the dealer was nice enough to drive his car off a cliff shortly after that. Then I just had to deal with the original source—the minister of culture in Egypt."

Paul felt like he was going to vomit. He gazed at the rocks below, wondering if he should just jump and put himself out of his misery.

"The minister was extremely cooperative, once I explained the situation. He admitted to everything. I had to explain to him the risks he was taking. That it would be best if he sold the entire lot to me, in order to ensure he received adequate compensation and kept his name and position safe."

Paul remembered the minister from the party at the Erickssons'. He could not imagine that person becoming "extremely cooperative" unless Harry had threatened him with death or disclosure. Likely both.

Harry pulled the keys out of his pocket and jingled them. "That's it in a nutshell. We should be off. I'll tell you the rest later."

Paul had tried to block everything out, but bits and pieces kept sneaking in. There was one question he couldn't help asking.

But Harry saw it coming. "You're still wondering why we chose you?" Harry put his sunglasses on. "Simple, really. You see, we needed someone to bring this shipment into America, someone with impeccable credentials and a spotless record. This one's too big to go underground. We can't ship it one piece at a time, hidden in containers. It would take years, and there would be more risk. No. We decided to go the full Monty on this one. This will be a crime in broad daylight, as they say. And now that you're the hot new celebrity dealer who always finds all the greatest treasures, you're the perfect man for the enterprise. No one would question the great Paul Klugman, would they? Congratulations, you're about to be even more famous than you are now. You could be the next Howard Carter."

Paul winced, the knots in his stomach getting tighter.

"Let's get in the car."

"You've destroyed my life," Paul said. "I'm going to spend the next twenty years in a twelve-by-twelve cell with a hole for a toilet."

"I promise that's not what the universe has in store for you."

Paul resisted the urge to rip Harry's tongue out.

They drove for thirty minutes in silence. Paul tried to force himself to relax. There wasn't any way out. He took a series of deep breaths, shut his eyes, leaned back in the seat. Maybe Harry was right: Maybe he should just go with it. Maybe it would work out the way Harry said it would. But maybe not. More likely, he'd end up in jail. Either way, it was out of his control. They drove over a hill; Torrento appeared below them.

"We're closer than ever, Paul. Isn't this exciting?"

"The night is fine," the Walrus said / "Do you admire the view?"

CHAPTER TWENTY-SIX

Kate couldn't sleep during the nine-hour flight, even though she had been awake for almost twenty-two hours before departure. She squeezed her eyes shut, but her mind was not cooperating. It kept jumping around, going over the plans she had made with Camilla before she left, what she was going to say to Luca, and telling herself everything was going to be fine, just fine. By the time she stepped off the plane in Rome, she had been awake for thirty-one hours.

She grabbed her luggage and walked through the terminal. Her second wind had come and gone, as well as her third. She was waiting for her fourth wind, but it didn't seem to be in any hurry. Kate made a quick stop in the washroom and glanced in the mirror. No one looks good after being awake for two days, but this was ridiculous.

Grabbing a makeup kit out of her bag, she did what she could with what she had. Brushed her teeth, applied an extra layer of concealer and lipstick. She tried to comb her hair, but it refused any attempts at rehabilitation. She changed into a new silk shirt she'd bought for this trip. Overall, the improvement was minimal. It would take a couple of days of hot showers and a few weeks of sleep to recover any semblance of the human she used to be. As it was, she was going to meet Luca for the first time looking like a three-hundred-year-old gremlin. Oh well, so what, she thought. This was a job, not a date. It didn't matter what she looked like. She stuffed everything back into her bag and left.

She saw Luca. He was standing by the doors near the exit, looking at his phone, glancing up now and then to see who was coming. Kate stood back, just out of his line of sight, looking at him in person for the first time. After all this time, it seemed strange to see the real thing. He wore a loose green jacket and white shirt she recognized, and that hair still looked perfect, but in every other way he looked different than she remembered. It was probably the fluorescent airport light or her almost total exhaustion, but he seemed older. A bit of a slouch, at least ten pounds heavier, a few wrinkles.

It was a relief, to be honest. He wasn't the perfect human specimen she had imagined, and that was not a bad thing. It would make it easier to say what she had to say.

The next time he looked up, their eyes connected. He smiled and they both waved. Kate felt a rush of blood to her face and wondered if she was blushing. She felt nervous, but she wasn't sure if it was because of what he looked like, who he was, or who she suspected he might be. Maybe all three—or maybe she was just tired. When they got closer she stuck out a hand, but he ignored it, giving her a big hug and a kiss on the cheek.

"Ciao! Benvenuto! Kate, I'm so glad you are here, so happy to finally meet you in person," he said. His eyes were big and warm, his smile wide. "You look amazing."

She laughed, a high-pitched laugh that went on far too long. He looked at her quizzically. "It's nice to be here," she said. "And I don't, but thanks for saying so."

"I have to admit, I've known you for almost seven weeks but I've been so nervous about meeting you in person. It is like I am back in high school. It is silly, but true. How about you? Not nervous at all, I bet."

"Nervous?" Then that weird high-pitched laugh again. Where did that come from? "No. No, maybe just a little tired."

They stood and looked at each other, seeing each other up close and in person for the first time. Kate wondered what he must be thinking. Was he happy or disappointed? Was he as nervous as he said? He didn't look nervous.

"Should we go?" she asked.

"Yes! Of course, you're right. Forgive me. Allow me to take your bags." He reached out and grabbed them before she could object. "The car is this way."

She followed him to the door and outside. It was a hot day for April, and a warm breeze made it feel almost tropical. A long water feature with eight brightly lit fountains shot streams of water into the clear morning sky. Kate stopped and looked around, breathed in the air. It felt like she'd walked onto a movie set. Through the fog of exhaustion and layers of anxiety and doubt, this was a moment she wanted to remember. Everything felt different. Frightening, but exhilarating. The deadweight of boredom that had pressed on her shoulders for so many years had lifted. It had been replaced with fear and excitement, which she preferred. It felt more like life.

Luca strolled ahead, pulling her bags. His walk had a confident, lumbering gait that seemed both relaxed and determined, as if he was comfortable with the way the universe was unfolding around him. He was good-looking, she admitted. Different than she thought, and not as good-looking as she had imagined, but still. And he did seem charming. And kind. Of course, criminals could be just as charming and kind as anyone, she supposed.

Kate had been working on ways to find out if he was guilty or innocent. There had to be some clever way to catch him, like the questions detectives on television always seemed to have ready that went something like "and if you knew this, you must have been there." and ended up with a full confession a few minutes later. It looked easy for them, but after all those hours on the flight she hadn't come up with anything. Now she was out of time.

He looked back and smiled. "Are you coming?"

Kate didn't move. "No. I don't think so."

His smile disappeared. He cocked his head to one side, confused. "You don't think so?"

She took a deep breath. "Did you take them?"

"Take what?" His eyebrows scrunched together. "What are you talking about?"

Kate stood still, looking at him as cars passed between them, eyes wide. It had never been her plan to confront him, not like this—straight up and unfiltered, blurting it out in a busy parking lot just a few minutes after meeting him. She knew it was a mistake. She should have waited, found a better time and thought of a better way to get to the truth.

"Did you take the earrings?"

Luca shook his head. "What are you talking about?"

"You took them, didn't you? It was you."

He walked back towards her, crossing the road to a cacophony of angry horns.

"You're telling me the earrings are missing?" His expression hadn't lost its confused look, but his voice had turned a shade darker.

"Yes. But you already knew that."

"No." His eyes were locked on Kate's, as if he were looking for something. "I did not know that."

"Yes. You did."

Luca crossed his arms and laughed. "You're joking. Of course." He looked at her again and stopped laughing. "You're not joking."

"Not joking."

He stared at her in silence for a moment.

"Perhaps you could tell me what happened to the earrings," he said. "And why you think I have them."

Kate wished she could go back, just rewind this scene and hit pause until she came up with a better approach. Something that was brilliant and cunning and all that. But she couldn't, so she just pushed away the doubts gnawing at her stomach and jumped right in.

"I almost fell for it, you know. At first, I thought you really did want to work with me. I believed everything you said. But now I know. It took me a while, but I figured it out. You were lying when you said I was doing such a good job, and I believed it because I wanted to believe it. Big mistake. The only thing you liked about me was that I was stupid enough to believe you."

He shook his head again, but didn't argue with her.

She cleared her throat. "It could have worked, you know. You could have fooled me. But you made a mistake. When I came up with that plan for catching the thieves with the earrings, you couldn't help yourself. All you had to do was send me these rare, priceless earrings, then you could steal them from me, and you'd not only have the earrings, but you'd also get the FBI off your case. It was too perfect to resist, wasn't it?"

Kate thought she was doing a good job at this confrontation thing, considering that she had never been one for confrontations. Her voice was firm and steady, her eyes were locked on his, and she hadn't apologized and changed the subject. Hopefully he couldn't see her knees shaking.

He looked at her blankly. "How did I steal the earrings?"

"You had Jacob call me late at night, knowing that I would meet him. It was easy from there. You knew my apartment would be easy to break into, so you had someone come in the middle of the night and take them. Does the name Leon mean anything to you?"

"Leon? No." Luca rubbed his chin. "I still don't understand why you think it was me."

"Why else would you send me such priceless earrings? You wouldn't do that unless you knew you'd get them back. And also—no one else had my address. So you see? It had to be you." She smiled. It felt good to say all this out loud. Just letting it all out, letting it go. It was, on second thought, a good decision to confront him straight away.

But if it was a good decision, why did she feel so sad? She remembered how she felt talking to him all those times on Zoom, how exciting his life seemed and how good-looking he was. She had convinced herself there was something between them, that they would somehow end up together—two famous art detectives, Kate and Luca, solving art crimes during the day and drinking Aperol on the Italian Riviera at night. Laughing at danger. Falling in love.

And then this.

Luca put his hands in his pockets. He looked around, making sure they had privacy, then leaned in closer and locked eyes with her. "They were fakes."

"What?"

"The earrings we sent you. They were fakes." He shrugged. "I'm sorry."

That was not possible. He was lying. "No, they were not fakes."

"Yes. They were fakes. Forgeries. Replicas."

Kate looked down, staring at the cracked sidewalk between them. How could they not be real? They had to be real—or did they? The realization that the FBI hadn't verified their authenticity struck her as a horribly foolish oversight. "No. No, they're not."

"They are. You would never have known. No one could. These days, the forgeries are as good as the originals."

The full weight of all those hours of sleeplessness crashed down on Kate, obliterating whatever was left of her ability to process thought. What did it mean? She struggled to put together a logical flow of events. Would the Carabinieri send fakes? If so, why? Actually, the answer to that was obvious—in case they got stolen or lost. Kate shut her eyes. If they were fakes, her theory about Luca being involved in this didn't make any sense at all. Did it? *Think, Kate, think.* But the only thing she could think of was how confusing everything was.

"I'm sorry," he said. "I should have told you."

A couple pushing a baby carriage appeared behind them. Luca and Kate moved to one side to let them by and didn't speak again until they had crossed the road.

"Why wouldn't you tell us when you first sent them?" she asked. "Why tell me now?"

He thought for a moment before answering. "If you didn't believe they were genuine, no one else would have believed it either. Could you have convinced this Jacob that they were the real thing if you didn't believe it yourself? An agent with decades of experience might be able to pull that off, possibly. But it would have put you in a more dangerous position than you were already in. I wasn't willing to risk that."

"If they found out, they could have killed me."

A man on the platform shouted for a cab.

Luca said, "That's true."

"And you were okay with that?"

He smiled and ran his hand through his hair. "Of course not. But we knew they would never find out."

"What about the vase I found in Customs? You told me not to work on that, even though you must have known it was being smuggled. Why?"

"The Amasis vase. We already had agents on that case. It has now been closed. The vase was recovered, and the thieves have been arrested."

For a few seconds, neither one of them spoke. The sound of cars driving by and people looking for buses and cabs filled the gap. Kate rubbed her face with both hands, trying to clear her mind enough to make this make sense. She couldn't. "I don't know. I just don't know."

Luca stepped forward and held his hands together as if he were praying. He spoke quietly. "Kate, please. Per favore. Listen to me. I don't blame you for questioning me. I told you myself there is corruption at every level here, and there is. In this business, you have to question everything and everyone. It can be the difference between living and dying. You were right to do that. But at some point, you have to trust someone. That's never easy. But none of us will ever get anywhere alone. The reason I wanted to work with you is because you are good. You are. And I need your help. And now I am asking you to come with me. Please." He put his hands on her shoulders, gently, his eyes peering into hers. "I know we can do this. But only if we do it together."

Kate looked up at him, hoping to find an answer in his eyes. She couldn't.

He stepped back. "I tell you what," he said. "If we solve this case, and if we save Alexander's treasures, and the guilty are arrested, and if we don't get killed in the process, and if we are awarded an Order of Merit of the Italian Republic . . . I will buy you an Aperol." He raised his eyebrows and smiled. "How does that sound?"

He'd said nothing to convince her, not definitively, that he was innocent or guilty, that he was on her side or not. But he was right about one thing: She had to trust someone. If she didn't, nothing would happen. She'd just go back to her old job and her old life. If she was ever going to do anything that mattered, she had to take a chance.

Besides, an Aperol sounded pretty good.

Kate silently nodded and followed him to the car. She was feeling a bit numb. "Where are we going?"

"I booked you a room at the Isola Sacra Hotel, about ten minutes away. You can sleep, have something to eat, shower. Then we get to work."

"But we don't have much time."

Luca waited for a car to pass and pushed ahead to the parking lot. "No, we don't."

"I mean we don't have any time. We have to go now." She couldn't believe she was saying that. She really needed sleep. But if they were going to do this, they didn't have time for sleeping.

"I don't know what you mean," he said. "Where are we going?"

"We're going to Torrento."

"Why are we going to Torrento?"

"Get in the car. I'll explain on the way." Kate had always wanted to say that.

Luca started to object, but she insisted. They climbed in the car, started driving, and Kate started talking. Once she started, she couldn't stop. The miles rolled by, and she kept talking. She told him everything. Luca listened, nodding now and then, interrupting only to ask questions.

"What do we know about the man in Torrento?"

Kate stopped to think. What did they know? "We know he's a dealer. And that he's Iranian, English, Turkish, Armenian, Swedish, or that he may not exist at all. So not much."

Kate looked out the window watching the city turn into country, the busy highways turn into quiet roads. Torrento was hours away. She was so tired, she felt like she was drowning. Maybe, she thought, she could shut her eyes for just a few minutes. She leaned her head on the window and was just falling asleep when her phone rang. It was her mother.

"You were wrong," she said.

Oh boy. At least she's speaking to me again, Kate thought. "I'm so sorry mom. I didn't mean to suggest that he was only—"

"You were wrong, but I wish you were right. Alejandro wasn't there to kidnap me. Honestly, I'd rather have been kidnapped."

Luca looked over at Kate with an expression of confusion. He could hear everything her mother was saying.

"What did he do?" Kate asked.

"He was taking advantage of me!" She sounded like she had been crying. "I should have known the first time he told me he'd lost his wallet. Then his credit card got canceled. It was always something. How could I be so stupid?"

Kate was relieved, in a way. "It's okay Mom, I'm sorry."

"He asked me to loan him ten thousand dollars. Just for a few days, he said."

"Did you?"

"No! How stupid do you think I am?"

"I didn't mean that. Just . . . good for you."

Kate waited for a minute while her mom pulled herself together.

"How are you doing?"

"I'm okay now. I'm flying back tomorrow. I'll call you later." She hung up.

Luca said, "Should I ask?"

Kate took a deep breath and looked out the window. "Nope."

"Got it."

CHAPTER TWENTY-SEVEN

Driving through the beautiful and busy streets of Torrento made Paul feel sick. People strolled along the tree-lined sidewalks, laughing, shopping, eating ice cream, enjoying the soft sun and gentle breeze, in no hurry to go anywhere. He saw bright pastel-colored shops and restaurants, crowded outdoor cafés, men and women dressed as if they were auditioning for a Milan fashion show. And then there was Paul, locked in this small car on the road to what he was certain would end in a jail sentence. Was this how prisoners had felt as they walked across the Bridge of Sighs, taking one last look at the glorious streets of Venice before they were locked up? Every smile he saw cut another slice out of his heart.

Harry had promised him a future of wealth and luxury, but Harry had lied to him since they'd first met. There were no five-star hotels and poolside drinks in his future. His future almost certainly contained nothing but hard beds, steel bars, and roommates with tattoos covering their heads. But. But . . . it was that "almost," that one-word qualifier, that left him with the slightest ray of hope that he could escape this horrible nightmare. A chance that maybe, just maybe, Harry's stupid, mad plan could work. There likely wasn't more than one chance in ten million that it could happen, but those were the odds he had to take.

Harry had made it clear that if Paul didn't go along with this, he was dead anyway. So what the hell.

They drove along the streets, turning this way and that, past the most obvious tourist areas to a part of town just outside the city center. Harry had continued to try and start conversations, and Paul had continued to refuse to respond. After a few more turns, they parked in one of the few spots available on the road. Paul looked up and saw a men's clothing store, a hat store, a small coffee shop, and a tourist-trap art store—Sarafian's Art Emporium.

Harry shut the car off. "We're here."

"We're where?" The store's window displayed T-shirts, coffee cups and landscape prints. A handwritten sign in the bottom corner read Day Tours Available—Ask Inside. "What is this?"

"This is where your grand new future begins."

Harry climbed out of the car. Paul would have liked to stay there, to delay taking this step towards his "grand new future" as long as he could, but knew it was inevitable. He opened the door, pushed himself out, and followed Harry inside. A man was standing at the counter.

"Paul, meet my friend Tigran."

"Welcome, Paul." Tigran walked around the counter, offering a hand and a big smile. "I am happy to meet you."

He seemed almost square, with the wide shoulders of a linebacker and a thick waist. His black hair was cut to the scalp, and a growth of stubble spread across his round face. He had wide, black eyes that seemed friendly but careful, as if he was used to keeping his distance.

Paul kept his hands in his pockets, ignoring Tigran, and looked around. The inside of the store was much like the outside window display. Just more trinkets and trash for the tourists. This wasn't any more of an art gallery than a strip mall gift shop.

This was the man Harry was counting on to execute his glorious plan?

"I'm afraid Paul is a little under the weather," Harry said. "Not his usual cheery self today."

"Sorry. No problem," said Tigran, nodding emphatically. "Would you like herbal tea?"

Paul folded his arms and stared at the ground.

Tigran turned to look at Harry and smiled. "Everything is in the back. Come with me."

Tigran and Harry walked to the back. Paul stayed where he was. Tigran had already opened the door and walked into the room when Harry stopped and looked back at Paul.

"Please, my petulant friend. You are about to lay eyes on one of the greatest collections of ancient treasures in the world, one of the masterpieces of all human achievement, and the answer to one of the greatest mysteries in history. So, and I hope you'll excuse me for saying this, but perhaps you could stop being such an absolute jackass and come have a look."

Paul was tempted to pick up one of the cheap metal teapots on the shelf and throw it at Harry's head, but he didn't. He clenched his fists together and followed him inside.

The light in the back room was dim, just one bulb hanging on a cord from the ceiling. It was chilly, damp and smelled of mold and dust. Thin metal shelves were scattered along the exposed brick walls, half-filled with more tourist trinkets. He turned to the right, where Tigran stood, and stopped breathing.

As his eyes grew accustomed to the light, he could make out the treasures of Alexander's tomb spread out over half the room. The biggest piece was a stunning marble sarcophagus, eight feet high and maybe twelve feet long, with a battle scene carved into the side. Was Alexander's body inside? Beside that he could see a chest, just a few feet high and maybe three feet long, glowing as if it were gold. He suspected it was.

On a shelf near the far wall was a bronze bust, about fifteen inches tall. Paul recognized the face of Alexander, that curly hair and proud nose, looking imperious, handsome and brave. It seemed like Alexander was looking right at him, challenging him. Wondering if he was going to put up a fight. Paul felt a throb of guilt.

Harry and Tigran ignored him as they wandered around the room, stopping to admire one object or another. Paul stepped closer, his mouth dry and his breath coming in spurts. Everything was in boxes or on shelves, still covered in centuries-old dirt and broken in pieces. Fragments of ceramic pots, the bright colors shining through. Swords, knives, and armor. Warrior's masks. Precious gems and jewelry, glistening in the dull light. Small cups, piles of cutlery. Silver and bronze vessels. A gold wreath. On the top shelf was a marble ivory sphinx, cleaned up, restored and resplendent, the one piece that appeared ready for the museum's display case.

Something shone on the floor, close to the sarcophagus. It was a small dagger with a curved blade and an ornate, carved handle. It could have been used, he thought, by Alexander the Great himself.

"What do you think, Paul?" Harry said. "Aren't you glad you joined us?"

Paul was awestruck. The treasures laid out in the room were glorious beyond words. Gifts to Alexander the Great, to honor him, to protect him, to be used in the afterlife. He felt sick at how he came to be here, sicker at what he knew was going to happen to these artifacts. But the significance of the moment was overwhelming. He couldn't speak.

"It's a bit chilly back here. Should we?" Harry headed towards the door.

They walked back into the store. Harry grabbed the only chair available, behind the counter, and the other two men stood.

"Isn't this exciting?" Harry asked.

"No. It's insane. And it's not going to work."

"I'm certain it will."

"So where did I supposedly find these pieces?" Paul asked.

"Excellent question. You purchased them from an anonymous source. You will claim you can't reveal any more information, that the seller has insisted on privacy. But everyone—including the press, investigators, the governments of Egypt and Greece, the public—will put you under great pressure to reveal your source. They will be extremely persistent. You'll insist you have to protect your source. But you can't hold out forever, and eventually, you'll give in. One day, you'll confess you got them from a man in northern Italy who discovered them in his grandfather's basement. The old man had been hiding them from the Nazis when he died. That won't be enough. They'll demand more. You'll hold back until finally, under mounting pressure, you'll have no choice but to give in and reveal your source. That anonymous source, by the way, is Tigran. And what will happen then, Tigran?"

"I will deny everything!" he said proudly, like an actor who had been patiently waiting to deliver his lines. "Until, under mounting pressure, I will break down and admit everything you said was true."

Harry smiled. "That was good Tigran. Thank you."

"I repeat, it's not going to work," Paul said.

"But Paul, you haven't even heard the entire plan yet! It's a beautiful thing. Have a seat and I'll explain."

Paul sat on the floor. He leaned on the shelves but they cut into his back, so he lay down. Stretching out on the hard floor, he put his arms behind his head and shut his eyes. Let the old liar talk.

"The minister of culture had them shipped here from Egypt. I have no idea how, but I suspect a lot of money was exchanged between a lot of hands. No matter, it's here now. Our challenge is getting them out of this country, across the ocean, and into the United States.

"We have let the border authorities know that there is an important shipment of major artworks arriving tomorrow. We've asked them to limit the information to as few people as possible, as we're concerned about alerting art thieves to the shipment. We've also asked them to increase security, if possible, while the shipment is coming through. Isn't that brilliant? They won't suspect a thing. It would be like calling a bank and telling them you were about to rob them. You can thank your friend Francis for that inspired bit of genius."

Francis too. It seemed like everyone he knew was aware of this plan but him.

"That's where you come in," Harry continued. "It's your name, your virtuous reputation, that's opening the borders for us. Your seal of approval has virtually eliminated doubts about the legitimacy of this shipment. The great Paul Klugman, famous antiquities dealer, a modern-day Indiana Jones, has uncovered these incredible treasures abroad and brought them to America, with audiences cheering and trumpets blaring, for the New York Museum to display. Who could question a man who was recently featured in *ARTetc* magazine?" Harry laughed, caught up in his own brilliance. "By the way, did you know the Ericksson twins own that magazine?"

Paul banged his head on the concrete floor. *That* was how he ended up on the cover. He was amazed at the depths of his own stupidity.

"Allow me to get to the practical side of things. Tomorrow, all these treasures will be packed safely into shipping crates, loaded into a truck, and driven to the airport in Rome. You will be supplied with all the paperwork required. You're to meet that truck at the airport and accompany the shipment to John F. Kennedy Airport. Francis will meet you there. Don't be concerned about media. It won't be until everything is at the museum that the official announcements will be made."

Paul knew that all it would take was one curious Customs agent, one bribe, one nosy journalist, and the arrests would begin. But what good did it do to think about that? He didn't have a choice. Just go along and hope for the best.

"Are you with us, Paul? You're not falling asleep, are you? We're just getting to the exciting part."

"No, I'm not with you. This whole thing is completely wrong. Why the New York Museum? Why didn't you just sell everything privately? You could have kept it quiet, out of the spotlight, and you might have had a chance."

"We considered that option. But it would have taken years to sell all this one piece at a time. We would have had to get every piece refinished, find the buyers, and negotiate prices, and every time we did our risks would grow. Francis and his rich friends, including the Erickssons, put together a consortium of buyers that will take the entire package as is. One shipment, one money transfer, and it's done. Then you and I, and our friend Tigran, can go off and have a well-deserved vacation. For the rest of our lives."

"Somewhere, somehow, someone will keep sniffing around until they find out the truth."

"A possibility. But that won't matter to us. We'll be long gone by then, in some faraway country with the money safely ensconced in foreign bank accounts and a drink in our hand."

There were a hundred things that could go wrong. Paul was sure of it. But he was too tired to think of them all. Listening to Harry lulled him into a state of semi-consciousness, and he couldn't focus any longer.

"We should probably retire for the night," Harry said. "It will, no doubt, be an exciting day tomorrow."

CHAPTER TWENTY-EIGHT

Kate opened her eyes to the disorienting vision of looking over the edge of a cliff. It took a few moments to figure out why she was there. She was in a car, she was driving on a road overlooking a huge body of water, there was a man in the car . . . Right, she was in a car with Luca, and they were going to Torrento. Even after she arrived at that conclusion, it still took a few minutes to believe it.

"How long have I been asleep?"

"Three hours, maybe?"

The thought that she had fallen asleep with a man she didn't really know driving somewhere she'd never been before struck her as something she should think was dumb, or weird, or dangerous, but she didn't. "Wow. Where are we?"

"Halfway to Torrento. Another few hours to go."

Kate tried to get her brain working again. A large cappuccino would be helpful right now, but there was no Starbucks anywhere near here. Nothing but water on one side and tree-covered hills on the other.

"I have so many things I want to ask you," she heard him say, but the fog in her mind hadn't cleared and the words faded in and out. "How do you like New York? Where did you go to high school? How do you like your eggs?"

She was thinking about her answers when her eyes closed and she fell asleep again.

Kate slept, woke up, and slept again. Every time she woke up, she'd discreetly look over at Luca, making sure he didn't catch her checking him out. He did look different. Not a lot, but different. Thin lines on his face she hadn't seen before, and his skin didn't look exactly the same. Not quite as soft or smooth. He was older than she thought—maybe thirty-eight? Forty? Or maybe he was just tired. She probably looked like she was eighty, so who was she to judge?

"I use a filter on Zoom," he said.

"Sorry, what? What did you say?"

"Va bene. It's alright, you don't need to be sorry. You're looking at me, wondering why I don't look the way I did on all our calls. It's because I use a filter. It softens the wrinkles. In real life, this is what I look like. I hope you're not disappointed."

"No! I'm not looking, I was just—"

"Yes you were, and it's okay. Why wouldn't you?" He shook his long hair. "You want me to be honest? I've had laser treatment done. When you get to be my age, you need a little help. Not everyone can look as naturally good as you do all the time. It seems like every day I need more work, just so I don't . . . spaventare? . . . scare children."

"Oh! Well, that's good! Everybody does that. Why not?" Everybody didn't really, but whatever. He still looked good. And did he say she looked naturally good? She certainly did not, but she would take it anyway.

"How about you?" he asked. "Now it's your turn. Tell me something about you."

"Luca, we have to figure out what we're doing, how this is all going to—"

"I know. We do. But we've still got some time. I am excited to meet you, and I don't know anything about you. Tell me something. Just one thing, un po, a little, something so I feel like I know you."

Fair enough. The hills of northern Italy rolled by, and Kate thought about what she could tell Luca. Maybe about the boys she had loved who had dropped her, three of them with a text message, or about how depressed she was after her father got cancer—no, not that—or the psychiatrist she gave up on after he hit on her, or that time she drank too much lemon gin, or when she thought she might be gay, or about hating herself for most of her teenage years. "It's stupid."

"You can tell me."

"I used to think I was gay."

"Bene! That's natural. Everybody goes through that. Thank you for sharing."

After a few minutes of silence, Kate fell asleep again. It only seemed like a few minutes, but when she opened her eyes again the scenery had changed completely. They were driving on a winding, gravel road, up a long, tree-lined hill with no signs of civilization anywhere. "Where are we?"

"We're going to visit Marco."

"What? Who is Marco?"

"He's a friend of mine."

She caught an inflection in his voice, something a little bit off. As if he were nervous about something. It did seem odd. Why were they going to visit Luca's friend? "Do we have time for visiting?"

"I told you before, this is a people business. You have to know people, and Marco is one of the people you have to know."

Kate summoned up all the mental energy she could muster and tried to think of a reason why this should be okay. But mustering that reason proved difficult. Five hours earlier, she had convinced herself Luca wasn't a criminal. No, that wasn't quite correct: She thought he *probably* wasn't a criminal, which was a long way from actually being convinced. What was she doing here? Where were they going?

"Luca, I'm really not comfortable with this. Can you tell me where we're going, and why? And exactly who this Marco is?"

"Of course. I tried to tell you before, but you kept falling asleep. We're going to D'Aquila. It's a small town about an hour north of Torrento. After you told me we were going to Torrento, I was thinking, I believe Marco may be able to help us."

"How?"

"He's a tomb raider."

Kate was tired, but she wasn't that tired. "Isn't that funny? I thought we were trying to catch tomb raiders, not make them our friends."

"We arrested him for raiding tombs years ago, and . . . accordo. We made an arrangement. In exchange for a light sentence, he keeps us informed about the smuggling business here."

Kate rolled down the window. They passed old brick homes and small farms appearing out of the tree-covered hills. A man was pushing a small plow through a field, slowly, as if this single row would be his life's greatest achievement and he wanted it to be perfect. The wind was stronger and colder here, and it helped clear some of the fog in her mind. A few minutes later, they pulled off the road and parked in front of a long, low, run-down brick building.

"Welcome to Da Vittorio," Luca said. "The best restaurant on this entire hill."

It looked more like an abandoned farmhouse than a restaurant. Six long tables, with benches instead of chairs, lined the walls. The glasses were plastic and the wooden floor was covered in dirt. A man in a stained T-shirt stood behind the bar, watching a soccer game on television.

Luca paused, looked around, and pointed at a man sitting at a table near the corner. He was holding onto a beer and staring at the wall, his back to the door.

"Marco!" Luca called.

Marco turned around and gazed at them without smiling. Luca and Kate walked to the table, sat down, and the two men started talking. In Italian.

Fine, Kate thought. I'll just sit here and listen to you two catch up in a language I don't understand. Don't mind me, I'll just entertain myself. She looked around, wondering what she was doing there and how long they would have to stay. They could have been in Torrento by now. Luca asked a lot of questions, and Marco answered in monosyllables and shakes of his head, looking as if he would like nothing better than to be somewhere else. After twenty minutes, Luca turned to Kate.

"Niente. He doesn't know anything."

"After twenty minutes all you found out was that he doesn't know anything? What were you talking about?"

Luca shook his head. "Just catching up on old times. Let's go."

He thanked Marco, who just turned away. A couple of minutes later they were back on the road.

"What was that really about?"

"He didn't want to talk to me for a reason. That man is terrified right down to his bones, and he's not a man that scares easily."

"Did you find out anything?"

"The only thing he admitted is that there is a dealer here trading in smuggled artifacts."

"We already know that. We need to know who. Nothing else?"

"That's about it. I'm guessing this person is very powerful, from the way Marco acted."

"Chief of police? Politician?"

"I don't know. I doubt it. But the other thing I found out was that Marco thinks he's Armenian."

Kate scrunched her eyebrows. Alfred at Hatchwell Art Restoration had mentioned that one of the dealers might be Armenian. She'd heard Paul Klugman mention an Armenian at the event at the museum. "What are we supposed to do with that information? Walk around town looking for suspicious Armenians?"

"We better come up with something. There isn't much time, and right now that's the best plan we have."

• • •

Frederic's Art Gallery was a small, crowded shop in Torrento's downtown that catered primarily to wealthy tourists. The gallery was filled with paintings and sculptures from area artists, Murano glass and all manner of mirrors, lamps, and furniture. The sound of soft classical music floated quietly in the air. Luca and Kate headed straight for the back.

"Why are we here?" Kate asked.

"Frederic has been in this business a long time, and he's well connected. If anyone here knows about an Armenian dealer, it will be him."

A moment later, Frederic shuffled into the room, hunched over a cane. He was wearing a black cashmere sweater that was three sizes too big for him, and he had big, friendly eyes and a warm smile.

"Ciao, Luca."

The three of them exchanged introductions. Right after Kate spoke, Frederic switched to English. But he spoke softly, his voice barely above a whisper, with a thick accent that still made it difficult for Kate to understand. After a few minutes of small talk, Luca explained why they were there.

Frederic spoke directly to Kate. "You're looking for an Armenian art dealer? In Torrento?" He leaned back against a table, crossed his arms, and thought for a minute. "No. There is no one."

"Maybe he's new?" Luca asked. "Or maybe you don't know he is Armenian. He could have changed his name, and you wouldn't necessarily know his background. Is that possible?"

Frederic paused. "I know everyone that is working in the art business here. The dealers, artists, curators, clerks. Everyone. I can tell you what they like to drink and eat. I can tell you their family history, their bad habits, who they've had affairs with, what church they belong to and how often they attend. There is no one with any connection to Armenia."

Kate said, "Maybe he's not a dealer. Maybe he's an agent, or a wealthy patron, philanthropist, or—"

"This is not a large community. The art world here is a close family. He is not one of them."

Even if she missed half of what he said, Kate got the message. This was a dead end. After a little more talk, they left.

"Now what?" she asked after they got in the car.

"We keep knocking on doors until we find what we're looking for. Someone has to know something."

"I hope somebody knows something soon. It's four o'clock. The galleries will close soon."

They drove around the streets, visited two more galleries, and came up with the same answer. No one.

"It doesn't make sense," Luca said. "He must be here. But everyone is telling us no one here fits that description."

"I don't know what else to do," Kate said. "I keep looking out the window for people I think could be Armenian. I don't even know what Armenians look like. Do you?"

"I think they have dark hair and dark eyes."

"So do most of the people on the street."

They stopped at a red light and watched the tourists walk past their car, a sense of panic building with every second that clicked by. They had driven every street and visited every gallery in the main part of town. It was five-thirty. Soon, the stores would close and the day would be lost.

"Should we call the Carabinieri? The police?"

"We're still in information lockdown. They won't change that unless we have a good reason. Which we don't."

"We know the artifacts from the tomb are here somewhere. We know there is an Armenian that has something to do with them. That's not nothing."

Another red light. Luca swore under his breath. "We don't really know that. It is all more like a strong suspicion, mixed with a lot of hope."

Another ten minutes went by. They had moved to the outskirts, heading towards another gallery, when Kate saw a store named Sarafian's on the other side of the street.

"Sarafian's Art Emporium?" Kate asked. "What kind of name is that?"

"A dumb name. Sounds like a cheap airport gift shop."

"I mean, what kind of a name is Sarafian?"

"I don't know. It is . . . wait. I know what you mean. Yes. Can you check?"

Kate searched for the name on her phone. "It is. It's Armenian."

Luca slowed down, turned around, and drove back. A minute later they were parked in front of the store.

"This is not an art gallery," Kate said.

"It's not even much of a gift shop. Another dead end."

She opened the car door and climbed out.

"Where are you going?"

"There's no time to go anywhere else. We may as well look."

A man who might have been in his fifties approached them from the back of store, flashing a big, toothy smile. "Hello, good evening, I am so happy to see you! What can I do for you today?"

To Kate, this seemed like exactly the kind of person they weren't looking for. He seemed too happy to see them, too unsophisticated, too *pure*. Not a speck of the polish art dealers have, or an ounce of the wariness a suspect would have. His clothes looked more like an office cleaner's than an art dealer's, and his expression seemed to suggest that Luca and Kate were the only visitors he'd had this week.

"We're just looking, thanks."

"Please take your time. I am here for anything you need."

He walked to his desk near the front and sat down, watching them, smiling every time they glanced over. Luca and Kate walked through the store, pretending to be interested in the cheap tourist gifts that filled the shelves.

"This can't be the right place!" Kate whispered. "We're looking for someone that's working in a global smuggling ring, and this guy has shelves full of coffee cups and shot glasses!"

"You're probably right. But on the other hand, we don't really know what we're looking for. What else can we do? Like you said, there's no time to go anywhere else."

Kate nodded, but she still felt like they were wasting time.

"I'll call him over and ask a few questions. You look around," Luca whispered.

"Look around for what?"

"I don't know!"

"Prego?" Luca called out. When the man jumped up and walked over, Kate headed towards the other side of the room.

She heard Luca making small talk, asking about gift suggestions for a niece, while she wandered about. Feigning an interest in tea towels, she picked up a few, looked, put them back. She walked past a closed door near the back. Glanced around to see if anyone was watching, and no one was. She reached out to see if it was locked and had wrapped her hand around the door handle when she caught the owner looking over at her. The smile on his face disappeared. She pulled her hand back.

Luca and the store owner were walking towards the back of the store, so she walked towards the front. It was after six now, and the chance of them finding anything today had all but disappeared. She went to the front and saw the store owner's desk. The two men were at the back and couldn't see her. She decided to go behind it and have a look around.

Today's newspaper, a half-finished cup of coffee, a pencil that looked like it had been chewed by a hungry dog. A few photographs, propped up in cheap frames. She leaned closer to the pictures. The owner on a fishing boat. The owner with someone she guessed was his wife.

She tried to pull open a desk drawer. It was locked. A second drawer was also locked.

There was one more drawer, under the other two. She pulled it, and it stuck for a moment, but she pulled harder and it gave way. Another chewed pencil, a chocolate bar wrapper, and a couple of photographs. She heard footsteps getting closer. There wasn't much time left. She picked up one of the photographs. It was old and faded, but she could see two men standing in front of an ancient Greek cup. It was a cup for drinking wine, with two rounded handles on either side and a mask, with wild eyes and a big, mad grin, painted in the middle. Kate recognized the cup immediately. It was the Kantharos

Cup, by Euphronios. She'd seen it in the Drake Museum. Researched it for an essay she'd written years earlier. It was rare, extraordinary, and priceless.

She looked closer at the two men. One of them was the store owner, although much younger, maybe ten, fifteen years. The other man she thought she recognized but couldn't be sure. He wore a white linen suit. She was almost certain she'd seen him somewhere before. But where?

Luca's raised voice warned her that they were heading back to the front. There were a few more photographs in the drawer. Kate grabbed them, pushed them into her purse and stepped away from the desk just as Luca and the store owner appeared. She hurried to a nearby counter and grabbed a T-shirt that read "I ♥ Torrento." After she'd paid for the shirt and thanked him, they walked out. Luca was shaking his head as he opened the car door.

"Merda. That was a waste of time." He pulled the car out of the parking spot and into the street. "This is hopeless. I have been working on this assignment for almost two months. Two months. And I have accomplished nothing." They stopped at another red light and Luca pounded his fist on the steering wheel. "Nothing!" The light turned green and he raced ahead.

Kate pulled out her phone and looked at the photograph. She remembered everything about that Kantharos Cup. It was one of the few red-figure vases attributed to Euphronios. Incredible! But how could it have ended up at the Drake?

"It could be too late by now," Luca said. "All the artifacts from the tomb could have been sold, shipped, and already sitting on some rich jerk's mantelpiece."

The other man in the photograph. The one in the white linen shirt. Kate looked closer. She'd seen him before. But where? When? It was from a few weeks earlier, maybe more.

Luca raced through a yellow light. "We should never have come here."

"That wasn't just a gift shop," she said.

"No, it's worse than a gift shop. It's a—" He glanced at her. "Wait. Why did you say that?"

"This photograph. It was in his desk. He's standing beside the Kantharos Cup, the one that's now in the Drake. There's something else going on."

Luca thought for a moment. "So if it's not a gift shop, what is it? Who is he?"

"I have no idea." She looked at the other man in the photograph again. "I know that face."

Luca pulled into a parking lot and shut off the car. "Whose face?"

She showed him the photographs. "These were in his desk. I took them. See this one? There's the store owner, and this other man, beside the Kantharos Cup. It's a Euphronios. The other man, though. I know him from somewhere."

Kate handed him the photograph and he looked at it closely for a moment. "Now that's what dealers look like. Not Sarafian."

Of course, she thought. That's who it was. "I remember now!"

"He's a dealer?"

"No. Maybe. I don't know. But he was the guy at the New York Museum."

"Where? When?"

"It was just after the earrings had been stolen from my apartment. I was looking for the man I'd met at the Four Seasons, Jacob. A totally desperate idea, but the museum was having a big event and I thought maybe, if he really was interested in ancient art, he could be there. He wasn't, of course, but this guy was. I remember his long, white hair."

They looked at each other, and back at the photograph.

"Do you know him?" she asked.

"No. No idea who he is."

"But this can't be a coincidence. I don't know what it is, but it's not a coincidence. He couldn't just happen to be at an art event like that and show up in a photo like this."

"I think," Luca said, "the Carabinieri may be able to provide some assistance."

A few minutes later they were sitting in an outdoor café. Luca had sent the photo to the Carabinieri and they were waiting to hear back.

"Now what?"

"We may as well have some food while we're here. They may take a little while."

They picked up the menus, ordered, and waited anxiously.

"How long?"

"Could be a few hours."

"A few hours? Why?"

"It's Italy, Kate."

Kate fidgeted and looked around. They didn't have a few hours.

"Do you think it's possible those two just happened to be standing, or posing, by that, what did you call it? The Kantharos? Or that, maybe, it's a fake?"

"No. I don't think so."

"Good. So we wait. And also . . . while we're waiting . . . how are you?" Luca asked. "You must be beyond exhausted."

"I don't know anymore. I'm afraid if I start to think about it, I'll fall asleep in this chair. It's better if I keep distracted." She remembered the other photographs in her purse. "Wait! I almost forgot." She pulled them out and laid them on the table. Luca pulled his chair over beside her.

There were four. In three of them, the store owner was posing beside different art and antiquities. Kate recognized two of the pieces from art history books she'd studied over the years. Francis Palma was in one of the photographs, shaking hands with Sarafian. Another photo showed Sarafian and the man in the white linen suit together with a woman Kate recognized. She was the head curator of the Drake. They couldn't all be working together, could they? If they were, that meant . . . but it couldn't. Not all of them. Kate tried to think of a reason they would all be together in these photos, but in her sleep-deprived state she couldn't come up with anything. "What does this all mean?" she asked.

Luca said, "It means that was not just a gift shop."

The food arrived and they sampled it without tasting anything. Luca checked his phone every few minutes, shaking his head every time he picked it up and saw nothing.

"What's taking them so long?" Kate asked.

Luca held up his hands. "I'm sure they're working on it."

Kate stared at the photograph. She couldn't help thinking he must be European. It wasn't just his long hair, or the way he dressed. She remembered the way he had hugged Paul Klugman. It wasn't a New York hug. Too huggy.

Kate's phone buzzed. A message from Natalie.

How is Italy?

Nice. Little busy now.

With Luca?

NVM

Ha. Call me when you're back.

Yes. No wait a minute.

Kate thought for a moment. She might know him. Natalie had been in London. She worked in museums. Wouldn't hurt to ask.

What?

Sending something. Hold on.

Kate grabbed the photo of the man with the white hair and hit send.

Any idea who this is?

The real Luca?

No! Do you know him?

A few anxious moments later she heard back.

Ugh. I do. That's Harold Lumley.
Was director of National Museum.
Met him once. Kind of a jerk.
Why?

Thanks! Will call.

Kate searched for Harold Lumley on Google. A few minutes later she said, "Luca. That man in the photograph. He was the head curator at the National Museum in London. Quit unexpectedly a few years ago." She handed her phone to Luca.

He read the article and looked up. "Wow."

"Yes, wow. Claimed he wanted to spend more time with his family. You know what that means."

He nodded. "He was forced to resign."

"So he's connected to the Armenian. The gift shop owner."

"Which likely means he's connected to everything."

Kate thought for a moment. "So Sarafian is the big, powerful, connected art dealer we are looking for?"

"Si. A seller of shot glasses. The perfect disguise," Luca said.

"If what we're looking for is anywhere, I bet it was in the back of that store. Behind the door I couldn't open."

Luca stood up and threw a few euros on the table. "Let's go."

They ran to the car and climbed in.

"This has been a such a nice date. Are you having fun?"

Kate smiled. Maybe she wasn't lying when she told her mother about Luca after all. "I am having fun," she said. "Thanks for inviting me."

CHAPTER TWENTY-NINE

Harry had booked a hotel for the night. Refusing his repeated offers of dinner and drinks, Paul went straight to his room and shut the door. It wasn't even eight o'clock, but he felt tired, sick, and just wanted the world to disappear. He took off his shoes and went to bed. Climbed under the blankets fully clothed, clamped his eyes shut, and hoped the world would obliterate itself.

Thirty minutes later he woke up to a gentle banging on his door. A soft three knocks, a pause, another three knocks. Steady, insistent, and infernally annoying. Paul shut his eyes and tried to will it to go away, but it kept coming back. He gave up, got out of bed, and walked towards the door.

"Go away. Just go away."

"You'll have to excuse me, Paul." Harry's voice. "May I have a word?"

Harry was back. Shit. He wanted to "have a word," as if he were giving Paul a choice, as if Paul could simply respond with "Would it be possible if we had a word in the morning instead?" and Harry would agree. Paul was learning to hate this phony British politeness, pretending everything was a friendly request rather than a thinly veiled command. He wondered if Harry himself was nothing more than an act, a personality he had appropriated from some old movie, and had stayed in character so long he'd forgotten who he was.

Paul opened the door.

"There's been an . . . an incident," Harry said. His voice, normally so gentle and melodic, was cold, curt, and businesslike. "I apologize for bothering you, but you'll have to come with me. I'll explain on the way."

"No. Whatever it is, it's your problem. I'm going to bed."

Harry pushed the door open and walked inside. "There is no choice, I'm afraid." Even in his half-awake state, Paul could see he didn't have any chance of getting out of this unexpected trip. He knew what would happen if he didn't follow orders, whether they came wrapped as a polite request or not. "Just a minute."

As he pulled on his shoes, he wondered what could have happened. The tension radiating from Harry suggested it was something big. Whatever it was, Paul guessed, the odds that this nightmare would end happily had just gone down by a significant degree. While Paul finished tying his shoes, Harry didn't even try to initiate any conversation. Which was very un-Harry-like. It wasn't until they were in the car, driving down the now quiet streets of Torrento, that Harry started talking and Paul knew he had guessed correctly.

"I just got off the phone with Tigran. He had a couple of customers today, a man and a woman. They seemed a bit off to him, he told me. Not like your normal tourists. They asked too many odd questions, like they were just pretending to be interested in buying something. One of them tried to open the door to his back room. Thankfully he caught them before they did. I don't know who the man is, but as soon as he described the woman I knew exactly who she was. Leon told me about her. It's the woman who was asking questions in the Hodges Gallery. The same one who was pretending to sell the earrings. And now she's here." Harry looked over at Paul. "Do you follow?"

Paul felt himself sinking further into the quicksand. "I knew it. I knew this stupid plan wasn't going to work."

"They didn't find anything out. Of that he is absolutely certain. But it does suggest the police are sniffing around. They don't know who we are, or what we're doing. Not yet. But they're out there, circling, getting closer. Which does complicate our plan."

"You mean the plan you called 'beautiful'?"

Harry didn't answer.

"What does it mean?"

"It means we have to make a slight pivot. Move on to plan B. You see, the border patrol, Customs, the police, will all be on high alert. Under these conditions, we won't be able to ship anything to the New York Museum. Francis can't be seen touching anything that carries the slightest cloud of suspicion. Not that he truly cares, but he is sensitive to the political winds that are blowing everywhere. It's a question of optics." A traffic light turned red and Harry drove right through it. "At any rate, the game has changed."

Paul realized they were driving to Sarafian's.

"In retrospect," Harry said, "I should never have listened to Francis. He's the one who talked me into shipping the contents of the site to New York. I let him convince me it was the best plan, hiding everything in broad daylight that way. With the reputation of the New York Museum and the great Paul Klugman heading up the acquisition team, I thought he could be right. My mistake." He was driving right on the bumper of the car in front him, and swore and honked before pulling over and passing him. "And he had that consortium behind him. They made a convincing argument." Harry shook his head and sighed. "I wish I had stuck to my original plan."

Paul was grinding his teeth so hard he thought they would crack. "Not such a beautiful plan."

"I suppose you're right. The New York Museum was to receive approximately half of the contents, so at least some of Alexander's tomb would have been available for public viewing. So there was an element of public good, wouldn't you say?" Harry half smiled. "You try and do something nice . . ."

"But—those two at the store—what if they're just asking questions?

We don't know who they are. Okay, no, we can guess they are police. What if they decide it's a dead end? What if they never come back?"

"That's a bit hopeful." Harry tapped his fingers on the steering wheel. "You sound disappointed, Paul. I thought you'd be happy to hear our plan had been compromised."

Paul would have been happy if Harry had been thrown in jail, or shot, or fell off a cliff, or was run over by a car. But the plan being compromised was not good news. It meant there was an even greater chance he would be arrested. He could feel the trap closing in on him, getting tighter than ever.

They parked in front of the gallery and got out of the car.

"So what are we going to do?"

"We? Are we a 'we' now? Have you actually joined the team?" Harry pushed a button by the door. "What we do is stay calm and carry on."

Tigran opened the door and they went inside. The gallery was dark, with just enough light coming in from the street to see where they were going. They walked to the back.

"Listen to me carefully, gentlemen," Harry said. "We have a lot of work to do. Our plans have been disrupted. This is obviously unfortunate, but we mustn't panic. The good news is, we do have a backup plan. It's not ideal, but that's where we are, isn't it? Everything will be fine." He looked at Paul, as if he was expecting some dissension in the ranks, but Paul was staring at the ground. "We'll take everything underground and sell it the old-fashioned way. One piece at a time, to the highest bidder. But first"—he opened the door to the back and walked inside—"we'll have to get everything packed up and out of here as soon as possible. The police could be here at any time. Tigran?"

"The truck will be here in a few minutes."

"Did we find any help?"

"Professionals," Tigran said. "Two guys. Big muscles."

"Wonderful. You've done a fine job. Paul, now that you're on our team, would you mind giving us a hand packing up? Time is rather tight, and I'd like to get started."

"Where is it going?"

“We’re moving everything to my residence in Greece. For the time being.”

But if that was the plan, Paul reasoned, why did Harry need him? If Harry didn’t need his sterling reputation as a dealer to bring all these treasures through Customs, what use was he? Harry wasn’t going to keep Paul around just because he helped them pack. And if Harry didn’t need him, Paul knew what his future looked like. It wouldn’t be in the jail cell he had been imagining, because he wasn’t going to live long enough to get there. Harry would make sure of that. Before long, maybe even tonight, Harry would decide that the risks of having him alive outweighed the rewards, and that would be the end of Paul.

In the meantime, all he could do was play along and make himself useful. He would avoid the inevitable as long as he could. Maybe an idea would come to him. “I’m here to help,” he said.

Paul started picking up the smaller items and wrapping them in the paper and bubble wrap Tigran had provided. Tigran and Harry tried to lift the sarcophagus, but it was too heavy. They tried to push it closer to the exit. As they were busy straining, pushing and pulling, Paul noticed the dagger he’d seen lying on the floor earlier. He picked it up and felt the blade. It was rusted and dull with age, but still solid. He slid it into his belt at the back, under his jacket.

A minute later Harry and Tigran gave up on the sarcophagus. “The movers can take it. Let’s gather up the smaller pieces.”

“Where does this go?” Paul lifted the box he’d filled.

“Put everything by the door. The truck will be here soon.”

He placed it by the door and started packing another box with jewelry. Five minutes later the rear door swung open and a large commercial truck was backing up towards them. It stopped and two tall, muscular men climbed out and mumbled a few words in Italian before starting to pack. The first item they moved was the sarcophagus, hoisting it onto a dolly without any obvious effort and loading it into the truck.

“How are you getting across the border?” Paul asked.

"We'll drive to Bari, on the southern coast. We've arranged for a ship to meet us there. That ship will take us to Albania. No one asks questions in Albania that can't be answered with a few thousand Euro. From there we drive across the country to Kastoria, where we cross the border into Greece. Kastoria is as isolated as it gets. There won't be anyone there to stop us."

The other men were working so quickly that Paul realized he was just getting in the way. He sat down and watched while they packed. A few hours earlier he had been trying to convince himself there might be a small fragment of hope he would come out of this with his career intact and maybe even money in the bank. He didn't really believe it, but that lie had helped him avoid dealing with the truth. He couldn't avoid it any longer. Now he knew, and it was worse than he had imagined.

There weren't going to be any hotel pools, fancy wine, Lamborghinis, or sharing his new couch with young actresses. There wasn't going to be anything, except total and eternal blackness. Somewhere, between here and the Greek border, Harry was going to terminate Paul's role in this enterprise and Paul would cease to exist. A bullet by the side of the road, a push off the deck of a ship, a large mover snapping his neck. He didn't know how or when, but he knew.

Paul touched the back of his shirt, where the dagger pressed against his skin. He promised himself that when that time came, he wasn't going to make it easy.

CHAPTER THIRTY

Luca raced through the streets of Torrento, speeding through red lights and passing cars in both lanes. The tires squealed as he turned a corner too fast and almost lost control. An elderly couple was crossing the street and he slammed on the brakes just in time. They hurried out of the way and he hit the gas again. Kate grabbed the door handle and held on, her stomach spinning.

He pushed the phone button on the dashboard.

"Luca," a woman's voice answered.

"Si. Generale."

"Dove sei?"

Luca said, "Torrento. Pensiamo che abbiamo trovato i manufatti di Alexander. Stiamo andando lì adesso." Kate heard the name Lumley and what she thought was the word for smugglers before the general cut him off.

"So chi é," the general said. "Qual è la connessione?"

"Abbiamo una foto di Lumley con il calice di Kantharos. E—"

"Una foto di cosa?"

"Il calice di Kantharos. È un vaso Greco, di . . . di . . ." Luca looked at Kate.

"Euphronios," she whispered.

"Di Euphronios."

"Ferma," the woman said. "Ferma. Ferma la macchina."

Luca was protesting, but it didn't sound to Kate like the general was listening. He pulled into a small parking space at the side of the road, the tires slamming against the curb. Kate watched as he squeezed his eyes shut and rubbed his face.

"Ho fermato. Generale."

The general said, "Aspetta. Non metterò a rischio tutto quello che abbiamo fatto basato su una fotografia di qualcuno con un vaso Greco. Ci stiamo avvicinando molto. Non roviniamolo."

Kate didn't understand a word of this, but the expression on Luca's face suggested it wasn't what he wanted to hear.

He took a deep breath and exhaled slowly. "Dobbiamo andare adesso. Se non—"

"Mi dispiace, Luca. Non è abbastanza. Hai bisogno di ottenere migliori informazioni." She hung up.

Luca stared at the dashboard for a moment, his eyes blank. He banged his head on the steering wheel. "Working in a big organization," he said, "is a nightmare."

Kate put a hand on his shoulder. "Are you okay?"

"No." He looked out the window, squeezed his eyes shut for a few moments, and opened them again. "That hurt."

"What are we going to do?"

"We're going to get better information."

"Like what?"

"I don't know," he said. "Why don't you ask the general?"

Kate knew they didn't have time for this. "We have to go. For all we know, Lumley and his gang could be packing everything up right now."

Luca rubbed his chin. "I am being told that I do not have enough evidence. As if I don't know what I have. Can you believe that?" He leaned back in the seat and stared out the window. "I have no idea what to do."

Kate felt as if she'd fallen off a cliff. Ever since she had first spoken with him, she had believed Luca would always know what to do. Even when she thought he was with the criminals, she never doubted his intelligence or abilities. Why? Because he had all that experience, maybe. Or because he looked like he did, or because he was so full of confidence. Or maybe it was something else.

Maybe it was just her deflecting her own anxieties and projecting her insecurities onto Luca. Maybe Kate wanted to believe he would always know what to do because she felt like she never did. She was just a junior agent from Chester, and she felt like an imposter half the time. What did she know? With the stakes this high, when someone really had to know what to do, it had to be him because she didn't think it could be her. But none of that mattered now, because now it was up to her. Whether she thought she could do it or not, it was up to her.

"Let's go, Luca. Let's go back to that shop."

"No. We can't."

"We can. We have to. If we don't, they'll be gone. Everything will be gone."

Luca shot her a questioning look. "The general told us not to go near the shop alone. I don't like it any more than you do. But she's not wrong. You know why? Maybe she's right, maybe we need more information. But also—because that's how agents end up dead. We don't know who's there. There could be two or three of them, there could be twenty. For all I know, they have machine guns and rocket launchers. We can't just go there and ask them to stop."

"So what are we going to do? Nothing? We're talking about the treasures of Alexander's tomb. What if no one ever sees them again because we didn't do anything?"

Luca crossed his arms and looked straight ahead. "I'm not risking my life, or yours, for a bunch of antiques. I don't care what they are, how old they are, or where they are from. They're just things." He turned to face her, his eyes wide and jaw tight, as if trying to convince both Kate and himself of something he didn't believe. And she didn't believe him, not one little bit.

She said, "Let's at least go look."

"Then what?"

How would she know? She didn't even know right now. "If we don't see anything, we can always leave."

Luca shut his eyes and put his fist under his chin. To Kate, it appeared as if he was just trying to think of a way to convince her she was wrong. Which was a problem, because she wasn't wrong.

"We have to go, Luca. If you don't, I'll go by myself."

He opened his eyes, pushed the car into gear and hit the gas. "Bene. Fine. We can drive by. We can look. But we can't get too close. You understand that, right? We're not taking any stupid chances."

Kate opened her mouth to say something and stopped. He was a chief sergeant, she reminded herself. This was his jurisdiction.

His eyes locked on hers. "You do understand that?" he asked.

"Of course."

Eight minutes later, they were driving by the gallery. The streets were empty, and a heavy fog had crawled through the empty streets. The whole block felt like it had been deserted. The gallery's lights were out, which wasn't a surprise. It was after ten o'clock. They kept driving, circled around the block, and drove by again. Luca found a parking spot as far away from the store as he could that allowed them to keep an eye on the door.

"There must be a back lane or something," Kate said. "Something behind the store, where they pick up the garbage and unload delivery trucks."

"There probably is. But we can't just casually drive down their back lane. What do you think the chances are we'd get out?"

"We could at least go look."

"No."

"Then I'm going." Kate opened the door.

Luca's head jerked backward. "Fine. Go."

She started to get out.

"Wait," Luca said.

She sat back down and shut the door.

"Tell me something," he asked. "Why does this mean so much to you? I know they're not just antiques. They're important, they're history, they belong to the world and all that. I get it. This is the reason I work in the Carabinieri. But this is reckless. I've never seen anyone so willing to risk their life, so quickly. Why are you doing this?"

"I don't know." She paused, twisting her lips. "Maybe it's not just about them. Maybe it's also about me. Your whole life, you've done things. You can point to all the art you've saved, the crimes you've stopped and solved. But I don't have any of that. This is a chance for me to do something that matters. To make a difference. Maybe that's a stupid reason, but I don't care. It's my reason."

For a few moments, neither one of them moved. Luca reached out and put his arms around her, she put her arms around him, and everything outside the car disappeared. It was another moment Kate wanted to remember forever. If they weren't in such a hurry, she might have been happy to stay like this for the rest of her life.

He leaned back and held up a finger. "First, I want to go on record as saying this is a very bad idea. Yes?"

Kate raised an eyebrow and shrugged.

"A very, *very* bad idea. D'accordo? Are we agreed?"

"Yes! I get it. You said it's a bad idea. Can we go now?"

Luca unbuckled his seat belt. "What are we waiting for?"

He opened the door, climbed halfway out and turned around. "I'll go first," he said. "And call you as soon as I know it's safe. Okay?"

"Oh . . . oh, sure. I understand. Absolutely."

"I'll be right back."

Luca got out and shut the door quietly. He crossed the street, walked along the sidewalk for a minute, and disappeared down a laneway.

Did he really think she was just going to sit here? Not a chance. Kate waited until he was out of sight, counted to ten, opened the door and got out of the car. If anything was going on in that store, she wasn't going to be left behind.

The street felt like a museum after dark. Everything was dead still, and so quiet that the sound of her feet seemed to echo off the store fronts. The gallery was on the other side of the street, still a few minutes away. Kate couldn't help thinking how nice it would be to have a gun right now. Every step she took increased the anxiety building inside her. Part of her wanted to turn around and run back into the safety of the car. But she knew she'd regret it if she did.

She stopped when she got to the front of the gallery, watching the store from behind a van parked on the street. Even from this close, it was difficult to see inside. There weren't any lights on, and she couldn't see past the front window display. This wasn't getting her anywhere. It was tempting to walk to the front. That was the only way she could see what was happening. Yes, that's what she was going to do. She stepped off the curb, almost slipped on a grate, and was about to cross the street when two men appeared from behind the van.

She took a few steps back, turned around, and tried to run. Where did they come from? One of the men grabbed her arm. She struggled to get loose, but he squeezed tighter and she couldn't break free. His hand felt huge around her thin arm. He pulled her back, sending a sharp jolt of pain all the way to her neck and spinning her around so fast she almost fell. She caught herself and steadied her feet. Two large, leering men stared down at her. They looked like truck drivers. One of them had long, dark hair, the other short red hair and a beard.

"You should have stayed away," the man with the dark hair said. He smiled, showing a row of gray, broken teeth. His breath smelled like stale beer.

Kate started to say something when the other man pushed a finger against her lips and told her to shut it. His finger tasted like dirt and grease; she jerked her head away and wanted to spit but thought better of it. They each grabbed an arm and twisted it behind her, turned toward the store and dragged her across the street. She held back a scream, afraid to make any noise. The only sound was her shoes scraping on the pavement. They kept her arms pinned behind her, twisting and pulling until the pain grew so intense she thought she could feel the bone separating from her shoulder socket. They reached the gallery door, and one of them let go for a moment to pull it open. She thought about running but knew she wouldn't get anywhere.

As soon as they were inside the store they let go and pushed her towards the back. Kate walked slowly, head down, wrapping her throbbing arms around herself. She pushed away the fear and pain that threatened to overcome her and tried to think about how she was going to get out of this.

The man with the red beard stepped in front of her and opened the back door. Three other men were in the room. One was loading boxes into a truck parked near the open loading dock. Another was sitting on the floor with his head between his legs. The third, the man from the photograph with the long white hair, was sitting in a chair. He turned around and looked up at her.

"What a wonderful surprise." He stood up. She saw the flat metal of a handgun's grip tucked into his belt. "You must be the one they call Judith. I don't believe we've met."

Kate steeled herself and somehow summoned up the willpower to stop shaking. There would be plenty of time to panic later. "You're Harold Lumley."

"Oh, please, call me Harry." He smiled, revealing a row of gleaming white teeth. "I'm afraid you have me at a disadvantage, the one they call Judith, because I don't know your real name."

Kate bit her lip. "I know what you're doing."

"It would have been better for you if you didn't." He looked over at the men in the truck. "Are we almost ready?" The men nodded. "Ideal. As you can see, we have another package to bring along. Could you pack up this young lady with the rest of the boxes? Then we can continue on our way."

The man on the floor stood up. Kate recognized him from the event at the New York Museum. Paul somebody, the one who made the presentation. He looked at her, and there was a flash of recognition when their eyes met.

"What are you doing?" he asked Harry.

"We're leaving, Paul. And this young lady is going to join us. Do you know who she is? She was the one asking all the questions in the Hodges Gallery. She tried to sell fake earrings to our friend Jacob."

Paul's eyes opened wide. "You can't take her. I know her. She's with the FBI. You know what that means, right?" He looked over at Kate, then back at Harry, his eyes pleading. "That's a capital felony. Don't do this. Let her go."

Harry folded his hands behind his head and leaned back. "Oh, Paul, it's nice that you're taking an interest in this young lady's well-being. But she's been following us for weeks now, and she knows who I am, who you are, what we're doing here, and a lot of other things she shouldn't. She will come with us. And if she happens to have an accident on the Adriatic Sea, well, we can't be blamed for that, can we?" He turned back to the men. "Let's pack it up, gentlemen. We have a long journey ahead of us."

Kate felt as if she were floating out of her body. The pain in her shoulders had been replaced with cold fear. The two men pulled her into a chair.

"You can't do that." Paul looked at the men and then at Harry. "Stop. Let her go. She's not going to say anything." He turned to Kate. "Tell them. Tell them you won't."

Harry laughed. "Paul, excuse me, but would you please shut the fuck up?"

One of the men held Kate from behind. She tried to get up, but he was holding her so tight she could barely move. The other walked over to a bench at the side of the room and picked up a roll of tape. He turned around and walked towards her.

Paul pulled the dagger out of his belt. Kate's eyes opened wide. The dagger was about two feet long, with a curved blade and carved handle. Did he really think he could stop these men with an old antique? Didn't he know Harry had a gun?

Paul held it with two hands, straight out in front of him, and pointed it at Harry. He said, "Fuck you, asshole."

Harry was still smiling. "I'm sorry?"

"Stop. Stop everything." Paul said. "You're not getting away with this. You're not going to take all this away. You're not going to kill me, or her, or anyone else." Paul swung the dagger back and forth in front of Harry. "I'm not going to let you."

The other men froze, their eyes on Paul.

"Oh, Paul." Harry was shaking his head. "What's happened to you?"

"I did not agree to this. This is all you. What you're doing is insane, and it's going to stop." Paul pushed the dagger into Harry's chest, the blade cutting into Harry's shirt. "It's going to stop now."

Harry swung an arm up, knocking the dagger to one side and leaving a tear in his shirt. Blood began to seep down the front. Paul tightened his grip on the dagger and lunged at Harry, taking a wild swing. Harry jumped back and it missed by several inches. Paul moved closer, raising the dagger over his head and getting ready for another lunge. By now the other men had forgotten what they were doing with Kate and ran towards Paul. He spun around and pointed the dagger at them, his lips curling into a hard frown and his head lowering, as if challenging them to attack. The momentary distraction was all Harry needed. He pulled a gun out of his pocket and pointed it at Paul's head.

"You know the old saying," Harry said. "Never bring a three-thousand-year-old knife to a gunfight." He turned to the men that had been about to tape Kate to the chair. "Wrap him up as well. We have another package to deliver."

The man with the beard walked over to Paul.

Paul pointed the dagger at him. "Come on. Let's go," the man said, knocking the dagger out of his hand with one swift kick. It skidded across the room. He reached out and grabbed Paul's arm, pulling and twisting it up near the back of his neck. Paul gasped in pain. Kate knew exactly how he felt.

"Why, Paul?" Harry asked, holding the gun and shaking his head, smiling. "Why? A few months ago you were practically homeless. Now . . . there are tens of millions of dollars in treasures here. You could have had a share of all that. Why the sudden crisis of conscience? I mean, you're already guilty of a dozen crimes. And you choose now to become a saint? That seems like awfully bad timing to me."

"Because . . ." Paul winced and cried out. "Because this is who I am."

Harry laughed. "Well, isn't that wonderful. Congratulations on this grand moment of self-realization. Now, if you'll excuse us, we have work to do." He looked at the men, and his smile changed to a sneer. "After you're done with him, finish taping her up and load them both into the truck. Hurry." He walked away.

"Are we ready?" Harry asked.

Tigran nodded.

The three men started to tape Paul to the chair. Where was Luca? thought Kate. Why was he taking so long? There weren't many artifacts left to be loaded in. Once they were done with them, they'd come for her. She'd be lucky if she had another minute or two before she'd be taped to the chair and tossed in the back of that truck. And that would be it. No one would ever see her again.

The door at the back, the one that led to the store, was still open. If she could reach it, she might be able to get away.

This could be her only chance.

She swallowed the fear and pain. The only thing that mattered now was getting out of there. The door was only twenty feet away—she might be able to make it. She jumped up and ran. Big strides, legs pumping, pushing hard. Fifteen feet. Amazing what adrenaline can do for you. She didn't hear anything behind her. Maybe they hadn't noticed yet, maybe they were still focused on Paul. Picked up speed. Ten feet. Halfway there. She had a chance. She surprised herself at how fast she could run. Faster, faster. She just had to reach the door. Almost there—

The sound of the gun came first. Then the sharp stab in her right leg. It felt like a red-hot poker had been jabbed into her thigh, and she fell face-forward. She hit the floor, her hands coming up too late to break the fall. Her face smashed into the concrete. Kate felt a flash of pain; she tried to get up but fell back down. She looked back and saw Harry pointing his gun at her. Blood was oozing from her leg.

"That was unnecessary," Harry said.

The pain was growing, taking over her entire body. Harry walked over and stared down at her, shaking his head.

"This is unfortunate," he said. "You would have enjoyed our cruise on the Adriatic Sea, at least for the time you were alive to see it. The view is beautiful this time of year. But now you'll never know, will you? Oh well. We're in a bit of a hurry now, so I'll have to finish you off and leave you here." He pressed one of his feet on Kate's leg, grinding his heel where the bullet went in, and she screamed. "I'd like to say I'll miss you, but I won't." He lifted his gun and pointed it at her.

Kate shut her eyes, trying to block out what was about to happen.

A gun went off.

She waited. Waited for the bullet to hit her in the head, the chest, wherever it was going. Waited a fraction of a second that seemed like an hour.

Harry's body fell on top of hers.

"Are you okay?"

Luca's voice.

She didn't answer. She couldn't speak.

It wasn't for a few long seconds, after she heard the sound of police sirens, that she could even open her eyes.

Luca was standing at the door, his gun pointed at the men standing behind her.

The blood from the hole in Harry's head was spreading across the floor. She tried to slide backwards to get away from it, but couldn't move. Tried to push him away, but his body was too heavy. Kate felt dizzy and lay down again.

"Are you okay?" Luca asked again.

"That blood," she said, "is never going to come out of this shirt."

CHAPTER THIRTY-ONE

In Chester, by ten o'clock the sidewalks had been rolled up and most people were in bed. In Portofino, Kate and Luca were just being seated and the restaurant was only starting to fill. Behind them, the small harbor area was lit up with grand white yachts and rustic fishing boats, busy boutiques and pastel-colored cafés. Scooters raced past and tourists wandered happily while fishermen cleaned their boats and mended their nets. The warm, still air smelled of sea salt and roasting fish, and a full moon looked down from a deep-purple sky. Kate sat down and leaned her cane against the chair.

"How is the leg?" Luca asked.

Kate said, "Nothing a glass of Aperol can't take care of."

She had been lucky. After a few days in the hospital and several weeks of physio, she was almost able to walk without assistance. It still hurt. A constant throbbing reminded her she'd recently been shot. One Aperol probably wasn't going to be enough.

Luca ordered. An older man sat alone at a table, reading a newspaper with a bottle of wine and full glass in front of him. A middle-aged couple were holding hands and whispering to each other over glasses of champagne. Kate browsed the menu, wondering whether she should have the Acqua Pazza or the Baccalá Mantecato: The menu, being in Italian, offered little assistance.

"Looks delicious. What's good here?"

"Everything. But I recommend the carbonara with white truffles."

"They don't serve that at Denny's. How about the Baccalá Mantecato?"

"A local delicacy, but it is an acquired taste. Only for the brave."

They put the menus aside and gazed at the rugged cliffs over the sea. A yacht, lights streaming in all directions, floated lazily by. The Ligurian Sea glimmered back at them, the moon bouncing off the small, soft waves. The restaurant was filling up with families, couples, large groups of friends. Like a busy Sunday afternoon in New York, but without the car fumes. She was struck with the sense that she didn't want this to end.

"The waiter is taking his time," she said.

"Remember, this is not New York."

"You should tell them an FBI agent has been shot. Apparently it's a good way to get help fast."

Luca laughed. "It worked with the Carabinieri. Why not here?"

"Did you find out what happened to Paul?" she asked.

"Paul is out on bail. He's talking, telling them everything. I'm betting he gets off with a warning. Apparently, he's working at an art gallery in Minneapolis. Does tours, works in the back room, packing crates and managing storage."

"So he tried to steal millions of dollars in antiquities and he just walks away, like nothing happened?"

"We might not be here if it weren't for him."

Kate remembered the expression on Paul's face when he ran at Harry. It was the look of a man who had given up, had nothing left to lose. "True. And the Ericksons?"

The drinks arrived. Luca sipped his drink and looked out at the sea. "They have a lot of money and good lawyers. I think this will soon be little more than a memory for them. Jacob seems to have vanished."

"Unbelievable. And Francis? Did you hear about the New York Museum?"

"That is a subject you know more about than I do."

"I know a little. Those photographs I found at Sarafian's have led to multiple investigations and claims for restitution. It seems like just about every article on the shelves of the New York Museum and the Drake is being reclaimed by the country it came from. The museums have both been avoiding repatriating artworks for years, claiming they obtained them all legally. They will have a much harder time defending themselves now—the investigations and lawsuits are piling up. Francis has resigned to spend more time with his family, so he says." Kate sat back in her chair. "So? What now?"

"First. Saluti! You helped save an important historical find from tomb raiders, and it is now safely back in Egypt. They are preparing the exhibition as we speak. Those photographs you found will lead to many more antiquities being returned to their rightful owners. Congratulations. Absolutely brilliant."

Kate let that sink in for a minute. It wasn't so far back that she was convinced she'd spend the rest of her life searching for Stanley Cup rings. Now, a new world beckoned. Luca was right. She was brilliant. Of course, she had always known that.

But she didn't do it on her own. "No," she said. "*We* did it."

He lifted his glass and smiled. "We make a good team."

"Saluti," she said, looking into Luca's eyes, the wind blowing his hair gently over his face. He looked like he'd been photoshopped. "In France they believe you must make eye contact during a toast or you'll suffer through seven years of bad sex. Is it the same in Italy?"

"In Italy, they believe you will suffer through seven years of overcooked pasta."

"Which is the worse nightmare?"

Kate smiled. "Best not to take chances."

Once again they toasted, staring straight into each other's eyes. He did have beautiful eyes. And they really were the longest eyelashes she had ever seen on a man. She wondered if he had a brother Natalie could meet.

Eventually the waiter came and broke the spell, but Luca's hand still rested on hers, and their fingers were wrapped tightly together.

"What's next, Kate?"

"I have to go back to New York to see my mom. She has a new boyfriend, who apparently is also quite suave, and they're leaving for Peru next week." Kate looked back at the sea, then back at Luca. "I started taking Italian lessons, you know. I finished my second class yesterday."

Luca raised an eyebrow and smiled. "Fantastico. How's that coming?"

She picked up the bruschetta in front of her. "Bruschetta deliziosa."

He raised a hand and shook his head. "Bene. But it's pronounced 'bru-sket-ta.' Not 'broo-shet-a.'"

"I think," she said, "I better move to Italy. How else will I ever learn?"

"Buona idea. It's the only way. And we need more people like you. I need you."

"Do you have plans for me?"

Luca nodded. "Si. I'm working on one right now."

Kate lifted her glass of Aperol, and Luca clinked.

She had already made her decision. And it wasn't what Luca had suggested.

She was going to have the Baccalá Mantecato.

ACKNOWLEDGMENTS

I am forever grateful to Ann for her encouragement, patience, and inspiration. Thank you to early readers Larissa Lawrence and Paula Aicklen, and Diane Young, who edited an earlier version of this manuscript. A special thanks to the wonderful people of ECW Press, including Jack David, Samantha Chin, Cat London, David Marsh, Emily Ferko, Michela Prefontaine, Alexandra Dunn, and the rest of their team.